Man Eating F*ckers

David Owain Hughes

A HellBound Books LLC
Publication

www.hellboundbookspublishing.com

Printed in the United States of America

Also by David Owain Hughes
Novels, Novellas and Short Story Collections:

All-Wound Up
Wind-Up Toy
Wind-Up Toy: Broken Plaything
Wind-Up Toy: Chaos Rising
White Walls and Straitjackets
Escapees and Fevered Minds
Choice Cuts
Walled In
Man-Eating Fucks
The Rack & Cue
Collision Course
Granville
Home Improvements
Puckered

Anthologies:

Shadows and Teeth Vol.3
Trapped Within
Hell of a Guy
Unleashing the Voices
Rejected for Content Vol. 4, 5 & 6
Crossroads in the Dark Vol.1 & 2
Fifty Shades of Slay
How to Cook a Baby
Madame Movora's Tales of Terror
Big Book of Bootleg Horror Vol. 1, 2 & 3
Shopping List
Depraved Desires
Easter Eggs and Bunny Boilers
Bah! Humbug!
Slashing Through the Snow
VS Vol. 1 & 2
Black Candy
Into the Abyss

Compiled & Edited Anthologies:

What Goes Around
Man Behind the Mask
Fuck the Rules

David Owain Hughes

Man Eating F*ckers

A HellBound Books Publishing LLC Book
Houston TX

Chapter 1

The clock's second hand *boom-boom-boomed* its way around the face, ticking the minutes off her remaining time with her therapist. Lying on the black, tougher-than-granite couch, Storm traced the thin cracks in the ceiling as she listened to the thunderous tick-tocks.

She'd never liked the clock, thinking the oversized object looked stupid on the wall behind her doctor's desk. The thing was flanked by Dr. Samantha Veech's framed medical certificates and family photos. Two filing cabinets stood directly beneath it, along with the clichéd Yucca plant.

Uniform grey walls surrounded her. Confined her to the box-sized room. At the beginning, she had felt breathless at the mere sight of them. However, over numerous visits, she'd got used to them, just like she'd got used to revealing her innermost thoughts to her doctor, who was now waiting for a reply.

She didn't know how to answer, though.

It seemed *too* personal.

"Storm?" Dr. Veech coaxed.

"I heard you," Storm replied. "But why would you want to know that? My mother has nothing to do with what happened to me…"

"It's still part of your past, Storm. It's important to discuss these issues."

"*No!*" she said, her voice raised and sharp.

"But Storm, please—"

"This *should* be about what those fucking animals did to me and my friends!" Storm interrupted. "If you saw the things I see when I close my eyes…"

"I know. But please, humour me about your mother?"

"*Ugh!*" Storm pained. She knew the woman wasn't going to let the matter drop. She conceded. "What would you like to know?"

"Tell me about her," the doctor encouraged. "Anything you'd like."

"She was a bitch. Ran out on me and Dad – I've told you this before."

"Yes, I remember. Do you still keep her letter in your bedside drawer?" Dr. Veech asked whilst writing in her notepad. Her half-rimmed glasses sat on the bridge of her slender nose, and she peered over the top of them as she scribbled.

She's crow-like. Her fingers are long and bony. 'Pianist's fingers', Dad describes them as, she thought, watching her doctor jot more notes. *And what's with the tight, black pencil dress she wears week-in, week-out? It does nothing for that scrawny body…*

"Storm?" Veech called, breaking the girl's thoughts once again. "Do you still have the letter?"

Scowling, Storm replied, "Yes."

"I see. Want to tell me about that?"

"Not really, no."

"Okay. So, tell me, how are you finding motherhood?"

Storm considered this for a moment. "I'm enjoying it. I can hardly believe Stevie is almost two. She…" she started, but stopped herself.

"Yes?" Dr. Veech pushed.

"She…I'll…How am I going to tell her...What…?"

"These are not questions you need to be asking yourself yet, Storm. Your little girl is just a baby."

"But—"

"By the time Stevie's old enough to ask those questions, you'll be in control of all your emotions – the trauma will be behind you. You'll be equipped to deal with the answers to your daughter's questions."

"I guess you're right. I still have and read Scuzz's text messages from two years ago… Isn't that a little strange? Shouldn't I try moving on?"

"It's perfectly fine. There's nothing wrong in holding on to certain things from your past. Things and events which made you happy, Storm."

She nodded. "I just feel guilty, you know? I'm here…he's not."

"Storm, you can't beat yourself up over that. People are killed daily. What happened to Scuzz was *not* your fault."

"I guess."

"There's no 'guess' about it. It wasn't."

Storm nodded. "I'm interested in a guy at Uni – I saw him today. I guess that's what triggered—"

"That's okay. It's healthy. You should explore those feelings – it'll be good for you."

"You're probably right. I'm just having difficulty in letting go, especially after how wild I became following the events in the woods. I never meant to fall pregnant – it was a one night stand…I loved Scuzz."

The good doctor nodded, thinking it best to change path. "Yes. Just try to move forward when you're ready. Remember – small steps. How's your dad?"

You like him, don't you? Storm thought, a laugh almost escaping her. "He's seen better days." The doctor looked up as though pressing for more. "He's still nursing his loss..."

Flicking through her notes, Dr. Veech found what she was looking for. "The death of Officer Pitman was not his fault."

Ever the professional, hey, Veech?! Storm thought. "*Fuck* you!" she blurted, startling the doctor. "Sorry, I didn't mean to..."

"Yes, you did," Dr. Veech said.

They both smiled.

"No, I *am* sorry – I shouldn't have snapped."

"That's okay, Storm. You're only trying to protect your dad. I get it. You miss her, don't you?"

"Mam?"

The doctor nodded, her pencil poised. "Uh-huh."

Storm wiped her eyes. "Yes, but I'm not sure I could ever forgive her."

"You still blame her?"

"Probably. I'm not sure. I just want to see her – to yell at her."

"Why?"

Storm shrugged. "I'm not sure, but it might make me feel better. She crushed Dad..."

"I see," the therapist said, making more notes.

"What do you write?" Storm asked.

Veech tapped the side of her nose with her pencil. "Comments about our conversations. Has Huw started dating the PC he used to work with?"

"Yes, I think so."

"*Humph*, that's good."

Storm detected a hint of something in the doctor's tone. Sorrow? Regret?

"Will you both be attending the re-opening of the recreational centre?" Dr. Veech continued.

Storm looked at the woman in amazement. "What do *you* think?!"

"I think it would be good for you – exorcise your demons. There's nothing to be afraid of."

"How do you know?!"

"It's been a long time, Storm. If he was going to come back for you, he'd have done it by now. He's more than likely dead. You told me his wounds were fatal."

Storm lowered her head. "I'm almost positive."

"Well, there you have it. I think you should go. Huw, too. It'll be good for you."

"I'll think about it," Storm said, more so to move away from the subject than anything else.

"Good. I think it opens in a few days. I could pop along if you wanted me to, of course?"

Storm looked at her doctor. "That would be nice. I could ask my neighbour to baby-sit Stevie."

"Great, then it's settled?"

Storm reluctantly nodded. Bile filled her throat. "We'll see. I'll ask Dad about it when I see him."

"Okay, fine. Let me know when we meet next, yes?"

"Yeah, cool. We're meeting Thursday?"

The doctor flipped to the pad's calendar. "Yeah, that's right – two days from now. Perfect. The re-opening is on Saturday?"

"Yes, it is," Storm said, trying to put as much enthusiasm as she could into her voice.

Dr. Veech smiled. "You'll be fine," she said, looking at her clock. "Not long left, I'm afraid. Is there anything *you* would like to discuss? Open floor."

"*Huh*," Storm sighed. "Nothing I can think—" she started, and then it happened:

'day-terrors' or 'waking miseries', she'd pet named them.

They were vivid.

Everything came alive.

Her senses awoke.

Storm didn't know whether she was sleeping, awake or something in between. It was weird. Fucked-up freaky. These worlds she entered were so imbalanced, she thought she was sat in a padded cell somewhere wearing striped pyjamas and a straitjacket. And, just like in ninety-five percent of her other waking miseries, *he* was in this one too.

Skull.

He was standing in front of the office door, blocking her exit route. In his left hand, he held a child's decapitated head by its hair. The swinging head spattered the floor with blood as it swayed; the splashing sound was thunderous. The air was thick with the smell of iron. Exposed cords flapped. The eyes were rolled back.

Skull was filthy; his naked form was caked in dry mud and blades of grass. Twigs were knotted in his hair.

He was vile personified.

In his free hand was a knife. A hunting knife. Eight inches of razor-sharp steel. Bits of skin, blood and hair clung to the metal teeth. The once-silver blade was coated crimson, as though it had been dunked into a bucket of red paint.

Even though it was Stevie's head he held, Storm didn't scream.

She closed her eyes and willed him away. *Count to ten. One, two, three, four…*She could still hear the patter of blood, which was audible over her doctor's voice. She was asking something, something along the lines of, "Is everything alright – is it another episode?"

Opening her eyes, she gasped – he was still there. Panting, she closed her eyes and willed it over. Counting to ten normally worked – it dispelled the dream and sent the demons away.

Skull stepped towards her. His mouth was set into a half smile, half snarl. A low, straight-from-the-pit-of-his-guts growl travelled up his throat.

She snapped her eyes shut.

Count faster!

...Five, six, seven, eight...

Her lips flickered with lightning speed.

"Go away," she said. Then louder, and louder still. *"Go. Away!"*

The smell of the woods was strong: wet grass, soggy bark, pines, even the shit from the wildlife.

Her body convulsed like a cluster of leaves when having their branches rattled. Her mind felt like it was crumbling.

Her eyes shot open.

He was *still* there, and advancing on Dr. Veech. He tore his knife down her stomach, cutting her open and spilling her innards onto the well-polished floor.

Her lungs burned as bile leapt up her throat. *It can't be, can it?* After two years, he'd finally found her. Tracked her down to end her.

No, he wasn't going to get her. Never. She'd beaten him once. She'd do it again, damn it!

Dr. Veech could only watch as her guts poured out of her. She hit the floor with a jarring crack, making Storm flinch.

"I come back for you..." he said. His child-like way of speaking spooked her.

"No..."

He threw Stevie's head at her, and she put her hands up to block the attack.

"Arrrgh!" she screamed, feeling rough hands on her arms. They shook her violently.

"Storm? *Storm*?! Wake up!" Dr. Veech yelled, shaking her, giving her patient a harsh slap across her face. This seemed to work, and brought Storm out of her dream-like state.

"Where…where…where am I?! *Daddy*!" she screamed. "*Daddy*!" Her ragged breathing was replaced by aggressive sobbing. Snot shot from her nostrils.

Dr. Veech cradled her. "*Shhh*!" she cooed. "It's alright. It's alright. It was just a dream."

"I want my dad!" she demanded.

"He'll be here soon," the doctor said. "Come on. Try to get off the floor."

"I *can't*!" Storm gasped, her grasp tightening on her doctor's sleeve. "He's here. I can see him!"

Dr. Veech looked about. "I don't see your father or hear his car outside," she said.

"No, not my dad," Storm said, breathing hard. "Him. *Skull*! He's over there. There, damn it!" she continued, nodding her head in his direction.

His feral eyes peeped back at her from behind the doctor's desk.

Chapter 2

He grunted as he dug the hole and threw the loose dirt over his shoulder. Beads of sweat trickled down his face and body – they cut glistening tracks through the grime which caked his naked torso.

This was the fittest he'd felt in a long time. His strength and stamina levels were almost back to normal. Skull's healing process had taken a little over two years – the injuries he'd sustained had kept him immobile for a year.

Had it not been for his Eight-Ball, he would have perished. *She keeped me alive*, he thought. *She fed, washed and treated my wounds best she could.*

As his strength returned she'd mated with him, leading to the birth of twin boys last summer.

Mother had been pleased.

Like Skull and Eight-Ball, she too had survived, but her serious wounds left lasting damage. She had never fully recovered and had died a day ago. Skull was grateful his mother had got to meet his baby boys before succumbing.

Sensing movement behind him, Skull turned and looked up. Eight-Ball stood over him, the twins cradled in her arms. She smiled. He smiled back.

Every day since their escape, they feared people would come for them. But nobody had.

After being beaten by that *girl*, Eight-Ball had rescued Skull and their mother. She'd managed to hoist them onto horses and they'd fled deep into the woods. They'd been lucky to live, let alone escape.

They'd ridden hard for a day, stopping only to feed and water the horses before continuing their arduous trek into the hills. That night, they'd come across an abandoned train tunnel.

It was deep in the woods, covered by trees, foliage and moss. Just enough of the structure had been visible for Eight-Ball to unearth more of it. She'd done it on her own. After putting Mother and Skull comfortable, she'd spent the day uprooting green in her fight to get to the bricked-up entrance.

Once she'd cut a path through and made it to the brickwork, she'd used all her might to pound at the blocks with a large rock. Most of the stonework came away with her first few hammer blows, but the rest had been stubborn.

When a big enough gap had been made, Eight-Ball had scooped her mother up and carried her inside. After this, she had aided Skull into the damp, dreary space. It had been as dark as a starless night, but their eyes were quick to adapt – they were used to living in such conditions. It had kept them alive for years.

Over the coming days and months, Skull and his mother had started their healing process. Eight-Ball was left to build their new 'home' single-handedly. She'd spent weeks clearing the opening to their new dwelling, providing easier access to the wounded members of her family.

Across from the entrance, she'd dug and built a fire pit. It had taken her most of a day to gather the stones needed. All the branches and green she'd cut down and pulled up were thrown into its centre. She'd started the fire by patiently rubbing two sticks together.

Eight-Ball had done a good job in making it feel like home.

She went out daily, hunting wildlife and scouring the area for what she thought useful. She couldn't attack people or raid homes alone. Skull had forbidden her.

After falling pregnant, Eight-Ball had continued to do as much as she could until Skull was finally recovered enough. He had then taken over duties whilst Eight-Ball rested for the remainder of her pregnancy. Like his sister, he hunted and scavenged daily whilst exercising and keeping himself fit. Slowly, his crippled body re-energised.

Throwing the shovel to one side and placing his hands at the top of the hole, Skull heaved himself out of the waist-high grave. He rolled his mother, who lay naked nearby, into the ground. His face was devoid of emotion as he began covering her corpse with loose earth. Eight-Ball stood at his shoulder, watching. The nameless twins slept.

When their mother was buried, they shoved a makeshift stake into the ground. This was not a tombstone, but a marker for Skull and Eight-Ball so they would know where to find their mother's place of burial. After spending a few quiet moments graveside, Skull signalled Eight-Ball to follow him.

It was time to go home.

Walking from the grave, Skull led his sister and babies back to camp, which was a few minutes away. He hadn't wanted to bury his mother too close or inside the base, because he didn't want the constant reminder. It angered him. He wanted revenge but knew the time was not yet right. He needed to become stronger.

He hadn't killed a man or woman in a very long time. Neither had Eight-Ball. He needed to make sure they were ready before returning for the girl. She, along with the men who had come for her, had killed his entire family. For that, she would die. It might take him a long time to find her, but find her he would.

The twins cooed and gurgled as Eight-Ball carried them through the woods back to camp. Skull pushed past low-hanging branches and bushes, holding them aside for Eight-Ball to pass. Nothing was said between them as they walked on.

As they approached their hideout, nearby voices disturbed their thoughts. Skull's heart raced. He'd not heard a person's voice other than Eight-Ball's and his mother's in a long time. Not that they'd spoken much over the past two years: Eight-Ball could not communicate as well as Skull, and his mother's injuries had kept her from being able to speak much.

Skull held his hand up, indicating Eight-Ball to hang back. She did as instructed and turned, heading quietly in the direction they'd come. She hid behind a cluster of trees. This pleased Skull, who crept forward smiling.

He drew his knife from the sheath at his hip. The steel was rusty. It wasn't the best weapon, but it was all he had until he could start scavenging in the 'outside' world.

When the tunnel came into view, Skull crouched. He could see people standing by his home. He peeked between branches.

There were three of them: Two men and a woman. They wore brightly coloured vests and helmets to match, which were inscribed with something. They held large rolls of paper and pointed at the tunnel and surrounding area. *Who they? What they? Warriors?* he asked himself. He wasn't sure he had the strength to attack them if they were.

The sight of the woman stirred something within him. The pit of his guts and groin burned. He *wanted* her. His grip intensified on his knife's handle.

Skull kept his distance as they rooted around his camp. One went inside the tunnel, whilst another poked and kicked at the ash in the spent fire. He could hear them laughing and talking but couldn't make out what they were saying.

Skull crept through the foliage, being careful not to rustle or disturb anything as he went. He crouched and listened.

Now he could hear them, but he didn't understand all their words. Nevertheless, he tried.

"So, what are you saying, Bill?"

"I'm not sure, Martin," the other man said, removing his helmet marked *Railroad Co.*, "but it definitely looks as though someone has been using this place as a campsite – they've even pulled the brickwork away!" He pointed at the tunnel.

"That much is clear, but it doesn't look as if they are here now. Does it? They could have left days or even weeks ago."

"Possibly, but the fire suggests different. I think it only burned out a short while ago."

"Well," said Martin, the bigger of them, "I guess we'll have to hang around and see 'em off!"

"You're probably right. We should have come out here sooner," Bill complained.

"Hey, we weren't to know. Besides, if the local council hadn't decided on re-opening this tunnel, then we wouldn't have had a reason to come out here in the first place."

The woman looked slightly embarrassed.

"True. Are you going to stick around, or will you head back and make your report?" Bill asked her.

The slight woman in a tight suit and wellies shuffled through her paperwork, which was safely fastened to a clipboard. She raised her oversized helmet to complete this task, which she huffed and muttered about, much to the amusement of the men.

"This look does nothing for me!" she said, smiling.

"Oh, I don't know," Martin said. "I think the colour of the helmet brings out the colour in your eyes. It also works well with your make-up and suit," he jested.

Bill laughed.

"Thank you, Martin," she said with a mock scowl.

"You're welcome!"

"No, I think I have all I need for my report. I can't see why we can't re-open this site."

"Good," Bill said. "I don't know why they closed it in the first place. You leaving, Paula?"

"I think I'll stick around whilst you strapping fellas see off the brutes who have been camping here," she said.

"Okay," Martin said. "Bill, I'm off to the jeep to get some signs and fencing. We better get this area closed off before other bums come marching through."

"Good idea."

"I'm off for another quick look inside – make some more checks," Paula said.

"Call if you need me," Bill said. "I'm going to start making room for Martin and myself to cordon the area."

Paula set off in the direction of the tunnel as Bill stood watching her arse swish. "If only I wasn't married," he muttered. With Paula gone and Martin nowhere in sight, he proceeded to break the campfire apart.

Skull gripped the haft of his knife as tight as he could. His over-grown fingernails dug into his palm, drawing blood. He breathed hard as his top lip twitched. His eyes darted from side to side.

"*Dead*," he mouthed.

But he didn't make a move. Not yet. His body was still weak, especially after digging his mother's grave, and he was cautious about having to deal with two men. Had there only been one, he would have attacked.

If he was going to strike, though, now would be the perfect time, as the three were split up.

He bird-whistled and then ducked behind the bush he was standing by.

Bill turned around. "Martin?" he called. When there was no answer, he went back to his business. He'd set the large rolls of paper to one side so he could clear the area.

Skull chirped again.

"Martin, is that you messing about? Come on. We have a lot to be getting on—"

Another chirp derailed him.

"What is that?" he said with a mystified look plastered across his face. He walked to where Skull crouched in waiting.

Skull peeked through the leaves, spying his target moving closer. His back was aching from his stance, but he remained still.

"Who's there?"

Skull chirped.

Bill scrunched his face up. "Birds," he whispered, putting his hands out to part the bushes in front of him. "Or dirty tramps who have been using this site to...*Ugggh!*" he managed as Skull's knife shot into his groin.

Bill tried to scream but Skull clamped his hand across the man's mouth, forcing the pained yell back down his throat.

Skull twisted the blade and ripped the knife upwards through the man's abdomen. He noticed Bill's eyes roll skyward – he'd either passed out from the pain or he was dead.

"Eight-Ball," he whispered. "*Eight-Ball*?!" he called slightly louder.

Bill's legs buckled, and he collapsed toward Skull, who was having difficulty in keeping the man off him. His arms weakened. He needed his sister's help.

"Fast!" he called. "Fast. *Help*!"

Sweat broke out across his brow and slid down his face. The salty liquid trickled into his mouth. The pain of trying to keep the body from falling and making a noise was punishing.

"Did you call, Bill?" Martin asked, making his way back through the bushes. His arms were filled with various materials. "I could do with a hand getting this stuff off the jeep, mate."

Skull muttered something on seeing the other man appear. He tried to fully stand, but lost his footing. The body collapsed onto him, pushing him and pinning him to the floor. The bushes shook.

"Bill, have you gone for a piss?" Martin asked, chuckling. "We have a lady present, you know."

Skull struggled to get the weight off him, but the man was too heavy to lift or roll. His energy was zapped.

"*Bill*?!" Martin called again, stepping closer to where Skull was hiding. "Are you okay, mate?"

Skull looked up and saw hands appear in the bushes, ready to expose him.

"Bill, are you playing hide-and-go-peep with me?" Martin sniggered.

At the moment the foliage parted, Eight-Ball removed the weight from his chest, freeing him from the ground. Staggering to his feet, he tackled Martin and propelled him backwards.

This left Eight-Ball to finish off the hapless Bill, who was choking on his bloodied vomit. She put her large hands to his head and twisted it to the left and then right. His neck bones popped and snapped. His body fell limp. She retrieved Skull's knife from his guts.

Eight-Ball could hear the woman exiting the tunnel. She had to be stopped.

"Bill? Martin? Are you alright? What's going on?" Paula said, her voice bouncing off the walls around her.

Before Paula could make it into the open, Eight-Ball positioned herself to the left of the tunnel's entrance, her hands poised. This was *their* home, and *nobody* was taking it from them!

"Will you two stop messing—" Paula put her hands to her mouth and gasped. She saw Martin rolling about the floor with another man, who could only be described as savage. He wore nothing. His body was bruised and battered; his face the same. He growled and spat as he fought to try and get the better of Martin.

"Get off him!" Paula yelled, racing out of the tunnel. She tripped and hit the floor with a hard thud – her chin connected with the ground, dazing her.

Eight-Ball rolled the woman over and straddled her. She slapped her about the face, trying to rouse her.

"*Arrgghhh*!" Paula screamed on seeing the deformed face of Eight-Ball looking down at her.

Eight-Ball smiled. *"Food,"* she bellowed, punching Paula as hard as she could in the temple, knocking her out and releasing her to help her brother, who was losing his struggle.

"I'll kill you!" spat Martin, who outweighed Skull and had managed to get on top of him. He wrapped his hands around his attacker's throat. "You're not supposed to…*Ugghhh!*" he gasped as a blade ripped across his throat. His hands sprang from Skull's throat to his own as he tried to stem the gushing blood.

He gurgled and gagged as he fought to stay alive. Crimson sprayed Skull as he tried to stagger to his feet, but he was pushed to the ground by Eight-Ball. She leapt onto the fat man and plunged the knife into his face before slashing it to ribbons.

Skull rolled onto his side and watched Eight-Ball's frenzied attack before getting to his feet and pulling her off the dead man. She continued to swipe at air until she found it pointless.

Putting Eight-Ball down, Skull pointed at the unconscious woman. "Tie her!"

She nodded.

Whilst Eight-Ball tended to her duties, Skull dragged both men over to the tunnel and placed them inside. They would be used for food, their remains thrown to the fire.

Once he'd regained his energy from having dragged the bodies, Skull built a new fire. He then stripped the men and fed their clothes to the flames. He took the opportunity to rummage in their van and stole their tools.

There was nothing he could do about the vehicle except push it off the road and into the foliage.

Once Eight-Ball finished tying Paula up, she fetched her babies, whom she'd placed in a safe spot behind a tree so she could rescue her brother. With her babies in arm, Eight-Ball shuffled into the tunnel to join Skull, who was using a saw he'd found to dismember the men's bodies.

"Dinner," he said.

She nodded.

"Next day, we go. People will come and look," he said, gesturing at the dead men and the tied woman. He pointed behind them. "We go into tunnel deeper."

Eight-Ball nodded. She knew her brother would keep her safe.

Moving further from the area was not something Skull had planned. He'd wanted to stay, recover, and then go looking for the girl who had caused him so many problems. But that would have to wait. For now, the most important thing was getting his sister and babies to safety; to keep building his family with Eight-Ball and now the woman they had captured – she would be good for fresh mating, he thought as he continued to hack the bodies apart. He put his bloodied fingers to the mouths of his children, who slurped and sucked at them greedily.

This made him and Eight-Ball smile.

Chapter 3

After regaining her composure and knowing Skull wasn't in the room, Storm had accepted Dr. Veech's help off the floor. She now sat in one of the chairs facing the desk, nursing a glass of water to her chest.

"I...I..."

"It's okay," Dr. Veech said, putting a hand to Storm's shoulders. "You had an 'episode'."

"Was I sleeping?" she asked, wanting to know the answer once and for all. It had never happened in company before.

"Not really. You entered a sort of daydreaming state. Zoned out on me. One minute you were chatting; the next, your eyes were clouded over."

"Oh, I see." Storm lowered her gaze.

"You've nothing to be ashamed of, Storm. With what you went through, it's not surprising."

"But it's been two years!"

"And it could take another two. Four. *Ten*, even. These things take time."

"Yeah," she said, forcing a smile.

"You've got plenty going for you, Storm."

"You think?"

"*Yes*! You have a loving dad, a baby daughter, University…Life goes on, so try living it. Think positive. We'll soon have these daydreams of yours under control," Dr. Veech said.

Looking up at the clock, Storm could see her time was more than up. "I'd better go," she said. "Dad's going to be waiting outside. Besides, I could do with the fresh air."

"Are you sure? You're more than welcome to wait here until he arrives. I don't have another patient until four…"

"No," Storm butted in. "I should get going. I'm going to give my legs a stretch," she said, pushing back her chair.

"Okay," Dr. Veech said. "I'll see you on Thursday?"

"Yep, you sure will."

"Good. And don't forget to ask your dad about Saturday night. I think it'll be a big step forward."

"I won't. I'll mention it to him as soon as I see him," Storm promised, reaching the office door.

"Great! Until Thursday, then?"

"Yes. Bye, Dr. Veech."

"Bye, Storm."

When Storm exited the building, sunlight bombarded her eyes. She sought shade by the side of the office and watched the traffic whiz by in both directions. The small valley was busy for a Tuesday afternoon.

I'm glad we never moved, Storm thought as she rummaged around inside her holdall. *I love it here – I want Stevie to grow up where I did.* Finding her smoke tin, Storm removed the lid and took out a joint she'd already started. She then thought about texting her dad to say she was off to the pub for one but decided against it. She needed to get home to start work on her University project.

Still shaken by the events in the office, Storm started walking. Checking her watch, she couldn't understand why her father was so late. He was usually on time.

"It doesn't matter," she uttered, looking at herself in a shop window. Storm gave her dreads a fluff – she'd had them done a year ago to remember Ruby. The memory of her best friend always brought a tear to her eye. Even though it saddened her, it also made her smile and giggle at some of the silly antics they used to get up to. "I'll always love you," she told her reflection before moving on.

Taking a drag on the weed, Storm began to relax – it meant some of her former self was returning at last. At the beginning, Dr. Veech had had to wait at the door with Storm until her dad turned up at the end of every session, which had gone on for months. But then Storm had found the strength to wait on the doorstep by herself. Then the car park. Some days, she would walk home, no longer scared by her surroundings. Deep down, she had a feeling the man who had taken her hostage and killed her friends was dead.

"Samantha's right – it's been *two* years. He would have come back by now."

After each session, she could feel herself getting stronger and stronger.

Starting University had also helped: she'd made new friends, spending most of her days wrapped up in her artwork and music.

Storm no longer felt timid or afraid of her own shadow.

The waking miseries knocked her back and made it feel as though he was close, but once reality kicked in again and the shakes subsided, she knew she was safe and he was dead. Him, and his sick, fucked-up family.

She drew closer to the turn for the recreational centre and took it. She wanted to see the building, which she hadn't clapped eyes on for over a year, when it had still been a burnt, hollowed-out shell.

Since then it had been sold – construction had commenced months ago.

Her dad had also been out to see the place a few times, telling her it helped with piecing his life back together.

Walking down the path, Storm noticed most of the foliage had been cut right back. The recreational centre no longer looked buried. The council had also chopped down most of the trees and added streetlights.

The building rose before her. The soon-to-be car-park was filled with lorries, vans and men running around in hard hats and overalls. The place looked completed to her untrained eyes.

"It looks much better than it used to," she uttered. Soon the place would be open. She felt fearless seeing the centre in the cold light of day, and could hardly believe how easily she'd managed to walk up to the place without a pang of anxiety or upset. Walking closer, she heard the men and women shouting back and forth to each other – some were yelling about paint, others seating. Stepping closer, Storm noticed she was standing by a massive lorry. Inscribed on the side was *Rigs' and Iain's Haulage Co.*

Truckers, who she guessed the truck belonged to, were offloading at its rear. She could hear them talking – something they said caught her ear so she tuned in.

"Another weird pub? You've got to be kidding me?!" the one wearing a hat said.

"Hold your water, dear – it's not like we're stopping, is it?" the other trucker said.

Storm looked away when the one wearing the hat stared at her. *What does he mean, 'another weird pub'?* she thought, turning her back and leaving them to it.

She strolled back up the path she'd come down.

Back on the main road again, she continued her walk home. Dragging on the last of her joint, she threw the stub over the side of the bridge as she crossed – her head was starting to feel muzzy, but it was nice. It was a feeling she could let herself slide into.

Storm picked up her pace. She wanted to be home. To be in her room and working. Digging her phone out of her pocket, she checked for any missed calls or texts from her dad. It wasn't like him to miss a pick up. Not these days, anyway.

Nothing. Her phone was void of any communication.

"Huh, looks like I'm walking the distance!" she told herself, not bothering to replace her phone. Instead, she flipped through her old texts from Scuzz. She liked rereading them. After her loss, the words onscreen had made her ache. Now, they made her smile. It brought him closer, along with Ruby, whose texts she'd also kept.

After the tragedy, most of her friends' families had moved away. Storm and her dad had been adamant not to go anywhere.

It was their home, and nothing was going to drive them away.

It's that kind of determination that's going to drive me to go to the opening on Saturday night with or without Dad, she thought.

She wasn't fully afraid of the shadows and dark nights any longer. Life had to move forward. Straight after the events, Storm's life had felt empty and meaningless, especially after the authorities had taken Claire's baby boy away from her and her dad.

"The child will be placed with his grandparents," the nice lady in a grey suit had told Storm and Huw.

She'd heard nothing since.

But then, she'd been busy with Stevie, who had been born from a one-night stand with a boy she couldn't even remember. For a few months after killing the life inside her, Skull's baby, she'd gone off the rails, drinking and smoking herself into oblivion. It had been her safety mechanism kicking in.

It took her father to get her on track.

To help her grieve properly.

When she approached Beth's Baps Café, Storm stopped and looked at the poster in the window advertising the recreational centre's big opening on Saturday night, but only the top half of the promotional flyer was visible.

She decided to go in.

The woman working the counter smiled, and so Storm approached her. Getting closer, she could see the woman's hair plastered to her neck with grease and sweat. All that was missing was a fag dangling from her half-open mouth as she chewed bubblegum.

She didn't wear a uniform, just an apron with bold red lettering etched into the corner of the fabric: *Beth's Baps Café*. The jeans she wore were too small, and the seams were at breaking across her broad arse and pale flesh wobbled where her T-shirt didn't quiet meet them.

"Yes, love?" she said, her valley accent cutting through Storm like a dentist's drill.

Her make-up looks as though it would take a jackhammer to remove it, Storm thought, stifling a laugh. *Nice. She has the classic slut-red lipstick, too. This woman's going places.*

"I was just wondering if you had any more of those leaflets from in the window?" she asked, her voice low and delicate.

"Table number four!" Lipstick growled. "Which one, love?" she addressed Storm.

"The one about the grand re-opening on Saturday night?"

"Oh, erm…Table four! Quick, Jasmine," she huffed at the young waitress. "It's getting cold, mun. *Quick*!"

"I'm coming, Mam. Give me five, is it? I'm rushed off my feet 'ere," Jasmine said, scowling at her mother.

"You can't get the staff these days!" she told Storm with a wink.

"Erm, yeah…" Storm said, letting her words trail off and smiling.

"No, love, we don't have any more of those flyers – try Paul across the road."

"Paul?"

"Yeah, you know – over in the newsagents."

"Okay. Thanks," Storm said.

"Try and get yourself one as it's fifty percent off the entry fee if you hand one in at the door."

Storm nodded. "Thanks." Before turning to head out of the café, she saw the chef standing in the kitchen doorway.

"Beth, are you going to gab all day or are you actually going to do something?"

Storm smiled as she left the two to compete in a slanging match.

Outside, she saw the newsagent's across the road. She was halfway across the road when she felt the vibration of her phone in her pocket. Removing it from her pocket, she quickly hit the answer button.

"*Dad*? Yeah, I'm fine. You'll be another ten minutes? Okay. No, it was okay with Veech. Well, there was a slight hiccup…No, I'm fine. I'll tell you about it when I see you. I'll wait by Paul's newsagent. What? You have something to tell me? Okay. No, I'll speak to you in a bit. Yes. Bye."

Now what? Storm thought. There had been urgency in her dad's voice – something was wrong. Her stomach flipped. Replacing her phone, she decided not to dwell on it. *I'll be seeing him soon. He's only around the corner. Best I get in there and find out if Paul has any flyers for Saturday*, she thought, entering the newsagent's.

The man behind the counter smiled. "Hello, little lady," he said. "I haven't seen you in a long time. How's your dad?"

Then she remembered him. Although Storm didn't really know Paul, he and her dad had gone to school together and were good friends. Smiling, Storm answered.

"He's good, thanks."

"That's great." Paul beamed. "Are you both over that awful business?"

Storm's guts dropped. She hated talking about it, especially to people she hardly knew. *But that's what the valley is like*, Storm thought. *Everyone knows each other and knows each other's business. People have been asking me if I'm alright ever since the damned episode finished. Dad, too! People won't leave it be.*

"Yes, we're pulling through it slowly," she told the shopkeeper.

"That's great to hear!"

"Thanks." *Now, hopefully that's the last I'll be asked about it!* she wanted to say.

"So, what brings you into my shop, apart from your legs?" he quipped, letting out a hearty laugh.

Storm chuckled and then smiled thinly. *How droll*, she thought, and then considered how mean she was being to him. *He's just trying to be friendly.*

"I came in looking for one of the flyers you have stuck in the window," she said. "Beth across the road said you might possibly have some?"

"Oh, right, I see. And what flyer would that be?"

"The one for the grand re-opening."

"For the recreational centre?" he asked, his eyes widening.

"Yes. Apparently, there's a discount if you hand one over at the door."

"But you're not thinking of going, *surely*?"

"Yes, why not?" Storm asked. She was starting to get annoyed with him. It was none of his business.

"Most people have boycotted the place. Nobody wanted it rebuilt. Plus…"

"Go on," she pressed.

"Wouldn't you…I mean…It would be difficult…?" His face turned scarlet.

"Actually, Paul," she said, "my doctor thinks it might be a good thing for me to exorcise my demons. To show me that there's nothing to be afraid of."

"I see. I didn't mean anything by it. I just…" He let his words trail off before digging his hole deeper. "I'll get you a flyer," he said, keeping his eyes lowered.

"Thank you, Paul," she said as he scuttled out to the backroom.

After a few moments, the shopkeeper returned. "I have a few, just in case you have friends…I mean a boy…*your dad* would like to go with you!" he said, stuttering. He handed the colourful papers over to Storm.

Turning to leave, she heard her dad's car pull up outside.

"Looks like my lift's here. Thanks, Paul," she said, heading out the door.

Opening the car door, she heard Stevie chuckle from the back seat.

"Hello, cheeky-chops," Storm said to her.

"Hey, love," Huw said. "How did it go today?"

"*Ugh!* It was okay, I guess. I had a waking misery whilst I was with Dr. Veech."

"Oh, really?"

"Nothing I can't handle."

"What have you got there?"

"These are for Saturday night's grand re-opening, Dad.

Dr. Veech thinks it'll be a good idea for us to go," Storm said, not letting him get the first word in.

He sighed. "Let me think about it."

"Dr Veech said she'd tag along for support, and that you should take your girlfriend," Storm teased.

"*Tut!* She has a name, you know." He started the car. "And besides, I haven't spoken with her in a couple of days."

"Trouble in paradise?"

"Maybe."

Alice Cooper filled the inside of the car as the radio came to life. He was singing about dead babies.

"Look, I need to tell you something without you flying off the handle," Huw said. "Okay?"

"*Gaaawd!* What is it?" she asked with playfulness in her tone.

"You're not going to like this, beaut. I don't. In fact, I'm annoyed. It's the reason I'm late picking you up."

"Oh?" Her joyful expression turned to that of a quizzical one. "What is it, Dad?"

"It's your mother, Storm."

"Shit. *What*?!"

"She's back, and she's waiting at the house to see you."

Chapter 4

As he waited, he did chin-ups in his cell. His back faced the solid steel bars. His roommate kept quiet, fearing he'd have another smack in the face if he disturbed Chester.

Chester's back glistened with sweat as he pulled himself up and then lowered himself down in rapid succession. His biceps rippled, making his muscles move his prison ink; they seemed to have a life of their own.

His head was shaved, but it hadn't always been like that. When he'd first 'moved in', his hair had reached his shoulder blades; it had led to being easily attacked. They'd yanked his head back from behind, leaving his body open for punishment.

Being raped was something he'd never forget or let happen again.

He'd been lucky they hadn't killed him. "We want to play with you," one of them had said. "This is the treatment rapists get in here!"

Playing rough was not a problem, especially after he'd learned their rules.

He cut his hair.

Made a shiv.

Soon it was them nursing broken bodies. Two died. The handmade knife had come in useful over the years, but it was the training that kept him safe and alive over the ten years he'd served.

After today, it wouldn't matter, because Chester was being released.

Not bad, he thought. *I only had to do twelve years out of sixteen to twenty. It would have been ten, had I not killed those two dickheads in here. Still, it was worth it.* Chester smiled. There was no way he was going to be a good boy when he got out. There was business to attend to, such as killing the fucking pig-cunt who'd put him away.

He let go of the handmade chin bar, dropping to his feet. For a man who was only five-foot-eight, he filled the box-sized room. His shoulders bulged with muscles which matched his equally impressive arms and six-pack. His top half was peppered in tattoos – most of them were of Swastikas and naked women, with female names randomly dotted here and there.

The clichéd *Mum* and *Dad* were inked across his fingers, with a single teardrop etched on his right cheek. He looked down at his cell mate. Chester wanted to hit him until he killed him. Why? For fun.

It would amuse him.

Not only that, he'd love to see what the man's heart looked like. Being good on the inside was hard: when you hurt an inmate there were minor consequences, making the violence moreish.

He wasn't even sure he wanted his freedom. He could do all the malevolent things his heart desired in prison, not to mention get his hands on anything.

"When I get back in 'ere, I'm going to batter the fuck out of you, Gary. I'll rip your fucking heart out, and paint the walls with your blood, piss and shit!" Chester said, getting in the other man's face.

Gary cowered on his bed. He wasn't one for confrontation.

"What's the matter, Gary?" He watched the man clutch his cock. "Are we going to play water sports?" He laughed.

"I 'aven't done anything to you, man. *Please!*"

"Oh, I'll leave you for now, but I'll be back, Gary. As soon as I've taken care of what needs to be done outside. There's a pig that needs its throat cutting!" He winked.

"*Aarggh*," he whimpered, as Chester put his hand on his face and patted it lightly.

"You will keep my cell tidy, won't you?"

All Gary could do was nod. "*Please*," he begged, holding his privates tighter. "I need to piss, man!"

"Then go! Toilet's there, *pussy!*"

Gary went to get up, but Chester pushed him back down.

"I *need* a piss!"

"You'll have to get past me first."

"*Nailfree!*" a guard yelled as he raked his keys along the bars to Chester's cell. "What the *fuck* are you doing, Nailfree? Jeopardising your freedom, is it?"

"No, sir," Chester said with arrogance in his tone. "I was helping young Gary to the toilet. Just doing my part, sir. That's all." He turned to face Thornebank, who was one of many warders at Cardiff prison.

"Over here, Nailfree, and be sharp about it!"

"Yes, sir!" Chester picked up his prison shirt and put it on. "Come to release me, sir?" Behind him, Gary jumped off his bed and dashed to the toilet. A gush of piss splashed the pan as he relieved himself. "Sounds like Gary was just in time!" He smiled.

"Any more lip out of you and I'll make sure you never leave this cave you call a home, lad!" Thornebank said.

"Understood."

"It better be! Now, come here," the warder demanded.

After being escorted to processing, Chester had been given his clothes and personal belongings back. He stripped out of his prison fatigues and changed into his jeans and T-shirt.

"Feels good!" he said.

Once he'd gone through the rigmarole, Chester had been led outside to the exit by three guards.

"On your best behaviour, lad," Thornebank warned. "If you come back, I'll personally see to it that you never walk or eat normal again!"

"Yeah, you little prick," one of the other guards uttered from behind the massive Thornebank.

"*Understood*?" Thornebank pressed Chester by getting in his face.

"Yes, Sir! But I have a feeling we'll be seeing each other sooner than you think, pal," Chester said, turning to walk out the open door to freedom.

Across the road there was a car waiting from him, its engine idling. Chester made his way over to it.

The heavy door to the jail slammed shut at his back.

Behind the wheel of the car was Janice – his fuck buddy.

In the back sat Griff, Janice's brother and Chester's partner-in-crime; the man who had helped Chester pull off many a daring and dangerous job over the years.

"What a sight for sore fucking eyes," Chester exclaimed. He leaned through her open window and stroked Janice's face.

She had this weird, yet sexy sixties look going on, complete with a scarf around her head and dodgy-looking white shades: she had Gothic sleeves down both her arms and her nose, lip and ear were pierced. Bright pink lipstick graced her blowjob lips. *The only downside*, Chester thought, *she wears too much make-up. Hell of a fucking body, though! Legs as long as a desert road.*

"Not so bad yourself, chick," Janice said, snapping her gum and winking at him from over the top of her shades.

"Gin, man?" Griff asked, taking a swig from the bottle before presenting it out of the window.

"Don't mind if I do, Griff!" he said, snatching the bottle off the buck-toothed man and guzzling the clear fluid. "Fuck, tastes good!" He threw the empty container over the car's roof. It hit a wall and burst.

"Ha-ha!" Griff bellowed.

"Shit, Chester! They'll drag your arse back inside if you're not careful!" Janice complained.

"Fuck, em!" he screamed, turning to face the prison and grabbing his balls. "You can suck on these, you fucking wankers!"

Griff laughed.

Chester turned and ran at the car, hopping onto the bonnet and sliding over it. He landed on his feet the other side and got into the beat-up Ford Fiesta. "I've missed you," he told Janice, giving her pert tits a squeeze and kissing her on the lips. "I bet your pussy's wet for me."

"Ha-ha! You'd love that, wouldn't you, you filthy beast?" she said, slapping his hand away from between her legs.

"Woooo-hoooo!" Griff screamed. "Tap that bitch!"

"*Griff!*" Janice said, starting the engine. "Where to?" she asked Chester.

"There's a few things I need to do," he told her.

"Right, okay…" Janice said. "Are you going to enlighten me, chick? We can't sit here all day."

"I know. I'm thinking. Griff?"

"Yeah, man?"

"Did you see that big fucking guard I came out with?"

"Yeah, he looked as though he was giving you shit!"

"That's the one. I want you to keep an eye on him – let me know when he leaves. Follow him home and get his address. Got it?"

"Of course. But why?"

"Because I'm going to kill the motherfucker, that's why. Have you got a mobile?"

"Yeah."

"Great. Do you have Janice's number?"

He nodded. "Yes."

"When that fucking screw leads you to his home, I want you to ring Janice and let her know where you are. Right?"

Griff nodded again.

"Okay, then get the fuck out and stay vigilant. I'm not going to be best pleased if you let him out of your sight," Chester said, putting his arm between the passenger's and driver's seats. He grabbed Griff by his hair and pulled him forward. "I'm counting on you, little man."

"*Aarrrgh*! I got it, Chester."

"Good. And no more texting your sister rude messages and pictures of your small cock."

"But…" he started, then turned red and lowered his head.

"She's told me everything, you fucking pervert! Now, get the fuck out. I expect to hear from you soon."

"Got it." Griff whined and rubbed his scalp. "You'll come and get me as soon as I get the info?" he asked Chester through Janice's open window.

"Yes, mate. Just give us a bell and let us know where you are. We'll be there as soon as possible."

"We get to have some…fun…?" Griff asked.

"Just like the old days," Chester said. This brought a smile to the other man's face. "Now, go! And keep watch. Love you, man."

"Love you too, Chest," Griff said.

"Janice, step on it," he told her, giving her thigh a squeeze.

In the rear-view mirror, Chester saw Griff standing in the road, his form shrouded in exhaust smoke.

"Killing *coppers*?!" Janice asked. "Are you out of your fucking mind, Chester?"

"He's no copper. He's a screw and a fucking *cunt*!"

"Come on, baby. We've never harmed a person with that kind of authority!"

"Well, maybe being inside for ten years has helped change me. So, you better get fucking used to it."

"Why?"

"I also have a copper on my hit list."

"Who?" Janice asked.

"The fucker who put me away. I need to find out where he lives."

"How are we going to do that?!"

"First of all, I need you to drive me to Bridgend. That's where he was based. You must remember him? He was at my trial."

"Vaguely."

"He was all smiles and dimples, the fucking pig. I'll cut that smile out of him!"

"How do you plan on finding him? He might not be on the force any longer. He might be dead or moved away."

"First things first, take me to Bridgend," he said, ignoring her. "I want to get some new clothes. Also, there's a spaced-out junkie living there who owes me a great deal of money."

Janice nodded. "Okay, baby. Then?"

"Then we grab ourselves a pig."

"Ha!" Janice said, and then squealed.

"What the *fuck*'s so funny?"

"We're just going to grab a wooden-top off the streets?"

"Have you got spuds in your ears?!" he snapped.

"In broad *daylight*?!" she pushed back.

"Yeah, sounds about right."

"Ha-ha, you're nuts!"

"That's why you love me," he said.

"True."

"We'll make sure to corner a lone officer. There's some pretty rough shitholes in Bridgend. We'll be fine, you wait and see."

"I'm not bothered. You know deep down it drives me wild, baby. Let's get to that friend of yours first. Sort him out," she said, pressing the accelerator harder.

Chapter 5

DI Dylan Cope sat in the passenger seat of his unmarked car. Officer Gregson was behind the wheel. In the back was Officer Peters. They were two fresh-faced PCs mere weeks out of training, and this was their first major assignment.

They sat opposite a large building that used to be a pub. Dylan could remember the place being operational, but knew the doe-eyed pair with him wouldn't.

He smiled at that thought.

"Do you know what this place used to be, sir?" Gregson asked. "It looks a right shitehole!"

His potty mouth went unnoticed by Dylan. He was no saint either. "It used to be a club. The Kit-Kat Club, back in the day," he said, looking up at the building's top windows. The unbroken ones were either boarded or concreted over. The lower ones and doors were covered by sheet metal. Chains, bolts and padlocks kept children, homeless and troublemakers out.

"Kit-Kat Club? In other words, a place for underage pussy to go!" Gregson said, breaking Dylan's thoughts.

"More than likely, Gregson," Dylan said, smiling at the young officer's way with words. Hell, he'd been a young cop once. *You can't rollock them for everything. Besides, Gregson's probably right – every tramp in Swansea would have fucked their way through this place on the weekends back when it was booming.*

"You really think it's a drug house, sir?" Peters chirped in. "I mean, wouldn't we have noticed by now?"

"Well, you would have thought so, Peters. I mean, surely there'd be a strong stench coming from inside. Wouldn't it waft up the chimney?"

"Exactly, sir. I'm not sure I buy it."

"The source I had it from was good. One of my best snitches."

"Must be right, then," Gregson butted in. "If not, we can lock him up for wasting police time. Maybe give him a few sly digs when nobody's looking?!"

"We'll do no such thing, Gregson."

"I was only joking around."

"I should think so, too," Dylan snapped. "We have to conduct ourselves in a professional manner, no matter how much we want to break their skulls." He could see Peters smiling in the rear-view mirror. "I see you agree, officer?"

The man bowed his head. "I believe in fair justice."

"*Fair*?! That's a laugh," Gregson blurted.

"What do you mean?" Dylan asked, not taking his eyes off the dilapidated building. He noticed that most of the roof had caved in. A rope ladder could be seen dangling down from a second-floor window that was uncovered. *Someone's definitely using the building, even if it isn't to cook drugs. Maybe Jack Snitch had it wrong?* Dylan thought. *Maybe the old nightclub is full of homeless people?* Or 'trolls', as he'd seen them referred to in books he'd read.

"Take this, for instance," Gregson said.

"This job we're on. If, and I do mean *if*, that place is crawling with druggies and drug dealers, then think about what they've been getting up to? Didn't your snitch tell you that they've been pushing to schoolchildren – sixth formers?"

"That's right," Dylan said. "School children. And any other person they can find to buy their rubbish."

"Then why should they get *fair* justice?" Gregson asked. "People like that – the scum – should be hung, if you ask me."

"And I agree," Dylan said. "But we have orders and procedures."

"Yeah, I know. It just makes me sick," Gregson said.

Peters said nothing.

"Most coppers feel the same, trust me," Dylan said. "Now, we'll give it another thirty minutes and see if anyone comes or goes. If not, we'll go knocking."

"Okay, sir," Gregson said.

"Do you have the warrant, Peters?" Dylan asked.

"Yes, sir."

"Good. Now, just a little bit longer, and then over we go. It would be handy to catch them dealing," Dylan said.

After another thirty minutes in the car, with little conversation between them, Dylan decided it was time to kick the doors down. Making arrests as big as this drove him – gave him plenty of vigour for the job.

At the start of his career, when he had been slightly younger than the two with him, Dylan had already climbed up the ranks. He'd made DI by the time he was thirty, much to the infuriation of most of his colleagues. He didn't care, though. The words of his mother would always echo in his mind, whenever he thought about people talking behind his back. "*You're not there to make friends. You're there to work. You don't have to live with 'em!"*

"So true, Mother," he uttered under his breath.

"Sir?" Gregson asked.

"Nothing, just remembered something. Right, Peters. Hand me the warrant."

"Here you go, sir," the young PC said, thrusting the piece of paper between the front seats.

"Thanks. Now, when Gregson and I leave the car, I want you to stay here. I may need you to radio HQ for back-up, if we should find anyone or anything. I'm still not totally convinced," he said.

Getting out of the car, Dylan adjusted his trousers. "Come along, Gregson," he called over his shoulder.

As Dylan approached the club doors, he noticed there was no getting in the front. "I don't think we're going to need that warrant," he said. "I'm not sure the owners of this place are going to be here."

"Agreed," Gregson said. "Maybe I should go around back?!"

"I'll come with you. There's nothing to see here, not even a window can be looked through. *Wait*!" he blurted, spotting the letterbox, which had most of its steel guarding peeled back.

"What is it, sir?"

"Maybe I'll be able to hear something from inside," he said, bending close to the letterbox. From inside, it sounded like a graveyard. Nothing. Not even a groan of a board or a whistle of wind.

Dylan shook his head. "Okay, around back we go."

Gregson nodded.

Finding an alley between the pub and the opposite building, Dylan was first down it. The track was smashed and lined with potholes. Muddy water filled the cavities. "Watch your step, Gregson."

The squeak of rats could be heard as they plundered nearby wheelie bins and rubbish which littered the floor. "What's that stench?!" Gregson blurted.

"*Shh!*" Dylan said. "Keep your voices low!"

Making it to the back of the building, Dylan noticed there were many openings to the structure. Half the windows mid-way up were uncovered, their glass smashed. All back doors and fire exits, along with lower floor windows, were covered. The building loomed over them, reminding Dylan of an old fort. Its corners were sharp, the brickwork worn and missing plaster in places. "Right, okay," Dylan said. "As quickly and as quietly as you can, jump onto the bin over there and get yourself through that open window."

"Okay, sir," Gregson whispered. "And then?"

"Once inside, use this."

"What is it, sir?"

"Lock picking tools. I want you to open that door," he said, pointing at the fire exit in front of them.

"Slightly unorthodox."

"Yes, so it'll be our little secret."

"Anything you say, sir." Gregson made his way over to the bin. Dylan watched as his man hoisted himself through the window like some cat burgling expert.

"Well done, that man," Dylan said under his breath.

After five minutes, Dylan started to wonder about his man. *What if Gregson has been captured? Or he's hurt himself? Possibly fallen? Shit, I should have thought this through before sending him up there. It doesn't take this long…* His raging thoughts came to a halt on hearing the rattle of bolts from behind the door.

Good lad, he thought.

As Gregson slowly and quietly pulled the doors apart, Dylan had to fight to keep a straight face. "It's

Casper the friendly ghost!" he whispered on seeing Gregson, who was covered from head-to-foot in chalk.

The PC said nothing, apart from briskly snapping his head backwards in a gesture of 'quick, come and see!'

Losing his grin, Dylan crossed to Gregson. The reek coming from inside the building was foul.

"I don't think we're going to find anyone. Well, nobody *living*," Gregson said, pointing his flashlight over to the other side of the room.

Crumpled in a heap, with a sack over its head, was a body. Another three lay by its side.

"Jesus Christ!" Dylan uttered. "Right, go and get Peters. We're going to need more man-power to search this place."

"Okay, sir."

"Also, tell him to call for back-up and an ambulance. I'll wait here until you return. Don't be long."

Gregson bolted through the door and into the lane they had used to gain access to the pub's rear.

Inside, Dylan walked close to the bodies. Removing the Hessian sack off the first one's head, he recoiled at the sight of brain matter and bone oozing from the three bullet holes. Most of the victim's mouth was missing. Using his torch, he found three tongues had been nailed to the floor, along with a matching number of scrota.

Using his light, he lowered it to the nether regions of the first victim. His lower half was bare. His privates had been hollowed out; so too had the bodies' privates next to it. Along with the scrota and tongues, fingers and toes were also missing.

"Who would do such a vile thing? I've seen some pretty sick and weird things, but this has got to be a first!" he uttered. He removed his handkerchief from his pocket and dabbed at his face.

Then he saw the beams from other flashlights as Peters and Gregson walked into the Kit-Kat Club. It appeared they were standing in a downstairs bar – most of the tables and chairs had been knocked over. Splashes of blood lined the walls and decorated the flooring.

"Oh, Jesus!" Peters gagged. He put one hand to his mouth and nose.

"Not quite," Dylan said. "Did you call for backup?"

"Yes," Gregson said. His face was scrunched into a painful-looking expression.

"You'll get used to this," he told them. "Try not to touch anything."

"What would you like us to do, sir?" Gregson asked.

"I want you two to seal off any escape routes until backup arrives, and then split up and search this entire floor. I'm going to the top. We'll meet in the middle. Got it?"

"Yes, sir," Peters said.

"Good. Now, off you go. And if you do find something, use your radio. I'll come to you."

He turned his back to the young coppers and made his way over to the stairs, which were situated by the bar. Glass, broken chairs and other debris littered the floor, crunching and splintering underfoot.

He shone his torch on the wall by the staircase and noticed a message written in shit. *"Revenge… Larceny will not go unpunished…"*

"I guess it didn't," Dylan said, placing one foot on the first step. The boards creaked and groaned under his weight. With his flashlight's beam leading the way. He was ready for an unseen threat.

The job had toughened him up to surprises, broken bones, abuse and blood.

Besides, backup wouldn't be long arriving.

Whoever did this, he thought, *was cold and calculated. We're either dealing with gang rivalry or this lots' boss got really fucking pissed off. Mind you, a few less junkies in the world is a good thing!*

Getting to the top of the staircase, Dylan stopped. He was met by another bar. This one was bigger, consisting of a massive dance floor and two sets of toilets. After inspecting all areas, including the abandoned DJ station, Dylan moved on. There was nothing of interest.

He climbed a second flight of stairs and took the steps two at a time. He was convinced the building was empty. Also, he'd not heard anything from his PCs down in the main bar. From outside, he could hear reinforcements arrive.

"Thank God for that," he said, reaching the second floor. "I was starting to think…" His words trailed off. Something was moving around up here.

Sweeping his torch from side to side, he noticed a handful of closed doors. Going to and opening the first one, he was greeted with a bare room. Leaving the door open, he went to the next. That too was empty, along with the third, fourth and fifth.

When he opened the door to the final room, which looked as though it had served as an office along with the growing and harbouring of drugs, Dylan was met with six bodies. A seventh was crawling away from the dead. Bullet wounds were evident in his back.

Dylan stepped into the room. A board creaked, and the injured person spoke.

"Please, l-l-leave…leave…" he managed. He left a slimy red trail in his wake. "I-I-I…" He coughed up a stream of blood. When he tried to speak again, his head hit the floor.

Dead.

"*Fuck*!" Dylan blurted. His heart galloped as he collapsed against the door he'd come through. On further inspection, he could see the poor bastards lying dead on the floor also had their entrails ripped out. More tongues, toes, fingers and privates were scattered about the floor.

The inside of the room stank.

Dylan pulled his radio free. "Get up here!" he barked at the two officers downstairs. "Quick. We have a situation. Bring help."

He heard footsteps thunder up the staircase.

"I'm on the top floor," he bellowed.

The rushing feet didn't need telling twice. Before Dylan knew it, four officers stood around him.

"Look!" he said, shining his torch on the massacre before them. "That one there–" he pointed at the body that had been moving "–was just talking to me. Get a medic up here, pronto."

"Right away, sir!" Peters said, rushing off.

"I just realised something," Gregson said.

"What?" Dylan asked.

"This lot – I know their faces. I've seen them before. One of their lot was released from prison earlier today."

"*Who*?!" Dylan asked.

"Chester Nailfree. That bastard's notorious. He dealt drugs here in Swansea, Cardiff and Bridgend. I think this lot were part of his crew. We were told about his release date."

"Good work, Gregson," Dylan said. "Get on the radio – I want to know everything there is to know about Chester Nailfree. I also want his movements since he was released this morning."

"I'll get right on it, sir."

"Good," Dylan said.

Leaving his team inside the building, Dylan made his way out to his car. By now, blue lights flooded the street and uniforms from every emergency service swarmed like ants on a carcass. He gulped in clean fresh air, not that the stench bothered him.

"Maybe I'm finally getting too old for this shit!" he uttered, then smiled. "Nah, never."

As he watched his men rush about the place to cordon the area off, the crackling of his car radio brought him out of his musing. "Now what?" he said, sighing.

Dylan bent into the car and unhooked the radio. "This is DI Cope, do you read me?"

"Sir, people have been reported missing. Two railroad workers and a member of the council," the female voice said.

"Have you sent a unit? Over."

"No, sir. Over."

"Then why are you calling this car?" Dylan said, annoyance in his voice.

"I thought Officers Gregson and Peters were closer to the incident."

"They're not, dispatcher. Send someone else. Officers Gregson and Peters are busy."

"Understood, sir," the dispatcher said.

"And another thing: how long have they been missing?"

"Since this morning, sir."

"This morning?! Good grief! Send a unit."

"Understood, sir."

The radio fell quiet.

"A building full of dead dealers and now three missing people. What next, a shower of toads? Rivers of blood?!" he muttered, throwing the radio's mic aside.

Chapter 6

Her father pulled up outside their house and her stomach sank. Storm didn't know whether to go through with it or not. She and her dad had barely spoken on the short journey home, and she could feel his apprehension, as he no doubt could sense her rage.

Her hands shook.

What am I going to say to the woman? Call her Mammy? she thought scornfully. *How could Dad put me in such a position?*

Huw sighed. "Look, I don't want to have to put you through this, but…"

"Then why are you, Dad? After everything that *bitch* has done to us!"

"*Shh*! Don't swear like that in front of Stevie, love."

"I'm sorry. It's just…I don't want to see her, Dad. I hate her for what she did to you. To *us*!"

"It was a long time ago, Storm. I've since moved on. I'd hoped that you had too," Huw said. "I'm certainly not doing it for her, love. I'm just trying to do the right thing."

"Why has she come back?"

"I'm not sure. I haven't got the full story yet. But it does seem like she's been feeling guilty for years. And, since her latest marriage has broken down, she thought she'd come and see us."

"*Huh*. Feeling a bit lonely, is she?" Storm said.

Huw shook his head. "I know how you must feel, Storm. What bloody right does she have, coming back into our lives, right? But it's not just that, love. She heard about the whole incident we went through. She was worried."

"Oh, how considerate of the woman!"

"She's still your mother," Huw said. "The only one—"

"That woman is no mother of mine!" Storm wanted to slap her father's face. *How could he let her back into our lives? Especially after everything that's happened. Now is not a good time for this. Dad and I have been through enough*, she thought. *Fucking woman*. "I need a smoke," she said.

"Weed for medicinal purposes, hey?"

"Now's not the time to get on my back about smoking, Dad. Please. *God*!"

"I wasn't going to say anything, apart from, 'Give me a drag!'" He winked.

"Did you lose your prudish ways all of a sudden?"

"I've learned life is too short to have a stick permanently stuck up my backside," he quipped.

She could see the pain in his eyes and so put her arms out for a hug. He pulled her head onto his chest.

"We'll get through this, love. I promise. All she wants is a chance to talk. To see if she can repair some of the damage."

"It's going to take a lot, Dad. I mean, she's a complete stranger to me. How did you react when you saw her?"

"I was shocked, and then I wanted to slam the door in her face."

"It's the least she deserves," Storm said.

"I know. I just couldn't bring myself to do it."

"Yep. You're soft. Especially in your old age!"

"Cheers!" he said. "Besides, we've got nothing to be ashamed of. It's all on her."

She sighed, and then looked at her front door. "I don't want her here long, Dad."

"That's fine."

"Does she know about Stevie?"

Huw nodded.

"Does she know…"

"I didn't go into it with her. You don't have to tell her anything–"

"It's not like she can judge!"

"I know," he said. "And, as far as anyone around here's concerned, now that Scuzz's parents have moved away, that little girl was his. And that's what we're going to tell Mam."

"Skye," Storm corrected. "You don't want her thinking your little girl is a slut for getting knocked-up by a guy she didn't know?!"

"I don't blame you for going a little wild, love. We were both going through a hard time."

Thinking she saw the living room curtain twitch, Storm shot a look in that direction. She could see a shadow behind the netting. "I don't think I can face her, Dad. Does she even deserve to meet her grandchild?"

"Questions only you can answer, love. If you don't want to go in there, then that's fine – I'll turf her out and tell her to never return."

"I think your days of roughhousing people are numbered, Dad. Especially with that gammy back of yours!" she said, snorting a laugh whilst continuing to wipe tears from her eyes.

"You think so, do you?!"

"Yep. You even failed to notice her keeping her beady eyes on us from beyond the living room curtains!" A snigger escaped her.

"*Where*?" He then pretended to desperately seek the woman out.

"She's receded further into *our* home, no doubt. We'll have to get Rentokil in to have her removed!" Storm said.

Huw stifled a laugh to let Storm know exactly what he thought of the idea. "Enough of that," he said, trying to sound serious. "Come on, let's get it over with. If we stay out here much longer, Skye is going to think we don't want to see her."

"You're hilarious," she said dryly.

Undoing his seatbelt, he then opened his door. The sun was starting to burn out of the day, which was a relief. Huw didn't like the heat. "Thank God it's starting to cool down," he said, wiping sweat from his brow. "I can't stick it."

"Same here," Storm said. Her movements were lethargic, and not because of the heat. She had no idea what she was going to say to Skye. To the woman who had abandoned them when she was a baby. *You never get over something like that*, Storm thought. *It's been three fucking years since I was snatched. I'd never call her in an emergency!*

Storm unfastened the belt from around Stevie and removed her from the car. She cradled her against her chest. "Dad, can you grab my bag and her things, please?"

The rage building inside her must have been clear on her face.

"Try not to tear into her too much in front of Stevie, love. Okay?"

"I'll try my best, Dad. But I'm not promising much."

"Perhaps it'll be best if I give Stevie a bottle, and then put her down for an hour. That way, we can all have a decent chat. To 'clear the air', as my mother would say."

"Sounds good."

Huw nodded and slipped his key into the door lock. Turning it, he pushed the door open. "Hello?" he called, edging his way in. "Skye, I'm back…"

Storm held her breath.

It was weird being back in the house again. It had been close to twenty years since she'd been behind these walls. Huw had told her, "Make yourself at home – you know where the kitchen is! Where the milk and teabags are kept." He'd taken her return well.

Serenely.

Her daughter would *not* be so forgiving.

Then again, she supposed Huw would have been more forgiving. He was aware of what was going on at the time – the arguing, the snipes and the cruel little digs…Neither of them had been prepared for a child.

She had been young and stupid, with Huw working hard to advance his career. When she'd first met him, he had been unsure about a relationship. But, like her, he had got caught up in it and fell in love. The following year, they had married.

She looked at the photos Huw had along the mantle-piece. Most of the framed memories were of him and Storm. They made her sad. She'd missed out on a lot. She was probably dead to her daughter.

"You're so pretty," she said to one of the pictures. Her daughter was no longer a child, but a young woman; a woman of striking beauty and intelligence. Huw had told her all about Storm's thirst for drawing, and how their daughter was in University studying art.

"I should have come back sooner," she told the image. The photo looked as though it had been taken at a gig. Storm was wearing a heavy metal T-shirt, her hair dyed many colours. In one hand, she held a beer. In the other, a CD, which appeared signed.

Skye picked the photo up. *I wonder if Huw would let me keep this one?*

Skye replaced it. She knew she didn't deserve anything concerning her daughter. Did she even have the right to refer to Storm as her daughter? She wasn't sure. She certainly wasn't going to refer to Storm as such to her face.

This will take time, she thought. *That's if Storm even wants to bother. I've been so foolish.*

She thought back to the day she left. She remembered it well. It was snowing – something it hadn't done in south Wales in over a year prior. Reports on the weather had said it would last for over a month, but it fizzled out after two weeks. After coming to the decision of leaving, Skye had left Huw and Storm a goodbye letter.

The coward's way out, she thought.

Huw had been due home at eight that evening, with Skye leaving the house at seven-thirty. She didn't feel guilty about leaving her daughter alone in the house for half-an-hour then, but had over the years.

Things had fallen apart between her and Huw. Damage had been done. And, with a young child in the house, Skye had come away at the seams. She should have spoken to Huw. Told him how she'd felt.

Young and stupid.

"They are the only words for it. Why didn't I just come back?!" she scolded herself aloud again, continuing to look at her daughter's photo.

As the weeks, months and years had passed, shame stopped her from returning.

Before Huw had got the telephone number changed, Skye had often rang, but she never spoke, just listened. She liked hearing his voice and the sound of her daughter chattering in the background. This often resulted in a teary night for Skye.

He'd known it was her calling.

Once, catching her by surprise, Huw had barked, "If this is *you*, don't call here again!" She'd detected hurt in his angry tone.

Shortly after that, the number changed and Skye had tried to move on with her life in Carmarthenshire – she'd always wanted to move to west of Wales. However, turning over a new leaf had not been easy.

After getting a job in a library and setting up home in a rented bungalow, things seemed to be going well for Skye, or so she had thought. She even met a man. Someone who she thought cared for her.

But it turned sour.

Ethan, much like Huw, had been a career man. A driven, focused individual. And when Skye had fallen pregnant, *again*, he'd become abusive. Had hurt her. Broken her jaw and right arm.

She hadn't had the courage to leave him.

Not even after six months of abuse.

After he found out she was not going to abort the child, Ethan had left her, taking the savings from their joint account and fleeing the country.

Once he'd gone, Skye had thought things would get better. How wrong she'd been. *I guess the past has a nasty way of catching up with you, especially when you've done something shitty*, she thought.

The stillbirth of her child had been fracturing. In the months that followed, she lost her job and home and had to move back in with her parents, who'd welcomed her with open arms. They'd been the ones to push her into getting in touch with Huw. To try and make things right.

When she heard the front door open, Skye's breath caught in her throat.

Suddenly, her head emptied, her planned speech lost. Sweat broke across her brow. Her palms were clammy. She heard Huw call, but she couldn't answer. She'd gone rigid.

Hearing them come through the door, Skye replaced a second photo she'd picked up. Turning, she faced them with a smile. A tear slid down her face. *She's even more striking in the flesh!* she thought. *Huw's heavy metal interests have clearly worn off on her. I love the dreads.*

"Hi," she managed to say. Her daughter showed little emotion. "I'm sure you have a lot of questions…"

"Dad, do you mind taking Stevie out to the kitchen and giving her a feed as planned, please?"

"Of course, love," he said, taking Stevie from off Storm. "You pair have a lot to talk about."

The slap Storm issued her mother was deafening.

"*Ow!*" Skye said, putting a hand to her face.

"*Storm!*" Huw blurted.

Storm turned on her father. "No, Dad. She's going to listen to what I have to say. I need to get this off my chest. So please, take Stevie out to the kitchen."

He nodded, and then left to let the women get on with it.

Chapter 7

He looked, unimpressed, at the view around him as he was chauffer-driven through Blaengarw in his Bentley.

He'd been putting the trip off for two years.

No man had ever had that kind of power of persuasion over him.

After all, he'd had a lot of money tied up in Lawrence, his ex-employee. One hundred thousand pounds, to be exact. Now, the money was not the point, it was the principle. If Lawrence *had* perished as told by DI Davies, then where had the hitman's personal belongings gone, such as the money he'd given him? *Someone must have scooped it,* Mr. Gibson thought.

But it wasn't about the money.

It was about the truth.

The DI had told him that Lawrence had died helping him recover his daughter. *I wonder*, Mr. Gibson thought, *if the DI knew he was a target just by being in the way?* He smiled at this.

After the loss of Lawrence, Mr. Gibson had been told the 'situation' was over, and that there was no need for him to travel down. As the months and conversations with Huw on the telephone had passed, Mr. Gibson started to accept the fact it was over, and that Lawrence was never coming back.

The loss of such a good employee had hurt.

Lawrence had most certainly been the best in my stable, Mr. Gibson thought. *A fine man, too. Polite. Well practised.*

"We're approaching, sir."

"How long, Ross?"

"Ten minutes tops, Mr. Gibson."

"Thank you, Ross," he told his henchman before raising the glass which parted the front and back of the car. As much as he liked the two up front, he preferred his own company. Besides, Ross and Ken had not been on his payroll for long. This was their first big outing. It was a risk, coming such a distance with new guards, but they needed bloodying.

Even though he was far from home, he had clients, workers and contacts everywhere. In fact, in Swansea, he had a drug factory in his pocket, which made him a pretty penny. This was one of many outlets across Wales he owned, or part-owned. He wasn't just into distributing drugs, but guns too, and trafficking women.

The weapons and girls were traded overseas, not in Wales. His empire had been growing since he was fifteen years old. "Good God. What a dump!" he uttered. He couldn't believe how rundown the south was.

Pushing the intercom, he spoke to his guards. "Gents, we need to make a stop in Swansea before heading home," he said, letting the button go on the intercom. "Best I call in on Carl, see how things are doing."

He removed his mobile from his pocket and speed-dialled Carl's number. It rang several times before it was answered. "Ah, Carl!" he exclaimed. "How the devil are…*What*?! When did this happen? They're all dead…? Do we know who's responsible? Yes, I see…I hope you haven't lost my money, Carl? That would be very disappointing…Good, I'm glad to hear it. Can the workers be replaced? The police are involved?! Damn it!" he cursed, slamming his fist against his door's interior. "This is most displeasing. I'll be making a visit later today…Make sure you have some good news for me." He snapped his phone shut.

The partition window slid down. "Everything okay, Mr. Gibson?"

"Not really, Ken."

"Anything we can do?" Ross asked.

"Yes. That call we have to make in Swansea? It's not going to be able to wait," Mr. Gibson said.

"Will it be a messy visit?" Ross asked.

"Rather possible."

"Good," Ross said, cracking is knuckles.

"It would seem my business in Swansea has been closed down by a heavy-handed third-party," Mr Gibson said. "After you drop me off, I want you pair to go to Swansea and find out what's happened, okay?"

"Anything, boss," Ken said.

"You'll report to me as soon as you've had a chat with Carl. Make sure the police don't see you."

"Got it, sir," Ross said.

"Is this the street we're after?"

Mr. Gibson looked out his window. "Yes, it is. I'm sure the good DI is going to be more than pleased to see me," he said, beaming.

Ken pulled the car over to the kerb and parked in front of the right house. "There you go, sir," he said, bringing the car to a complete stop. When the engine died, Ross hopped out and opened his boss' door.

"Thank you, Ross," Mr. Gibson said. "Please, wait by the car a moment. I can't see there being any trouble, but stay close just in case."

He stepped away from his car and knocked on Huw's front door. Something caught his attention. There was shouting coming from within. He put his ear to the door. "Oh, dear," he uttered. "I do believe I'm about to burst in on a domestic." He chuckled. "Good." He gave the door five more hard cracks, which made the letterbox rattle.

The noise from within stopped.

Silence.

"Jesus, how long does it take these people to answer their front door? Have they no manners?!" he raged. He was about to knock again when a large male opened the door. He was younger than himself, but not by many years. "The good DI, I presume?"

"Look, mate, I'm not sure what you're selling, but best come back," Huw said. Over his shoulder, the row continued.

"Where the fuck were you when I needed you, *Skye*?!"

"Don't call me that – I'm your mother!"

"'Mother'. That's a fucking joke!"

Huw winced. "See what I mean?"

"It would seem you have your hands full, Mr. Davies."

A strange look came over the ex-DI's face.

I think he's worked it out, Mr. Gibson thought.

"Do I know you, mate?" Huw asked. "Your voice sounds…Hang on…You're…No, it can't be!"

"Believe it, Huw, because it's me. Mr. Gibson. Lawrence's boss. Well, *ex-boss*, I should say," he said, trying to push past Huw.

"Hey, hang on a moment," Huw said, putting his hand firmly to the gangland boss' chest. On doing this, Huw noticed the heavies by the Bentley, which was parked outside his house. "You can't just come barging in here. You didn't even let me know you were coming!" he said, removing his hand from the man's chest.

"I didn't think I needed permission to come, Huw. I have unfinished business."

"What business is that, exactly? I told you, everything was taken care of two years ago. Lawrence and I sorted it. He helped me massively, in fact. I've told you all this time and again," Huw stressed.

"I would much rather discuss it in the comfort of your home, DI"

"It's not DI any longer," Huw said.

"Promotion? You never said—"

"I quit," Huw said flatly. "After what happened, I couldn't bring myself to go back."

"I see. Well, we can chat about it over a cup…"

"Look, Mr. Gibson, I don't wish to be rude, but I've had an unexpected surprise today, which you can hear going on in the background."

"I'm not really concerned about that, Huw. If I may call you Huw?"

"Of course. Not that telling you no would make a difference."

"I have matters I need to iron out. Things I didn't want to discuss over the phone. I've put this trip off long enough. Now, let's talk it over inside," Mr. Gibson demanded. "I've come a long way. Please don't disappoint me."

"Fine, but I'm not one of your dogs' bodies. Someone you think you can push around."

"I'm sure you're not, Huw. Please, may I?"

"*Huh*," Huw sighed. "Okay, I guess so."

"Thanks. I'll be right back," Mr. Gibson said, stepping away from the ex-copper.

He went back to his car and spoke with Ken. "Right, you pair. I want you to make your way to Swansea.

When you get there, find the old Kit-Kat Club – it's on South Street. You can't miss it."

"I think I know it," Ross said. "Didn't it close down around ten years ago due to a fire, sir?"

"That's right," he said. "Get there and don't make yourselves known. The place is probably jumping with police. Once there, call Carl. His number is on my phone." He gave Ken his mobile. "Tell him who you are, and that you want him to meet by the club. That you'll be parked close by. Got it?"

"Yes, sir," Ken said.

Mr. Gibson watched the car pull away before turning to face Huw once again. "We have much to talk about, Huw. I want to know everything. I also want to know what happened to Lawrence's personal belongings." He walked past the ex-copper and into his home. "A cosy little place you have here."

"Thanks," Huw said, closing the door.

Chapter 8

Looking up at the clock, Dr. Veech decided eight o'clock was late enough. Her last patient had left her office over an hour ago. She'd spent the time in between writing up case notes for the morning.

"Why can't you have a nine-to-five job like everyone else, Samantha?" She smirked. "Because Daddy would have been highly disappointed, that's why!" She huffed as she gathered her files on Storm and Huw Davies and stuffed them in her bag. She also picked up her notes from today's meeting with Storm – she would see what could be gleaned from them over a glass of wine.

"A doctor's job is never over," she said with a sigh.

Rolling her chair back, she closed the desk drawers before getting up and moving over to the coat stand. Once there, she took her jacket off one of the wooden pegs and then proceeded to the office door. Before knocking the lights off, she put her coat on and then locked the door.

Walking away from her office, she smiled at passers-by. The sound of songbirds in the trees and children at play around her made her feel good. She loved the summer nights. How time seemed to drag out with the sun in the sky for hours. *Not many more weeks of summer left,* she thought. *October looms!*

She saw mothers on their doorsteps, chatting as they watched over their children in the street. This had become common, ever since the incident in Blaengarw two years ago. And, even though her office was situated in Bridgend, it still scared the people here, close to ten miles away from where it had all happened.

She'd heard plenty of whispers. Whispers about the father and daughter she treated, and how they were harbouring a bastard child. Whispers about how the "monsters in the woods will have their day again."

"Poppycock," Dr. Veech muttered. "They're dead. Dead and gone. There's nothing out there. Not any longer. Huw and the others took care of business."

Getting to her car, she unlocked the driver's side door and threw her bag onto the passenger seat. Dr. Veech then got behind the wheel and put the key in the ignition. The small, one-point-four diesel engine kicked to life. She revved it, and black smoke coughed out. Before pulling away, she clicked the radio on, bringing the CD player to life – Lady GaGa started singing "Paparazzi".

Dr. Veech sang as she pulled her car out of her parking space. With both directions clear, she moved. The drive was a short one to her home. She was looking forward to getting in, kicking her shoes off, and having a hot soak in the tub. Wine, Chinese and chocolate called.

Then Storm popped into her mind. The incident in her office earlier today had been unusual. The girl had said it happened to her often, yet it was the first time she had experienced it with her patient.

"Odd," escaped her lips. "I'm not sure there's much more I can do for that child. I wonder what her dad has to say about it? If he's not going to pay me a visit, then maybe I should go to him? It's not like I'm embarrassed," she said, looking at her reflection in the rear-view. The crow's feet gathered at the sides of her eyes depressed her.

"You're getting old, Samantha. Is it my age? Is that what drove him away? I wonder if he's told Storm? Maybe that's why she's icy towards me…"

GaGa continued to drone on.

Slowing the car down, Dr. Veech took a left turn, and then a right. This brought her onto her quaint street, where the houses had low wooden fences and potted plants out front. It was a street where the neighbour's dog shit on the lawns and their cat was known by all.

Driving up her street, Dr. Veech waved at a woman jogging, then to a man tending the weeds and gnomes around his pond at the front of his house.

Bliss, she thought. *Even though I'm not quite home yet, just being on the street feels good. I've entered my bubble!*

She drove onto her driveway. Her home was the only bungalow on the street, which was envied by many, especially her next-door neighbours.

She killed the engine and removed her keys. Dr. Veech then opened her car door and grabbed her bag off the passenger seat. Once free of her car, she went into her house.

For a moment, she stood in the short, dark hallway and listened. She embraced the silence. The darkness. The heating had clicked on. The house was warm. Comfy-cosy warm.

Content, she flicked the light switch. The hall filled with a blinding glow. Dumping her bag, she took her heels off and rubbed her ankles one at a time. Once done, she walked into the bathroom to her left. There, she opened the window and started the bath before sitting on the toilet.

After relieving herself, she let the bath fill with hot water and went into her office. Dr. Veech placed her bag on her desk before unzipping her dress. Getting out of the garment, she then hung it on a hanger and placed it on the door.

She then removed her bra and knickers, and slipped into her robe. Happy, she switched her PC on and left for the kitchen. Once there, she put the kettle to boil and picked her phone up to order a Chinese meal.

She was told the food would take up to an hour to arrive, and so the doctor thought it best to bathe first. After pouring herself a mug of coffee, she went back to the bathroom, which was engulfed by steam, and switched off the hot tap. She then started the cold.

Taking her robe off, she tested the water by dipping her toes in. Pleased with the temperature, she got in. Before lowering herself, she put the lid to the toilet down and placed her mug on top of it.

"*Ahh!*" she gasped, laying back. "Now, what's to be done about Storm and her dad?" She closed her eyes. "Ah, the lovely Huw…" she mused, letting her mind drift. How she had *loved* him. If only he knew it. *Well, he had known it – I'd told him. Left him messages on his answer phone. Sent him texts, most of which went unanswered…*

His words still resonated through her: "*Samantha, I think what we had has run its course…*"

She flushed.

He'd bruised her.

Hurt her.

"*Look, I think we should keep this between us. I don't think Storm should ever know about our fling,*" he'd continued.

Fling! she thought. *How could he have said such a thing? It was love, pure and simple.* After splitting from Huw, she'd let it go, and stuck to her word. She hadn't told Storm – it would have been unprofessional. Her job could have been put at risk.

No, tactical play is the best.

As time passed, her feelings towards Huw had waned slightly, until Storm had told her that her dad was seeing a copper. *How could he? After only six months of parting from me!*

This had rekindled her feelings.

She'd forgotten how much she wanted him.

Needed him.

The old saying is true – out of sight, out of mind.

I must visit his room later, she thought. *That'll make me remember, even though it will hurt. After all, I love him. And you can't turn your back on love.*

Dr. Veech sat up, grabbed her mug and placed it to her mouth. She drank half its contents and then replaced it.

Best I start washing – food probably won't be much longer.

Taking the bottle of Radox off the edge of the bath, she uncapped it and squirted a load of green sludge into her hand. She lathered her body – moulded the aromatic liquid into her medium-sized breasts. She moaned with pleasure. Huw was still on her mind.

She wanted his touch.

Now.

Maybe I could call him later – pretend I need to speak with Storm about today's events. Yes, that's a good idea!

Lying back in the bath again, she pulled on the cord by her side, which started the jets in the tub. Bubbles popped and fizzed as she put Radox on her pussy. She stroked herself, teased herself into a mild orgasm, and then slipped two fingers inside her.

Huw had been the last man she'd had in her bed.

She writhed with the thought.

Her face flushed as she started gasping and panting.

The warmth about her aided her enjoyment.

Biting on her lip, she shuddered as a second orgasm rocked her.

"Oh, Huw," she uttered.

Stopping, Dr. Veech gave it a couple of moments before draining the water. Her thighs quivered, her breath short. After the giddiness subsided, she pulled the plug and stood.

Grabbing a towel from off the back of the door, she stepped out of the bath and secured it around her wet body.

"*Ugh!*" she blurted, draining the remainder of her tea, which had become cold. She exited the misty bathroom.

Going to the kitchen, she placed her mug in the sink, then turned to the fridge and removed the bottle of wine that had her name all over it. She poured herself a large glass just as there was a knock at her front door.

"Perfect timing," she said, smiling. Looking down at herself, she thought that maybe she should put some clothes on, but decided against it. "I could give the deliveryman a thrill!"

Taking her purse out of her bag in the kitchen she proceeded to the door which was now being thumped. "Hang on, hang on, I'm coming! Actually, I've already done that," she uttered, and then giggled like a schoolgirl.

When she reached the door and switched the hallway light on, a silhouette of a large figure could be seen through the glass. Turning the key in the lock, she pulled the door wide.

"At..." the delivery guy started, but his words fell short.

"Mmm, lovely!" Dr. Veech said, ignoring the roving eyes of the fat, balding deliveryman.

"You can say that again!"

"Excuse me?"

"Er, that'll be ten-pounds-fifty, please," he said. The poor light spared his blushes.

"That's fine." She put the food down by her side so she could dig the money out of her purse. "There you go." She handed the man a ten and five-pound note. "You can keep the change, dear," she said, poking a leg out from behind the towel. This gave him a glimpse of her neatly trimmed pussy.

The expression on his face was priceless.

She slammed the door on him. "What a pervert," she said, knocking the hallway light out as she left for the kitchen. "You can't seem to get away from them!" She chuckled. "Not like my Huw – he's a gentleman."

After finishing her Chinese meal, Dr. Veech turned the television off. The news was starting to depress her, what with the beheadings in Syria, missing schoolgirls, famine, The YES Campaign, etc.

It's enough to make you want to do a Sylvia Plath, she thought, putting her dish in the sink for washing. "I'll clean up in the morning," she uttered, picking up her glass of wine and heading to her office.

In the hallway again, she pushed at the latch in the ceiling, which dropped down, exposing an aluminium ladder. She drew the steps out and clicked them into place. She then headed into her office and picked up her laptop and case notes on Storm and Huw.

Going up the ladder, she knocked the light on in that room. Placing her things down on the desk up there, she sighed, then drank some wine. "Hello, Huw," she said, looking at the photos of the ex-policeman which graced her walls. Not an inch of space was uncovered.

She had taken the pictures herself. Some were from the time they'd spent together, but the majority had been captured when Huw had least expected it. They'd been hard to take, but well worth it. *If only he knew the love I harbour for him*, she thought, kissing one of the photos closest to her.

"My angel of love," she said, rubbing one hand against a breast. She quivered. She felt excited – *alive*, even. "You're mine. All mine," she whispered.

She needed to hear his voice. *Had* to. Looking at the clock, she saw it was almost ten o'clock. If she was going to ring, it would have to be now. It was going to seem weird, but that could not be helped.

Dr. Veech picked up Storm's file and went over to the only chair in the confined space. Her dad had converted the room for her to add more freedom to the small house.

She placed the file on her lap and entered Storm's home number – she had to check the 'personal details' section of the girl's file to make sure she was entering the right one.

It rang six times before Huw answered it. She couldn't believe her luck. He sounded disheartened.

"Hello?" he said flatly.

"Oh, hello – Huw?"

"Yes?" he said, his tone not changing.

"Hi. It's Samantha. Storm's doctor." She didn't know why she added the last part – maybe to make it look as though she knew he'd forgotten who she was.

"Oh, hey. A bit late to be making house calls, isn't it?" he said with annoyance in his tone.

"Erm, yes, well, I need to speak with Storm. It's rather urgent," she protested.

"Right, okay, but make it quick."

I knew I shouldn't have rung tonight. I've pushed my love further away, she scolded herself. "I'm sorry for calling at such a late hour, but…" She let her words trail off – she was speaking to nobody. Huw had gone to call his daughter. "Damn it!" she blurted, then fought the urge to smash the receiver against the desk.

Instead, she gripped the receiver as tight as she could, digging her nails into her palm. She then pulled her hair and slapped her face.

Storm's voice boomed down the phone.

"Hello?!"

"Oh, hey, hello. It's—"

"I know who it is. What do you want?!"

"Oh, I…" The mood which seemed to be coming from that household threw the doctor. "Is everything alright there?"

"Yes, I guess," Storm said.

"You know you can talk to me."

"I know. Look, what do you want?"

"I was just ringing to see how you were, after today's episode, and to see if you'd decided on going Saturday?"

"I've been better, but it's not to do with today at your office. My mother's back in town, and, to top it off, some heavy from the north of Wales has come to see my dad – it's all in connection with what happened to us two years ago."

"Oh," was all Dr. Veech could say.

"Yes, so it's been a bit of a strange day. Don't think our offish behaviour is a slur on you."

"That's okay. Look, I won't keep you – I'll see you Thursday. We can chat about it then?" Dr. Veech said, smiling.

"Cool. Oh, and regarding Saturday, we're going, as far as I'm concerned. I think you're right – it will exorcise a lot of demons," Storm said, hanging up.

A dull '*deeeerrrrrrr*' noise flooded the doctor's ear.

Standing, she screamed. "What the *fuck* is that *fucking cunting whore* of a mother doing back?!"

Dr. Veech hammered the phone against the desk until hunks of plastic, wiring and phone innards flew across the room. Bits ricocheted off her chest, face and forehead as she continued to yell and fume.

A huge shard of wood cracked and broke free from the table, making her smile. On seeing Storm's file on the floor, she went for that next. "I'll fucking show you, you little fucking tart!" Dr. Veech said, taking handfuls of notes from the file and shredding them. A guttural and somewhat primal snarl-growl pushed its way up from the pit of her guts – she threw the ripped paper about like confetti.

Not content, she went for her laptop. Not thinking about the work which was needed on it, she gripped the adaptor lead, which was plugged into the machine, and swung it around and around above her head. The light bulb smashed into tiny bits. A lamp was swiped off the desk.

"Fucking bitches! They're probably conspiring behind my back – that bitch PC Huw is seeing too! Probably having a right old fucking laugh. Wankers. *Fuckers*!" she continued to spit and seethe.

She let go of the cable. The laptop smashed against the wall – the screen instantly cracked. Going to it, she jumped up and down on it as though it was a bouncy castle. The plastic cracked, chipped and broke.

Breathless, Dr. Veech stopped, and looked at herself in the mirror perched on top of the desk. A rivulet of blood trickled down her face. She then noticed the huge split in the glass, which had probably been caused by a stray plastic missile.

Her tits heaved as she struggled for air. Pulling down her nightie, which had risen to her waist due to her flailing, she spoke to her reflection.

"They can plot as much as they like. Come Saturday night, Huw will be mine. He'll be reminded of the love he has for me. Of the love I have for him. And if anyone cares to get in the way, then they will be removed!"

Chapter 9

When night finally settled, Skull and Eight-Ball cooked the two men over their campfire. The roaring blaze rapidly heated the meat throughout, allowing them to devour as much as they could; their twins also greedily ate the fresh meat.

Their new member, however, refused.

Enraged, Skull stripped and beat her before lashing her hands together with rope and tying the other end to a high branch.

She would soon learn their ways and also breed with Skull, whether she liked it or not.

After his hearty meal of meat and blood, Skull felt much better. As though it was what his diet had been missing. *Maybe I not as weak as I thought*? he mused.

In the morning, he planned to go hunting. To see what he could find for their trip down the tunnel. The workers' tools and tool belts would come in handy. So too would the flashlights and other bits they'd found, such as satchels and hard helmets.

They would be able to protect themselves.

Skull planned to fill the bags with fresh kills from his hunt in the morning. They would need food for the journey, which could be long. It could take them days to find the other end. Also, there could be pitfalls, such as fallen walls. Making it to the other side was not a guarantee.

Skull had his babies to think of. He needed them to grow up, so keeping them safe and fed on the unknown path was pivotal. Skull longed for his clan to go on after him. To rebuild. Right now, they were the last of his kind, making himself and Eight-Ball vulnerable.

Tomorrow, he decided, he would start mating with the new woman.

She will make perfect children, he thought.

No defects.

No weaknesses.

She would fight him at first but that was of no concern to him. He would beat her. Whip her into shape. Break her, just like he'd broken many others.

Apart from one.

The one who had managed to escape and murder his family.

She will die, he thought, getting up from the ground. The cold night prickled Skull's arm and neck hairs as he left the fire. He went to his captive. She whimpered on seeing how excited he was.

"Please!" she begged.

He smiled. "Soon," he told Paula, then stroked her face with the back of his hand.

She pulled back. Bile leaped up her oesophagus and burned. Tears stung her eyes. A slow trickle of piss ran down the inside of her thigh. Her body quivered. "No," she whispered. "Please…let me go. I have children. A husband…"

Skull issued her a hard slap.

The smell of her urine mixed with her fear excited him further.

He wanted to take her now, but there were things to do. They had to be prepared to go tomorrow.

Skull headed over to Eight-Ball. He told her that she and the twins needed their rest for the morning. That they needed to go before the sun got too high in the sky.

Nodding with a grunt, Eight-Ball headed into the tunnel with her twins. Once there, she settled for the night. Skull would sleep by the dwindling fire to keep watch over their prisoner, who appeared to have cried herself to sleep.

After watching her for an hour, he was satisfied she wasn't going anywhere. He didn't want to take chances, not after last time.

Settling on the floor, he continued to watch her until he fell asleep.

Throughout the night, Skull woke several times to find Paula sleeping. She hadn't tried to escape. Now, with light breaking, he thought it best to get up and wake Eight-Ball so she could prep the twins.

Stirring on the floor, Skull arched his back and stretched. The feeling he'd had after the meal last night was still with him. Could it have been that simple? Was that all he'd been missing? Had his body been longing for human meat? He didn't know, but he planned to eat more of what remained before heading off to hunt.

Rolling onto his side, he noticed Paula was awake.

He smiled at her.

She looked away.

"Eight-Ball!" he called. "Food. Water!" He heard his babies cry and got to his feet. He wiped the sleep from his eyes. "Eight-Ball! Food. Water!"

From within the tunnel, Eight-Ball snarled and growled and appeared at the opening. She cradled the infants.

Skull nodded. "I fetch," he told her, picking up the bucket. "You. Food."

He stalked off into the woods and headed down to a stream close by. Getting to his knees, Skull cupped his hands and placed them into the ice-cold water, which ran down from the surrounding mountains. He then drank greedily. Once content, he straightened and wiped water from his chin. Some dripped onto his chest. He dunked the wooden bucket into the stream, filling it to the brim, and then returned towards camp.

Walking through the woods, he looked about him. The early morning sun cut shafts of bright beams through the trees and surrounding foliage. Wildlife frolicked nearby – everything seemed at peace. He loved his surroundings. A smile graced his face as he continued to walk.

Back at camp, Eight-Ball was taunting the woman by poking her in the ribs with a large stick. This went on until the woman opened her mouth and swallowed the food Eight-Ball had presented to her.

Skull's sister knew the woman needed to eat and drink if she were to survive. They would need her strong, not just for breeding, but also to keep moving at pace when travelling. If not, then she would be left to perish.

When she accepted the food, Skull took it as a good sign. *She become used to it. To the taste. She crave it soon*, he thought. *Soon, others come looking for her and the men. Maybe today. We need to move soon.* He looked at the sun – it was fully up. Morning had settled.

"*Humph*," he grunted, walking over to Paula. "*Drink!*" he commanded, holding the loaded bucket to her lips. Some sloshed onto the floor, splashing her feet.

With greedy gulps, Paula drank and drank, trying to wash the awful taste of human flesh from her mouth. The very thought of what she'd eaten made her stomach knot.

"Enough!" he barked, taking the bucket from her.

She pined for more, but meat was forced into her flapping mouth.

Gagging, she chewed on it. It was dry yet tender. She wanted to spit it out, knowing it was one of the men she had come here with. But she didn't want to die or be abused by the woman any more.

Eight-Ball giggled like a child as she continued to overload Paula's mouth.

Skull grabbed his sister's wrist and shook his head.

Backing off, Eight-Ball went to the campfire to get Skull's breakfast. He watched her go, and then helped Paula take another drink from the bucket. She gulped and gasped.

The meat was salty. Salty, yet tasty. Her stomach rumbled. She couldn't remember the last time she'd eaten. *Not since coming into the woods yesterday,* she mused. Last night, she had thought of escaping. But she had been too tired, and weak from lack of food and water.

For now, she would comply.

Someone will come looking for me, she thought as the bucket was removed from her mouth again.

"*No,*" Skull growled. "*Enough!*"

"More. *Please!*" she begged. "I'm very thirsty!" Her guts had started to cramp due to the water's coldness and her gluttony.

Skull shook his head.

Paula began to weep. "I'm so thir—"

Her words were cut short due to a backhand off Skull. "Quiet!" he snapped at her.

She swallowed her whines and tears. She didn't want to anger him further. "Will you untie my hands, please? I won't try to escape, I promise!"

Skull tried to gauge her face. Was she lying? She could have tried to escape last night, but hadn't.

"Soon," he promised.

She didn't argue. Instead, she smiled and said, "Thank you."

Skull nodded, and then turned to face Eight-Ball, who had touched him on the shoulder. She had in her hand an aluminium dish containing meat. "Eat," she told him.

He took it from her and rammed the food into his mouth. His wet, loud chews made Paula turn away. She felt queasy at the sound of his smacking chops and grunting pleasure.

"*Ugh*," she moaned.

Licking his fingers clean, Skull took a drink from the bucket before offering it to his sister. She too was devouring a meal. Grunting, she took a drink.

"I hunt. Pack," he told Eight-Ball.

She shook her head. "No hunt. Enough food." She grunted, holding up what was left of the two workers.

After inspecting their stock, Skull was happy to go along with what they had. He nodded, and thought he could hunt when they got to where they were going.

He fastened the tool belts around his waist as he watched Eight-Ball pack the bags with food. Once the belt was in place, Skull left his sister to get on.

Going to Paula, he reached up and undid the rope from around the branch above her. He would keep that part in his hand. "Ready?" he asked Eight-Ball, who grunted and made her way over to the tunnel.

As they were about to leave, they heard a slamming noise, followed by voices.

"*Huh!*" Eight-Ball gasped.

Skull put his finger to his lips. He shoved Paula in the back. "Move," he whispered.

They walked over to the tunnel and entered. From the darkness, they watched. Skull drew his knife. Eight-Ball took the screwdriver and hammer from her brother's tool belt.

"And you say they came out here yesterday, Mr. Grace?" Dan, the young PC, asked the older-looking man, who was dressed in bright green clothing. A hard hat graced his head. The yellow helmet bore the words *Railroad Co.*

"Yes. It was only a routine thing. They came out here with a woman from the council. They shouldn't have been gone more than an hour. Two, max."

"Odd," said the second PC, Philip, who appeared slightly older than his colleague.

"I don't care how odd it sounds. Their jeep is still here, for Christ's sake!"

"Please, calm down, sir. We'll find out what's going on," Dan said.

"Should we call this in, Philip?"

"Not just yet, Dan. Let's see if we turn anything up.

"Please wait here, Mr. Grace," Dan stated.

"Fine," he said, scowling. "But they're my men out there!"

Neither PC responded, but both removed their foldaway batons.

"Ready, Dan?"

"*Yes.*"

Slowly, they entered the woods. Leaves rustled and crunched. Twigs snapped. They found their way into a clearing and a tunnel came into sight. Looking about, the young officer could see that someone had been living there. Something had gone on here, as a fire was dwindling. Plus, there were splashes of blood everywhere.

"I think we should call this in, Philip."

"Wait, we don't know anything yet, Dan. Get your flashlight out. We'll inspect the tunnel first."

"No way. That thing could run for miles."

"Okay, I'll call it—"

Dan lost his chain of thought when a naked woman ran out of the tunnel. Her skin was caked in mud, her hands bound by rope.

"Help me!" she screamed. "They're going to kill me! They killed Bill and Martin. Please!"

"Jesus Christ!" Dan bellowed, watching as the woman crashed into Philip. Going to his partner's aid, he didn't see Skull and Eight-Ball rush out of the tunnel. "Are you okay… *Urgh*!" he cried. Someone shoved him from behind. Hard. He flew forward and shoulder-charged a nearby tree.

Before Philip knew what was happening, someone removed the naked woman from off him and jumped onto his chest. He bellowed on seeing a hugely disfigured woman straddle him. She then screeched in return as she mercilessly and repeatedly stabbed at his chest with a screwdriver. It ripped through his tunic, shirt and flesh.

Blood squirted up the feral woman's face, and then Mr. Grace was suddenly there, kicking her off her victim.

Eight-Ball sprang to her feet like a cat and pounced. She jumped on the fat worker and wrapped her legs around his back. Her weight took him off-kilter, causing him to stumble about.

As Eight-Ball attended to her victim, Skull rolled about the floor with Dan, managing to get his knife into the man's gut.

"*Huh!*" the officer said, feeling the blade puncture his skin.

The steel rotated and ripped up his stomach.

Entrails roped around Skull's arm as he pushed the copper off him. He then aided his sister by plunging his blade into the fat man's back. The green-suited man gasped. His arms fell limp, leaving him open for further attack.

Eight-Ball clamped her teeth on the man's throat and ripped his gullet out. She swallowed his blood and flesh and pushed the dying man to the floor. He gargled and wriggled. Crimson spurted from his lips.

Rolling him over, Skull pulled his knife free and sought out Paula.

She was cowering by the cave.

Skull smiled at her shaking form. She'd been too scared to make a break for it.

He kneeled in front of her. She couldn't look at his blood-spattered features. "Good," he told her. "You stay." He then addressed his sister. "Take what we can. Hide the rest. Fast. Need to go," he demanded.

After spending the rest of the morning carving and burying the bodies, Skull and Eight-Ball finally left camp with Paula leading the way down the tunnel with a flashlight. Skull was directly behind her, holding her leash in one hand and a torch in the other. He helped guide Eight-Ball, who had their twins nestled in the crux of her arms.

Their beams of light grew smaller as they ventured further into the tunnel.

Chapter 10

After leaving Griff behind to keep an eye on Thornebank, Chester and Janice drove to Swansea. The man he needed to see there was a drug lord by the name of Carl Hendry, who ran a drug factory on the outskirts of the city close to his home.

He's a regular kingpin among druggies, Chester thought.

Not only did he have his factory, Carl also had major connections to heavy hitters in Cardiff, north Wales, London, Manchester, Liverpool, Glasgow and Paris. However, he had a boss. A boss who was feared and loathed. A man Chester knew well. A man who fancied himself as a Godfather: Mr. Gibson.

Nobody knew his first name, not even his goons.

Chester had worked for him as a lapdog under Carl for many jobs, until he'd been sent to prison for rape, GBH and selling. Before he'd gone down, Chester had stashed a large quantity of drugs and money at Carl's. A huge haul he wanted back.

Before visiting Carl, Janice had taken him into the city for some new clothes. The stuff he was wearing had been outdated ten years ago, never mind now.

"You're in need of an update, babe," she'd told him. "Maybe we could get you some nifty Hawaiian shirts!"

"Sounds good. Nothing more I like than walking around looking like I've thrown up on myself, Jan, baby."

"Ha-ha! Light me a ciggie, babe. I'm gagging for one."

He reached into the glove box and drew her 'coffin nails' out. "These fucking things are going to kill you," he said, screwing the box up in his hand and tossing it out his window.

"*Chester*!" she whined.

"*No*! So get fucking over it!" he snapped at her. "You told me you'd quit. Why lie?"

"It was only a white lie, baby."

"Well, it stops now!"

She nodded. He scared the fuck out of her when he yelled at her. "I promise," she said.

"Good."

After shopping and grabbing a bite to eat, Chester and Janice had jumped back into her car. He felt great in his new clothes: a tailored suit with new shoes, making him look every inch the businessman he thought himself to be.

Leaving the city, they'd then driven to Carl's home, which was a low-key, two up, two down affair. Parked outside was a Mini Cooper, which was a few years old. It all matched the quiet image he was trying to set to remain inconspicuous. With his money, he could afford any car or house he wanted.

Chester had told Janice to park opposite the house, which was where they sat, watching and waiting.

"Are we going in?" she asked.

"Not yet."

"What are we waiting for?"

"I want to see if anyone comes or goes. Besides, I need to ring that dipshit brother of yours. It's been two hours, and still nothing."

"Well, Griff isn't the brightest," she admitted.

"You can say that again."

"I—"

"*Shh!*" he told her. "Look, Carl's by his window. It seems he has a couple of gorillas with him."

"Well, maybe it'll give me a chance to use my new toy!" she said, pulling a snub-nosed .38 Smith & Wesson from her purse.

"Where the hell did you get that?!"

"Griff got it for me."

Chester shook his head. "After this, you get rid of that fucking thing. You know my policy about guns. Knives, yes. Guns, no."

"Okay! Bloody hell, I'll get rid of it—"

Chester put his hand up her skirt. Her knickers were wet. He kissed her hard and fast, their tongues slapping.

"Wow! Slow down, you animal!" she said, pulling her face away from his.

"Why? I've not had a bit of arse in years. My dick is fit to explode!"

"We can't. Not here," she pleaded.

"Why the fuck not?!"

A smile flashed across her face. "Back seat?"

He nodded.

They got out of the car and into the back. Before Janice knew what was what, Chester was at her knickers – he ripped them in an effort to get to her cunt. She grunted as the material cut into her.

"Easy, *easy!*" she told him, but he paid no attention.

"I want your pussy, Janice!" He inserted two fingers into her.

She started to pant, her hot breath smashing against his face. Janice parted her tattooed legs and draped them over the front seats.

"If we weren't in such a tight space, I'd be down there eating that gash of yours," he told her.

"Just get your dick in there, Chester!"

"Were you a good girl while I was away?"

"Yes, of course! I'd never cheat on you, Chester. I love you."

"So no other dick?"

"No, I swear," she said, her teeth clenched, breathing ragged.

He continued to rub her G-spot. "Okay, I believe you."

They switched positions, with her sitting on his lap and then riding him as hard as she could.

The car rocked; the windows misted. People passed by but Chester and Janice only giggled like schoolchildren. The fling lasted a handful of minutes, leaving them breathless.

Shaking, she got off him.

"Fuck, I needed that!"

"How romantic," she said, smiling.

"Get your knickers on. We need to get over there."

"Yes, sir! On the double," she said, laughing.

He slapped her arse. "Cheeky bitch."

"You love it."

Chester took Janice's phone out of her bag and dialled Griff's number. After the fourth ring, the phone was answered.

"Hello, Griff? Yeah? That's good. Where is he now? So you've found his house? Who does he live with…Alone? Even better. Look, how are you fixed there? Have you got shelter for a few hours? Nice! Look, lay low and keep your eyes peeled. I'll see you in a few. I have something to sort out. Good. Don't let that fucking screw out of your sight! Later, mate."

Chester handed the phone back to Janice, who put it in her bag. "Let's get this fucking shit over with," he said.

Janice concealed her gun behind her back by tucking it down her skirt. She then got out of the car and met Chester by the bonnet. Together, they walked to Carl's front door and Chester rang the bell.

After a few more *ding-dong*s, Chester told her to look through the window.

"Looks like he's organising his troops in there. His fucking gorillas are coming to the door."

"So, he's going to try and fuck me, hey!"

"He won't get the chance," she said, standing in front of the door.

As soon as it opened, she barged in and hit the one bodyguard off balance. Before the second knew what was happening, Janice put a bullet through his cheek. The slug tore out the back of his skull, spraying Carl's face with blood and bone matter.

Whilst the other guard regrouped, Janice stood over him and shot him four times in his barrel-like chest.

"Holy fuck!" Carl cried. "Why did you kill them?!"

"I love you, babe," Chester told Janice. "But did you have to cause such a mess?"

She chewed on a fingernail in a provocative way and giggled. "Whoops. *Sowie!*"

Chester smiled. "That's my girl." He turned on Carl and grabbed the smaller man by his tracksuit top. "Were you trying to get the drop on me, you piece of motherfucking shit?!"

"No, I *swear!*"

"Where's my shit, Carl? I want it, and I want it *now*! You hear?!"

"Yeah…*Arrrghh*! You're hurting me!"

"I'm going to hurt you a lot fucking more if you don't get me my stuff. Pronto!"

Janice giggled.

Things hadn't meant to get bloody – Carl had promised Chester his drugs and money were safe. That they were waiting for him. This had been two days ago, whilst Chester had been in prison. He'd used his one phone call that day to ring the crime boss. He'd told him he'd be out in a few days and he'd be coming to visit.

"I-I-It's at the factory. We can go and get it—"

"You told me it was here, Carl! You lied?!"

"I didn't lie – it *was* here! I just moved it, you know. For safe keeping."

"*Carl*?!"

"I swear. Please, don't hurt me," he begged. His bodyguard's blood ran down his face and into his mouth. He spat crimson as he spoke. "I would never shit on you, Chester. I looked after you whilst you were inside…"

This earned the drug boss a hard punch to his guts. "Don't you ever say you looked after me. I looked after myself, you piece of shit!" Seeing red, Chester hammered Carl's head with lefts and rights, knocking him to ground.

Carl awoke an hour later and found himself tied naked to his bed. A gag had been stuffed in his mouth. Between his toes were bits of paper.

"What a titchy cock," Janice commented. "And it's hard!"

"I'm going to ask you once more, Carl. Where's my stuff?!"

He grunted and growled under his gag, and so Chester pulled it free.

"It's at the factory, I *promise*! I had to move—"

"Why?" Chester asked, putting a lighter close to the paper between the man's toes.

"*No*! Don't, please – I'll take you to the stash. Untie me."

"I think we should pour fuel over him, and then set fire to him!" Janice said. "Maybe cut his wee tool and balls off first?!"

Chester laughed. "You're a right cunting little tramp!"

"Ha-ha, that's why you love me," she said.

"I can't argue with you there."

"Please!" Carl protested. "Let me up! I'll take you to the factory. I'll give you half of what I've got too. Please!"

"Why did you move my stuff?!" Chester demanded.

"The police were sniffing around."

"Why?!" Chester pushed.

"There's been an incident over at the factory – all my men are dead. The police think its gang warfare. The place is crawling with coppers – Mr. Gibson's in town, too!" Carl blurted. "I had to move your gear – the cops came here."

"Okay. Janice, untie him," Chester said. "And put a fucking robe on," he told Carl.

Once Carl was decent and able to stand, Chester went for him. He punched and kicked him senseless, but didn't stop until he was breathless. "Tie the fucker's hands behind his back, baby."

Once Carl's hands were secure, Chester dragged the semi-conscious man to his feet and shoved him out the front door. On the doorstep, he gave Janice a kiss. "Clean this place up, babe. I'll come back to get you once I'm finished."

Ken and Ross were parked opposite the ex-club. The police had come and gone, leaving behind their yellow caution tape. Two bobbies had been left to guard the place.

So far, they hadn't been able to reach Carl on his phone.

After they had relayed the information to their boss, Gibson had told his men to stay and watch over the place. He'd also told them that he'd arranged to stay with Huw for the evening, and that the ex-DI was willing to drive Gibson out to them in the morning.

It was now ten AM. Ken and Ross had been parked in the same spot for more than sixteen hours. They'd taken it in turns to sleep. At nine AM, Ken had sent Ross to get them some breakfast from a little café close by.

"Anything from the boss?" Ken asked.

Ross checked his mobile. "Nothing, mate. He must be working some serious issues out with that ex-copper."

"No doubt. Maybe we should give him a ring after breakfast, just to check in? You know how much he likes that shit," Ken said.

"Yeah, true."

"I'll do it if you want? I've finished my grub."

"Okay, but I think you should try Carl first. That fucker's so dead. Nobody ignores Mr. Gibson," the bald man said as he chewed his food. "I hope I get to break his neck."

"Huh," Ken said. "I thought you may have wanted to use that new hand-cannon of yours?"

"The Magnum? Nah – I like to strangle. It's more personal. But don't get me wrong," he continued, jamming the remainder of his sandwich into his mouth, "I like using a gun from time to time."

"I know what you mean. I used to work with a guy who liked to use cheese wire. He liked to see if he could pop his victim's heads off like a bottle cap. It was amusing to watch," Ken said, giving Carl's mobile a ring. It rang twenty, thirty times. "Nah, naff all. I think that little fuck knows what's happened here and has made a run for it."

"More than likely," Ross said. "Especially with Mr. Gibson in town."

"Best thing he can do."

"Yeah, but he won't be able to hide."

Ken nodded and tried Mr. Gibson's phone. On the second ring, it was answered. He told their boss about not being able to get in touch with Carl and that they wanted to go looking for the man.

When he disconnected the call, Ken turned to Ross. "Seems there's a change of plan for me and you, mate."

"How come?" Ross asked, spitting crumbs and bits of food from his mouth.

"He wants us to give it another hour, and then go to the guy's address. He said it's stored in the phone."

"Brilliant," Ross said. "Did he say what we should do with him once we find him?"

Ken smiled. "He did. Mr. Gibson wants us to beat the full story out of him. Then, 'take care of him'," he said.

Ross smiled back. "I'm cool with…What the fuck was that?!"

"What? Where?!" Ken asked, looking out his window.

"I just saw two people go down that lane. One looked as though he had his hands tied behind his back."

"*What*? Isn't there coppers inside?"

"Yeah. Come on, let's get over there and find out what's going on."

"What about the pigs?"

"We'll cross that bridge when we get to it. If something goes tits up, it'll be our bollocks on the chopping block!"

Getting out of the car, they dashed across the road.

After entering the lane and going to the back of the old club, Chester shoved the battered, bruised and semi-conscious Carl behind a giant wheelie bin.

Had it not been for Carl stashing his cash and drugs at the factory, then he would have killed the fucker back at his home. By dragging the bastard out here, it guaranteed he'd get his hands on what belonged to him. He was determined to have it – fifty-k was a lot of dosh to someone who had just been released from the clink. He needed it – the fix, also.

All he had to do now was take care of the two pricks sat in the expensive car across the road.

He was hoping they'd seen him. It had been his intention.

It had taken him a little over forty minutes to get Carl to the factory, a walk that would've taken a non-battered person ten minutes at most. On approaching the building, Chester had spotted the car. He'd known right away that the men inside it were Mr. Gibson's.

They must be new, he thought, *because they stuck out like a pair of sore thumbs!*

Chester had quickly decided on luring the two men into the alley by letting his presence be known. The only thing he worried about was if the cops inside would hear. He needed to tread carefully, and be sure not to alert them.

With Carl behind the bin and barely with it, Chester got ready to surprise the goons, who he hoped had taken the bait. Peeking around the bin, he saw the gorillas making their cagey way towards him.

"That's it. Come into my parlour, little flies!" Drawing a knife from the waistband of his trousers, Chester gripped the haft tightly. "I'm going to carve me a steak!" he uttered, looking at the fatter of the men.

A glint of light caught his eye. He looked under the bin and saw a piece of lead pipe. He nabbed it and holstered his knife. He clubbed his open hand. "You fuckers are going down," he said, watching them draw their guns now they were in a concealed environment. "What amateurs! They must have come cheap!" Chester let out a sly laugh and then leaned back into the shadows.

"Are you sure you saw something?" Ken asked. "There's nobody here."

"If you keep talking, someone's going to hear us!"

"Are there even any bobbies left in there?"

"You saw that pair get left behind as well as I did, Ken."

A bottle rattled, causing both men to turn and come face to face with a wheelie bin. With a flick of his hand, Ross indicated that Ken should go to the left. If there was anyone behind the bin, then they would be trapped in a pincer movement.

At that moment, rain started falling. It gushed from the heavens and reduced all form of sound around them.

Ross rushed around the bin and stuck his gun out. "Freeze!" he said, his voice slightly raised. On seeing the unconscious man on the floor, he was thrown. "It's clear, Ken," he told his partner, who appeared on the opposite side of the bin. "It seems this guy stumbled around drunk and hit his head." He kicked the empty brandy bottle by his foot.

"Aye. Shall we leave—"

Ken's words were cut short as Chester's lead pipe smashed through his skull. His mouth sagged. His tongue lolled. Letting out an *"Oomph!"*, he crashed to the floor and his face slammed against the concrete.

With Ken's bulk removed, Ross could see his target. The man was hunched, a lead pipe between his open hands.

"One down," Chester uttered to Ross, who raised his gun hand.

"Wrong tool for the job, arsehole," Ross said, but was taken by surprise when the lead pipe was thrown at him. *"Shit!"* he said, putting his hands up to block it.

This gave Chester enough time to draw his knife and bull charge. He kept his head low and rammed it into Ross' guts. Ross doubled over and collapsed to his knees. He dropped his gun and grabbed his belly.

Chester pulled Ross' head back by his hair, exposing his throat, and prepared to slit the guy's windpipe open, but Ross elbowed him in the groin.

Half blocking the assault, Chester then took the impact of a rugby tackle, which ploughed him up against a wall.

Surely the cops inside have heard something? Bins have been knocked over, glass smashed. Are they deaf? he thought, as Ross laid blow after blow into his midsection. Chester tensed his stomach muscles and absorbed them before getting bored and sinking his teeth into the back of Ross' head.

He bit a chunk of flesh loose, which induced a glass-shattering screech from Ross. A part of Chester's front tooth snapped and gave way in the attack. Spitting it out, he ran at Ross and ploughed his shoulder into the man's chest.

This took both men off their feet, with Ross going for Chester's eyes with his thumbs.

"You dirty fuck!" Chester said, chopping at his opponent's throat, which was futile.

"I'll fucking kill you!" Ross choked out.

"Not if I kill you first," Chester said, seeing his knife which he'd dropped during the struggle. Grabbing it, he stabbed Ross in his side.

"*Argh!*" he bellowed, punching Chester in the jaw once, twice, three times, causing him to fall backwards. "You bastard!" he said, pulling the knife free. The steel was buckled due to it having hit a rib. Throwing the knife to one side, he went for Chester again and wrapped his massive hands around his throat.

The bodybuilder tried flexing his neck muscles, but he was too slow. The punches had him slightly dazed. He felt the bodyguard's hands strengthen around him. His windpipe started closing.

"*Huuuh!*" Chester wheezed, sucking in as much air as he could.

"Die, motherfucker!"

Chester didn't struggle or panic, knowing this would cause him to lose air faster. Instead, he focused.

"Hey, pigs!" Ross screamed for the police inside the building.

"Out here!"

Gripping Ross' wrists, Chester used his brute strength to prise his opponent's hands off him. He smiled on seeing the effort on Ross' face.

"Keep straining like that and you'll crap your knickers, lady!" he grunted, and then head-butted Ross on his nose.

Going to ground, Ross was powerless as he held his shattered nose. Kicks rained down on his ribs, head and back. Chester then took to stamping on his guts and face, trying to cause as much damage as he could.

He then went for the buckled knife.

"Fair play, big boy…" Chester huffed. "You gave me a good fight! I've not had such a battle since my first few weeks inside."

"Fuck you!" Ross slurred.

"No, thanks. I've had cock before and it's not pleasant." He lunged at Ross with the knife and stabbed him in the throat five, six, seven, eight times.

Ross gargled and choked. His body skipped and thrashed as though electricity pumped through him.

"*Adios, amigo*," Chester said, looking down at the dying man.

There was nothing quite like witnessing the demise of another.

When Ross' lights went out, Chester grabbed the man by his ankles and dragged him behind the bin. He left him with his dead colleague.

Mr. Gibson will be upset!

Before leaving the bodies, he rooted through their pockets. He took their wallets, guns, IDs and the car keys. The Bentley would come in handy.

He looked at Carl and gave him a few slaps about the face. "Wake up, you piece of shit!"

"*Uhh!*" Carl groaned.

Before trying to rouse him further, Chester thought it best to check the inside of the club first. *Isn't there supposed to be officers in there? Isn't that what the bodyguards said? If so, why haven't they come running – me and that dead fuck were making plenty of noise. Especially him! Probably sleeping on the fucking job. Oh well, it'll make things easier for me if they are…*

"Hey, wait a minute," he uttered, standing over Carl. "I could take one hostage and torture info out of him. See if he knows anything about my beloved Huw Davies."

Firstly, he made sure Carl wasn't going anywhere, and then made his way over to the club. He found the door to be unlocked.

Opening it a crack, he listened. Not a sound came from within.

He stepped inside. The building was deceiving from the outside. It was comprised of four floors – two above the ground level, and one below.

He saw chalk lines on the floor. *I wonder who attacked this place?* he thought. *Probably the fucking chinks – they've been trying to cut in on Carl's business for years. Fuck, I bet Mr. Gibson's pissed. Wait until he finds out his new dogs are dead, too.*

This made him smile.

Walking further in, Chester started to think he was alone. That maybe he should go back outside and drag Carl in. Make him get his stuff before executing him. *I could make it look as though whoever did this came back – that would explain the dead bodyguards, Carl and anyone else who may be in here.*

Kicking an empty bottle, he mouthed "shit" before standing still. A floorboard above creaked. A voice followed.

"Did you hear that?" Gregson asked, stepping out of a room on the top floor.

"I did," Peters said, keeping his voice low. "It sounded like a bottle or glass falling."

"Think we should investigate?"

"It's more than likely a stray tom, but I guess another sweep of the building won't harm."

"You know they say a perpetrator returns to the scene of his crime…"

"You've been watching too much Poirot, mate!"

"Ha-ha," Gregson said dryly. "You really should be on stage... Sweeping the bastard, that is!"

"Thank you. I'll consider a career change. Anyway, you lead the way," Peters said. "I've got a bad back."

"A fibber, to boot!"

"Hey, I'm not a liar, man. I jolted it in my sleep last night. Besides, you're the younger officer here. I take authority."

"Whatever," Gregson said, switching his torch on and then carefully leading the way down to the second floor.

"Good man. I'll make sure you get a recognition for this!" Peters joshed.

"Knock it off. I—"

"What was that?"

"Stop it!" Gregson said.

"I'm being serious. I heard something!"

The sound came again – it was like someone was scratching a wall. And then more glass broke on concrete.

"Shit! I heard it that time. It's either a cat or someone's found their way in," Gregson said. "Maybe we should call for back up?"

"*What*? No way! We'll be the laughingstock of the station. I can hear them now: 'The newbies were scared off by a horny queen'," Peters said. "Or a gin-soaked bum."

"I thought you'd locked the doors down there?"

"I thought I had."

Getting to the second floor, both officers swept the landing with their lights. Nothing could be seen apart from a rat that scurried along the left skirting board.

"*Ugh*!" Gregson said. "I bloody hate rodents."

"Me, too," Peters confessed.

"Come on, let's keep going. I don't think the noise was coming from this floor."

"No, I think it came from the bottom floor. Possibly near the bar."

"Yeah," Gregson said, taking his time going down the next few steps. The bare planks were rotten in places, with some missing completely. Nails jutted from them, making it a danger. "Watch where you're treading."

"This place needs knocking down! How in the hell could anyone work in here?"

"The sacks of shit probably loved it. Loved working in filth," Gregson said, stepping off the bottom step.

"More than likely.

"Right, shall we check around the bar area first, and maybe call out a warning?"

"I'm not sure about alerting someone to our presence. But then again, it could only be a bum looking for a place to sleep."

"True," Peters said, and then addressed the bar. "If there's anyone in here, please leave this instant. There is a police matter at hand, and it is against the law for anyone to be in here!"

No answer.

After a couple of minutes, Gregson said, "Maybe it was just a cat?"

"Yeah, because I think a bum or squatter would have answered. Unless they've fallen asleep."

"Come on, let's check it out."

The officers stepped around spilled tables, chairs and an abundance of smashed glass as they made their way to the bar.

"We're going to look so stupid when a tom comes dashing out from behind that counter," Peters said.

"I'd rather feel like an idiot than end up losing my job for negligence!" Gregson said.

Both men stood in front of the long dusty bar. Years-old glasses still stood on brown, dishevelled drip trays. The cloths looked as though they'd never been washed in their lifetime. Lipstick marks could be seen on the tumblers and wineglasses that stood on upright tables. Cobwebs that housed spiders decorated the shelving behind the bar. The wall mirror there had spider-web cracks in it.

"Reminds me of a saloon out of a forgotten western town," Peters said.

"Yeah, but it's missing the tumbleweed and dodgy-looking coffin maker. Come on, this way," Gregson said, leading his colleague around the bar.

They made another sweep with their lights. A few more rats scurried over bottles, half-smashed glasses and debris in the coppers' searching torch beams.

"Well, there's nothing here," Peters said, making his way back to the staircase.

"Hang on. Look." Gregson pointed his light towards the floor. "There's footprints in the dust."

"Anyone could have made those. There's been coppers and forensics in and out of here all day, man!"

"True, I never thought of that."

"Come on, let's get–"

"What?" Gregson asked, looking at the silly expression on Peters' face.

"There," he said, pointing his flashlight.

Looking, Gregson saw a silhouette of a person standing behind them, which was reflected in the cracked mirror behind the bar.

They turned, but not fast enough.

Chester clotheslined them. The hard, brutal attack took both officers off their feet.

"Which one of you pigs do I spare?" Chester asked, looking at the coppers as they struggled to regain themselves.

As Gregson tried to get up, Chester kicked him as hard as he could in the side of his head. "Lights out, boy!" Gregson hit the floor and disturbed a pile of dust. "I guess you're going to die," Chester told Peters, who was getting to his knees.

Chester smashed a bottle he'd found on the floor over Peters' head, who crashed back to the floor. "Fucking pig," he said, sticking the broken end of the bottle into Peters' neck and twisting it. He retracted it and stabbed at the officer's face, chest and throat.

Not bothering to watch Peters die, Chester turned his attention to Gregson. He tied the man's hands and feet with wire he'd discovered whilst hiding in the dark. It had also dawned on him that Carl may have had the upstairs soundproofed.

It would make sense as to why nobody heard anything from the outside, he thought.

Leaving Gregson where he was, he exited the club and carried Carl in.

Throwing the drug lord down by Gregson's side, he kicked the man until he came around. "Carl. Carl! Get your fucking arse up!"

"Ugh, ugh," Carl groaned. "Stop kicking me. There's no need for any of this! I told you I would...*Argggh!*" he screamed as a rib snapped.

"Get. The. Fuck. Up. Now!" Chester screamed and kicked Carl. "I want my shit!"

"It's behind the bar," he slurred. "There's a loose floorboard. I stashed everything under there."

"You better not be shitting me!"

"I'm not!" Carl said, squirming on the floor.

Chester used one of the coppers' flashlights to search the floor behind the bar. The loose board was easy to locate, especially when stepped on. Bending, he dug his fingers into the side of the slack plank and ripped it free. Rusted nails jutted out of the splintered wood he held in his hand.

He scooped the clear bag out of the shallow hole and looked inside – all the money appeared to be there. The drugs, too. Janice would be pleased. She knew how good Carl's cocaine was.

"Bingo." He threw the bag into the air and caught it. "Thanks, Carl," he said, walking over to the drug lord.

"The pleasure was all mine."

Chester loomed over him.

The plank cut through the air with speed. The four nails smashed through Carl's skull, killing him outright.

Chester smiled and grabbed Gregson by his arm. He tugged the copper off the floor. "You're coming with me."

Out in the lane, Chester propped the copper against a wall and checked to see if there was anybody around. The streets were dead. It was the perfect time to move the pig.

So he did. Getting Gregson to Mr. Gibson's car, he threw him into the boot.

Chester jumped behind the wheel and adjusted the rear-view mirror. He smiled at his reflection. There was blood everywhere: in his hair, on his teeth, in his ears, up his nostrils…

"I'll have to get Janice to give me a good scrub when I get back to Carl's. And this fucking copper better know something about Huw Davies," Chester muttered, starting the car and pulling off.

Chapter 11

Voices from below caused Storm to stir. She rolled onto her back and turned her head, noticing a mug of tea on her bedside table. This was her dad's doing – his morning ritual.

She smiled.

The sound of her father talking to Mr. Gibson was muffled. The TV was on – cartoons played in the background, along with Stevie, who was no doubt in her cot.

Good old Dad, she thought, looking up at the ceiling. Alice Cooper looked down, his wicked smile comforting her. She snuggled under the blanket, not wanting to get up. Not yet, even though the sun was high, with its beams pushing through the crack in her curtains and splashing the floor with a golden spread.

She couldn't believe her mother was back in her life. Why? What for? What on earth did the woman think she could possibly achieve by coming back now?

She shook her head and nestled down further in her bed. The warmth was pleasing. Also, the thought of not having to do anything today was lovely. No University class and no Veech until tomorrow. She had the whole day to do what she pleased.

Think I'll crack on with some coursework, she thought.

Even though she was ahead and nothing needed doing, she was working on her end-of-year project. The big one – coursework for her Independent Study class, which meant she had to choose something to do, run it by her tutor, and then crack on with it throughout the year on her own. However, there were regular meetings with her professor, which suited her.

But she wasn't going to get up yet and face the work. She knew it would help distract her, what with her mother being back, her dad pissed off and that bloody mob boss being under their roof. There was a lot to deal with.

Luckily, Skye had made reservations at a B&B in Bridgend when she'd arrived, and wasn't staying, even though her father had offered her his bed.

After everything she's put him through! He's too decent, she thought. He could forgive easily, but she couldn't. No way. The woman had ripped her world apart. Had hurt her dad. And for that, she could never be forgiven. She was glad she'd given the bitch a hard crack across the face.

Storm had wanted to give her more, but her father had stopped her. And with the intrusion of Mr. Gibson, Skye had left, saying she would call again today to see if things could be worked out. There was nothing to say as far as Storm was concerned.

Her thoughts turned to Veech. How strange had that conversation been last night? *What was she was ringing for? Oh, yeah, the episode in her office. Why not wait and talk to me about it tomorrow? Weird. I'm sure she still has the hots for Dad, but he'll have none of it*, she thought. *Oh well, he does have Sue on the go – or so I think. He plays his cards close to his chest…*

A noise outside her door derailed her thoughts.

A floorboard creaked.

When had the voices stopped?

Panic seeped through her.

Then came a knock, followed by her dad's voice. "Are you awake and decent, love?"

"Yes, Dad," she said, stretching. "Come on in."

The door opened and he stepped in with Stevie. "I picked her up this morning and have changed and fed her, love."

"Dad, there was no need to do that. Honestly."

"Well, you had a tough day yesterday and I wanted you to get your rest." He smiled at her.

She smiled back. "Thanks, Dad." He plonked Stevie on Storm's bed. "Hello, little lady," she said to her daughter.

"What are your plans today?" he asked.

"Well, there's no Uni or Veech so I was going to chill and push on with coursework. Probably take madam here to the park after lunch."

Stevie smiled at her mother, her blue eyes shining. She gurgled and cooed.

"Okay," Huw said. "Your mother…*Skye* may pop over at some point—"

"*Dad!*"

"Come on, love, be nice. You don't have to be her best friend but she is trying. I'm like you – I don't want anything to do with her either, but she's got nobody, apart from her parents."

"*Huh!*" Storm sighed.

"Just be nice. For your old man, yeah?"

"Okay, but if I don't hear the door or I'm out, then that's her tough luck."

A chuckle escaped Huw. "Fair enough."

"Where are you going, anyway?"

"Mr. Gibson wants to go to where it all happened so he can have a look around and see if anything jumps out at him."

"*Dad*! No! You can't…" Storm said, tears forming at the corners of her eyes.

"Hey, shhh! Don't be silly. There's nothing out there. The place has been swept time and again. You know that, love."

"Then why go?!"

"He just wants to look around, you know – satisfy his needs."

"Then why doesn't he do it without you?"

"Because he doesn't know the area."

"But there's nothing there!" she said, having to stop herself from yelling. "I've already lost so much. I couldn't take losing you, too."

"Don't be daft. That's not going to happen, Storm. We both know they're all dead…"

"But *he* was never found. What if he comes back? What if he's waiting for his chance?"

"It's been over two years. He's not coming back. The wounds he sustained where enough to kill any man. He probably dragged himself off to die somewhere."

"His body was never found, Dad."

"I know, but he's dead. I promise. Just trust me – it's a cop thing." He winked.

She and Stevie sighed. "Okay, you do what you have to do. I've got to get on here anyway," she said. "Could you bring her cot up for me, please?"

"Of course," he said, leaving the room.

Putting Stevie on her back on the bed, Storm got up and pulled on some clothes from the growing pile on the floor besides her bed.

All the while she kept her eye on her daughter, who was playing on the bed. Stevie was obsessed with her feet and legs these days. *They seem to amuse her*, Storm thought.

As if reading her mind, Stevie let out a hearty chuckle, making Storm smile. "You're a crazy little monkey, aren't you?" she said, grabbing a clean T-shirt from out of her wardrobe without looking. Once it was on, she turned to the mirror to do her hair and the logo on the top startled her. She put her hands to her mouth and gasped.

She hadn't worn the T-shirt in almost two years.

The words *Raining Spear*s were splashed all over the black top in big, bold green writing. It had been Scuzz's. He'd given it to her as a gift.

She started to remove it, but changed her mind. "Dr. Veech is right. It's time to forget the bad things and remember the good," she told her reflection. She ruffled her dreadlocks before tying them up – it was hard work drawing with them down, as they fell in her way. "Right, good. I'm ready." She turned to face her daughter. "How about a cuddle with Mammy first, Stevie?"

She picked her daughter up and padded around the room with her cradled to her chest. "Are you going to watch Mammy get creative? Maybe I'll inspire you to be creative when you're older?" she said. "That would be nice."

She went to the curtains and drew them back. "A glorious day, Stevie. When I'm finished with what I'm doing, maybe we can go to the park and feed the ducks? I bet you'd like that."

There was a knock at her door. "Only me, love," Huw said. "Are you decent?"

Rolling her eyes, she giggled. "Yes, Dad."

"Good," he said, carrying Stevie's cot, which doubled as a playpen, into the room.

"Thanks," Storm said, placing her daughter into it. "I'm sure she'll be happy in there while I get things done."

"Are you sure you're going to be alright?"

She put a hand to his face. "Yes, I promise." Before he turned to leave, she straightened his tie. "You know, you're not on the force anymore. You don't have to put on a shirt, tie and trousers."

"And what would you have me wear?"

"Busted jeans and a metal top, of course," she said, grinning.

"As I thought. I know I should, but these make me feel worthwhile, love. It's hard to ditch the routine."

"Well, you look smart." She brushed fluff off his shoulder.

"Thanks. Take care of each other," he said, looking from Storm to Stevie.

"Of course." She gave him a kiss goodbye.

"I'll see you both later," Huw said, leaving.

Storm heard her dad rally Mr. Gibson. A few minutes later, the front door slammed. From her window, Storm watched the high-spirited pair get into her father's car before turning away and looking down at her daughter. Stevie was busying herself with her toys.

"Right, maybe I can get some work done now," she said, going to her CD player and switching it on. The room filled with Whitesnake. *Ruby's band*, she thought, but she didn't let this faze her. She turned the volume down so it wouldn't hurt Stevie's ears.

Storm then hurried downstairs to make herself a cuppa, some toast and use the toilet. Once done, she took her breakfast upstairs. She was happy to see her daughter crawling around inside her little prison and playing with a set of bright plastic keys.

"Nice," Storm said, setting her tea and toast to one side. Beside her bed, she got to all fours and pulled her coursework out from beneath it. She put the oversized bag on her bed and unzipped it. The piece she was looking for was at the rear.

"Got you," she said, taking the huge sheet of paper out of her folder. She took it over to her easel, which her dad had bought her, and placed the portrait on it. She stepped back and drank in what she'd done so far. The piece was titled *Friends*.

Etched on the paper were rough sketches of her lost loved ones: Ruby, Scuzz, SS, Tev and Z.

She fought back her tears and emotions, even though they helped her when working. She'd already shown her tutor what she had so far. He was pleased with her.

"You could be looking at a two-one, possibly a first, if you can maintain this level, Storm," he'd told her when they'd met last.

She'd been pleased with his comments, because he knew how far she wanted to take her work, and how she hoped to do it as a profession one day.

"Right, okay." She got her pencils and rubber at the ready. "Once all the outlining and detail is done, it should be all downhill from there," she said. "I'm definitely not putting colour into it. Well, maybe one: Ruby's hair or lips. The rest can consist of shading."

She allowed the music to sweep through her body as she took to the piece. She'd practically finished Scuzz, Tev, SS and Z. Today she planned on finishing Ruby, the centrepiece of her work and her friends.

After working on her project for the best part of two hours, Storm decided to stop. Her daughter had fallen asleep and the music had finished. She put everything away, picked Stevie up and headed downstairs.

In the living room, she changed her daughter's nappy and then dressed her. "Mummy is going to make us some food to take to the park, baby."

With the food packed and under the pram, Storm was ready to head out the door when she noticed the TV had been left on. "*Tut*, Dad!" she said. "He has enough to say when I've left lights on."

She went to switch it off when an image popped up onscreen and chilled her. The hairs on her arms, legs and nape stood on end. The picture showed police and forensic tents at a wooded location.

She turned the volume up.

"Police say that the two men and women whose names have not yet been released went missing in these woods near Swansea yesterday..."

Everything went black as Storm's vision tilted. "He's back..." she whispered, holding her stomach as it lurched.

Her lights went out and she collapsed.

Chapter 12

After leaving his new PCs at the club the day before, Dylan had headed back to the station. He'd wanted to know more about the people who had been reported missing.

Once he'd been given the details on the railway workers and the woman from the council, Dylan had stuck by what he had told the dispatcher earlier in the day: he didn't want anyone going out there on a wild goose chase. *Hell, for all anyone knows, they could have gone for a gangbang in the woods*, he thought. *A cracking reason to skip off work for a few hours!*

But now, standing at the site, he knew his judgement had been wrong. Someone should have come to investigate sooner. The officers who had been sent along with a supervisor from the railroad company had also gone missing, and it was clear a struggle had taken place. Leaves and bark were covered in blood, and strips of flesh and guts had also been found.

This harks back to the incident in the Bridgend area some two years ago. Could it be the same people? he wondered as men in white suits and masks combed the scene for prints and other bits of information. All PCs had been ordered to keep away from the area to ensure case evidence wasn't disturbed or destroyed. Also, they were to guard the perimeter and stop journalists from entering.

Even though the zone had been sealed off, it wouldn't stop the local press from somehow getting in.

Dylan shook his head as he tried to fathom what may have happened. It was clear they were up against someone or something powerful. Something dangerous. Something the likes of which Swansea PD had never encountered before.

"What a fucking mess," he said, scanning the location. Dylan drank it in. "Hmm…A strange place to be hanging around, unless the person who did this was a passer-by? If that's the case, why stick around?"

Dylan removed his notebook. "No, I think the person or persons that did this may have been camping or even living here." He wrote this down, along with *'Check online when I get home. See what can be found on the killings two years ago. Are there any matches to what's happened here? Also, find out who was investigating the case back then. See if they can be contacted.'*

He closed his pad and took a step closer to the tunnel. There was something not quite right with the brickwork.

"Please, inspector," one of the masked men said. "We can't have you back here!"

"Okay." He turned and retraced his footsteps. "Something's not right with that wall," he said under his breath, looking back at it.

He went to his Sergeant and addressed him. "Hardy."

The chubby man turned to face his superior. "Yes, sir?"

"I'm heading off. I want officers posted here throughout the day and night in case they come back.

Make sure you pick vigilant ones. I don't want more people going astray."

"Yes, sir."

Dylan walked to his car and got in. He needed a fag, but he'd gone cold turkey two weeks ago. "Damn it!" he said, thumping the wheel. "Never mind, a few tinnies when I get home will sort me out."

He started the car and drove off.

He decided to call back to the station to see if anything else had come in. With no leads on the case, the trail was cold for now. He needed to wait and see what forensics dug up. Hopefully there would be something to go on soon.

There was also the mess at the Kit-Kat Club to sort out. *Maybe I'll drop in on Gregson and Peters before I head home for the evening,* he thought.

Then something niggled at the back of his mind: the tunnel's wall. There was something odd about it. It hadn't looked right. He had seemed to be the only one who'd noticed it though.

"No idea," he said to himself, turning his car radio up and drowning out the police one.

Once at the station, he checked in. There were no updates from the murder site or the Kit-Kat Club. The officers posted there had not yet reported in.

"Has anyone checked on Peters and Gregson?" Dylan asked one of the dispatchers.

"No, sir. We did hear of one of them earlier, but nothing since."

"Okay, don't bother sending a car. I'll check on them on my way home. If I'm needed, call me," he said, heading out the door and back to his car.

Pulling up opposite the Kit-Kat Club, Dylan thought the place looked quiet. Still, even. But that was silly – of course it looked quiet. The area had been cordoned off, with just the two PCs left inside.

He shook his head, killed the engine, got out and crossed the road, half-jogging as he went. Once on the other side, he noticed some of the police tape had been trashed – some lay on the floor, with more hanging loose.

"Bloody kids!" he grumbled. "I'll get Laurel and Hardy inside to sort this out – that's if they haven't fallen asleep. They should be out here patrolling, not hugging and touching each other's dicks in the warmth!"

When he neared the end of the lane, movement behind a bin caught his attention. He stopped, narrowed his eyes, and patted himself down. He wasn't carrying anything he could use to defend himself. *"Shit,"* he muttered. He moved closer and called out, *"Police*! Stop what you're doing and come out from behind there. This is a crime scene!"

Dylan heard shuffling feet on asphalt – a wet, sloppy chewing sound ensued.

"Police!" he said, raising his voice.

Nothing.

He took a step closer, his heart rate increasing to that of a galloping horse. Once he was directly in front of the rubbish bin, the sounds stopped. "Come out. *Now*!" he demanded, giving the bin a kick.

Birds took to flight.

Dylan laughed. "Silly bastard!" He pushed off the wall he'd jumped back against and walked around the bin.

His smile vanished.

Two men lay on the floor, dead.

"Jesus," Dylan said, placing a hand on the wall.

They'd clearly been cut open with a blade or something as sharp. Birds had plucked their tongues and eyeballs out, leaving behind gory pits. Parts of their

120

faces had been pecked and nibbled, and their teeth could be seen through holey cheeks – the flesh had been scavenged from their bellies.

The crows had picked at one of the guy's exposed guts – his entrails had been stripped out. Chunks of flesh and blood spatter covered the concrete.

Dylan turned his back to it. "I need to call this—" His words derailed. "Gregson! Peters! *Fuck*!"

He ran to the back door of the club and kicked it open. A cloying stench hit him immediately. Standing in the crushing darkness, he couldn't see much – he relied on the light coming from behind him. "*Gregson*?! *Peters*?! Where are you?! *Hello*!"

Dylan turned to his right and saw a pair of fresh bodies on the floor. "Oh, God."

One was his man, Peters. He wasn't moving, his face ashen. Luckily, the wildlife had not been at him. His eyes remained and were unblinking. However, rats scurried about – it wouldn't be long before they started to chew at him.

"*Shit*!" he bellowed, his rage and frustration exploding to the surface. Dylan grabbed his radio and called for back-up and an ambulance. He took Peters' flashlight and lit the second body.

He recognised the man. It was Carl Hendry, the local drug dealer.

Well, looks like he pissed the wrong lot off this time, Dylan thought. *Hendry thought he was smart and that the police weren't on to him – that the right ones were paid off. He was wrong, stupid, and now he's dead.* Dylan didn't give a fuck about him or the suits outside. His only concern was his men. Good, honest men.

Not scumbags like Hendry.

Within minutes, he heard the sound of sirens in the distance. Soon he could see the flicker of blue lights through the open doorway.

Dylan craved nicotine. It had been a long, tiresome day. Stress was kicking in – he needed a release, or otherwise he was going to bury his fist into someone or something.

He paced. *I need to get away from here*!

After informing one of the forensic team members he was off and that he wanted to know what they found as soon as possible, Dylan got in his car.

Destination: home.

When he entered his home, he couldn't remember the last time he'd finished so early. *I'm due a bloody break!* he thought. The heating had kicked in at some point, as the house was warm. After removing his shoes, he wandered into the messy lounge area. An open box containing a half-finished pizza lay on his coffee table, surrounded by mugs, tall glasses and empty beer cans.

The stale air choked him.

"God, it bloody stinks!" he said, fanning his nostrils.

He went to the kitchen window and threw it open before grabbing a recycling bag from under the sink. Dylan proceeded to empty the dregs out of the tinnies from off the table and then threw them into the clear bag. He dumped the leftover pizza into the food waste and tossed the box.

After a quick shower, he made himself a cuppa and checked his mobile and pager. Nothing.

He then went to his PC and plonked himself in the seat. While he waited for it to load, he recalled the day's events.

That wall… It was the bricks. Yes, something about them. What are we missing? Damn it! Think, man.

Think! The railway guys and councilwoman were out there to talk about the re-opening of the tunnel. The tunnel runs from Swansea to Treherbert in the Rhondda Valleys, but what's that got to do with anything?

Nothing, that's what.

Wait a minute! The fucking bricks were disturbed. Lopsided! That entrance was bricked up tight years ago! Someone dismantled it and made themselves a home. A... cave!

Excitedly, he turned to his internet. "I need to see what I can dig up from those murders a few years back. There might be a link...I'm sure there were bodies recovered—*Ah-ha*! Bingo!" he exclaimed, discovering articles on the incident.

Skim-reading, he found out that DI Huw Davies and his daughter, Storm, had been at the heart of the grizzly murder spree. Most of the stories, however, had been removed. "Strange. It's not giving full accounts. Why?" he said aloud. "Was it too graphic? Or maybe they didn't want to start a panic?"

Reading the one article posted by the *Rhondda Leader*, Dylan discovered that most of the events had taken place in and around Bridgend, and that a club in Blaengarw had been razed to the ground by fire, which had claimed many lives. Some who had perished in the blaze had been Storm Davies' friends, including her boyfriend.

"It was reported," he kept reading, "that not *all* violent parties were found in the woods after DI Davies went searching for his daughter. The DI was aided by firearms officers, a local PC and an unidentified third party.

"Details on this third party, who has remained nameless, are sketchy. It is, however, stated that the person was involved in illegal activity throughout the UK. This baffled his superiors. Why would a high-ranking officer of the law want the help of a felon? It is understood that the troubled DI will stand down in the coming weeks…"

Frantically, Dylan scanned more newspapers. There was no mention or photos of this mysterious third party, even though there was plenty of information and pictures concerning the victims, including Storm and her father.

"I should be able to get a number for him. Call Bridgend station? Better still, call mine!" he said aloud. Dylan scribbled some notes, shut his PC down and then headed to check his home phone answering machine and mobile – there were still no messages, and his beeper remained silent. "It must be quiet out there tonight. Thank God!"

He picked up the phone and dialled the number for his station. "Jayne?" he asked the woman who answered. "Good. I'm glad you picked up. Has there been any word from the crew at the old tunnel? Yes? All quiet? Great. What about at the Kit-Kat Club? Even better! Inform the Sergeant over at the tunnel that I'll be there at some point tomorrow. Yes. Thanks, Jayne," he said, about to hang up. "Wait – Jayne! Are you still there? Good. One more thing: can you dig a number out for me? It's for a DI Huw Davies. He was stationed at Bridgend. I want his home number and any information you can gather for me." He paused, then smiled. "Yeah, you're a sweetheart too. I promise! Okay, I'll say it - we'll go for *that* drink!"

After hanging up, his smile lingered. He liked Jayne, but not in that way. Still, he'd take her for a drink.

Gathering his notes, Dylan threw himself into his lazy chair and pored over them. He was convinced the recent 'disappearances' at the tunnel were connected to the same people from a few years ago. He was also certain that they'd made their escape down the old passageway.

Maybe alert the police department in the Rhondda Valleys? he thought. *No, not without some concrete proof.* He needed to get to that site as early as possible in the morning. With or without the ex-DI.

He put the pad and pen to one side and pondered the events. Who were the dead men behind the Kit-Kat Club? Were they Carl's heavies? Was there a connection between the killings at the tunnel and the club? Where the hell had Officer Gregson gone? Was it all tied together somehow?

Dylan had sent cars to search nearby areas, including Carl's house. More dead heavies had turned up at the drug lord's home. Things had gone from quiet to bat-shit crazy in twenty-four hours.

Dylan heard his pager buzz. A message. He picked it up and noticed it was the station. "Fuck, I knew it! Not two bloody minutes to be 'ad!" he said, getting to his feet and going to the phone. He punched in the required number. Jayne answered. "Hey, it's me. Yes, Jayne, *your* DI! I know you were only joking! Look, what is it? I have a beer and a meal for one going to rot, so I'd appreciate some info. Am I dragging my arse out again or not?! You've got his number and address? *Great.* That was fast work! Good girl, Jayne. Let me grab a pen," he told her as he reached for his pad.

He wrote down the number and address.

"Anything else? Good. Let's hope it stays quiet. If there *are* any updates or leads, contact me immediately. Thanks. Bye," he said, hanging up.

He picked the phone back up and dialled the number he had jotted down. He let it ring a dozen times before hanging up. He tried once more. This time, he got an answer. It wasn't Huw. The person was female. She sounded young.

"Hello?" she said.

"Hi. Is DI—*Huw* there, please?"

"No, he's gone out, I'm afraid. Who's this?"

"I'm a police officer," he said. "Are you Huw's daughter – Storm, is it?"

"How do you know my name?"

"I'm a police officer," he said cryptically.

The line was silent for a while. "He's gone out. Can I take a message?"

"Erm, yes. Tell him DI Dylan Cope from the Swansea force called, and that I'll be calling again early tomorrow morning."

"*Why*?!" she asked.

"That is something I will have to discuss with your father." This was met with silence. "Are you sure you have that all down?"

"I'll remember. DI Dylan Cope from the Swansea force," she repeated.

"Thanks. Good evening," he said, replacing the phone on the receiver.

Pleased with himself, he went to the freezer, took out a pizza and opened a can of beer.

"One or two won't do any harm," he said, putting the food in the oven. "Hopefully I'll get a peaceful night – no bloody callouts."

Looking at his pad, he thought, *Yes, Huw will be my first stop. I'll be taking him out to the old tunnel. I'm sure he's going to find all this very interesting.*

Chapter 13

How long have we been walking? Four, five, six hours? More?! Possibly. My legs are killing me, Paula thought. *Are we ever going to stop for another break? Those babies must be starving!*

It wasn't just her legs that ached, but also her feet. She had been forced to walk barefoot across sleepers, debris and gravel – her shoes had been lost in a struggle back at camp.

The stones and splinters had shredded her bare feet. All her yelps, pleas and tears went ignored by Skull, who had either mumbled under his breath or hissed at her. Once, he had even backhanded her.

Even though her whole body screamed with fatigue and hurt, she dared not ask to stop again. They'd stopped after a short walk, but since then, nothing.

Maybe the babies are sleeping? she thought. *How the fuck can they see where we are going? It's as black as a mine in here, even with the torches. And it's cold. So fucking cold!*

In parts, water could be heard cascading down to form deep pools they had to walk through. *This abyss seems never-ending*, Paula thought. Rats squeaked and scurried – some tried to scale her legs, but she hit them away, much to the others' amusement.

During the one stop they'd taken, Paula had heard crunching and slurping. It hadn't taken her long to work out that they had been eating the rodents.

They're probably biting the heads off and drinking the blood! she'd thought, and then had a rat thrust into her face. She'd smacked the offered food away. However, the small, decimated body had still touched her lips, leaving behind a slimy trail of God-knows-what on her mouth. She'd gagged.

That had been hours ago.

Had the rat been offered to her now, she probably would have eaten it. They didn't even offer her water, not even when they drank.

They're trying to break me! she thought. *It will never, ever happen!* She was determined. *Someone will come for me sooner or later. That's if we ever get out of this tunnel.*

"*Move!*" Skull growled when Paula slowed down.

"Water! Food!" She was exhausted. Spent. "*Please*! I have little energy."

She heard that awful growl in his throat. She felt he was about to strike her. She cowered when she realised he'd moved closer.

"*Please*! Don't hurt me anymore. I beg you! I'm willing to cooperate, but I need food and water."

"*Sit!*" he ordered.

She painfully lowered her shivering body and felt for the floor below. She managed to avoid sitting in a pool of water, but couldn't evade the sharp stones and rats. The wind whipped her, causing goose flesh to prickle her arms.

"*Cold!*" she said, her teeth chattering.

Something moist was jammed into her face. Using her nose, she detected meat, and hoped it wasn't rat. She opened her mouth and allowed the offering to be placed inside. At first, she closed her eyes, knowing it was one of the dead men from camp.

When she bit into it, the juices that escaped almost made her gag, but her stomach was grateful for the provisions. Then she surprised herself. "*More*," she demanded. Another hunk of meat was placed to her open, waiting mouth. Once that was gone, she pleaded for a third and then fourth helping, but her supply was cut off.

"*No*, walk now!" he said.

"*Drink*," Paula insisted.

Water was given to her, but not much.

"Walk now!" he commanded

She got to her feet and allowed Skull to pull her along. Her dry and cracked lips felt much better.

I can't believe I ate human meat! Disgusting, she told herself. *No more. I won't touch another bite. I should be able to make it to the other side without needing anything else. I'll figure out an escape plan once there.*

But deep down, she knew she'd want more food. *Would* need *more food*, she corrected herself. *It could be days or weeks before anyone finds me, or I get the chance to escape. Months, even. Will I be brave enough to make a run for it given the opportunity? I'll* have *to be. If I'm caught trying to escape, they will kill and eat me.*

That thought scared the hell out of her. She didn't want to die.

No, my best plan is to stay put. Make them think I'm going to be a part of them. He plans to mate with me! she suddenly remembered. *No, that can't happen.*

She wanted to sob. Her guts went instantly cold. She shivered again. Only this time, it was more violent.

I can't let that fucker violate me.

"Move!" he yelled.

Again, she'd slowed down and displeased him, so she got as close to him as possible – she could now feel his flesh against hers. He was just as cold, but seemed unaffected by it.

Those babies must be freezing! Poor things.

Paula had to trot to keep up with him. The weakness she had been feeling had now subsided. The short break combined with the food and water had given her a surge of energy to help her walk.

"Skull?" the woman called out, startling Paula. "Can't walk. Blocked."

"*Humph*!" Skull growled, yanking on Paula's leash. They passed Eight-Ball, who'd somehow managed to take the lead. "What's wrong?"

"Blocked," she said again. "Stones. Dirt. In way."

"Hold," he told his sister, giving her Paula's leash and the torch. "Get back."

When he had adequate space, he moved some of the smaller stones aside. He seemed to struggle, but didn't ask for help. Once most of the gravel had been removed, he scooped the earth out of the way. When a slender gap was created, he told the women to move forward.

To Paula's surprise, they slipped through with ease, but Skull had to suck his gut in.

He didn't quite get through unscathed, as sharp stones ripped at his stomach and chest. In the flashlight's beam, Paula saw blood trickling down his abdomen. He shrugged it off and took the rope from his sister.

"Come," he said, his tone softer.

They continued walking for what seemed like hours, making the trip appear endless. *What time did we leave?* Paula wondered. *Has a day passed?* They could be on their second or third in the tunnel for all she knew. She couldn't remember. She was losing track.

Up ahead, she heard loud splashing sounds. Before she knew what was happening, a sharp coldness started to rise slowly up her lower half. Gasping, she suddenly realised she was now almost waist-high in freezing-cold water. Bits of wood, loose stones and rubbish bobbed about her in the still water.

Something brushed her legs.

Paula bit down a scream and closed her eyes. She let Skull lead her. "I want to go home," she whispered aloud. And then, as fast as she'd stepped into the water, it began to recede. It lowered to her knees before dropping dramatically to her ankles, where it stayed for a short walk until she was on dry land once again.

They moved with a frantic pace, giving her the sense that Skull and his sister wanted the journey over. That maybe they were anxious. Perhaps scared. *No, not scared. Never scared. Nothing could frighten them. Nothing,* she decided. But they could be uneasy – worried that there was no end to the tunnel, or that they were lost or would need to turn back and meet with their fate.

Paula prayed they'd run into another blockage – one that couldn't be overcome. But it never came.

Finally, Skull called for a stop. A rest. Making her sit, he gave Paula some water before pushing food into her face. At first, she kept her lips pressed tight, but he slapped her, forcing her mouth open in shock so he could push the food in.

Not wanting another smack, she swallowed it and was surprised when she didn't wince at the thought of what it was. She embraced the taste and hankered for more, just like the first time. Her stomach growled.

"*More*," she insisted. He placed a second helping in her mouth and she scoffed it down. She was so ravenous, she licked his fingers clean. He seemed to like this, and gave a grunt of pleasure.

She felt something push against her arm. A shudder cut through her. *Is that what I think it is?* she questioned, chewing greedily. "Water!" she gasped.

When she thought he was going to deny her and make her walk, she wrapped her hand around his dick and slid the skin back and forth. He seemed powerless. She wanted him to think she was going to comply, and it worked, as water was handed to her.

She stopped stroking him and drank heartily. "Thanks," she said.

He snatched the water from her grasp. "Up. *Move!*"

Without argument, she pressed on. *I just need to comply*, she told herself. *If I do that, I'll live long enough for someone to rescue me. Unless they run out of food…No, he won't kill me. He wants me. Needs me. I had him under control just by stroking his dick.* She smiled. *He might be easier to fox than I first thought!*

"*Wall!*" Eight-Ball called, breaking Paula's thoughts. "End?"

"*Huh*," Skull grunted.

The thought of making it to the other side of the tunnel made Paula giggle. She covered her mouth, not wanting to provoke a slapping.

What's wrong with me? she thought, stifling more laugher.

"*Hold*," he told his sister, giving her the end of Paula's leash again. He then put his hands flat to the wall and moved them about the surface. It felt just like the wall at the other end of the tunnel. Was this the exit? Their way out?

Skull smiled and grabbed the hammer which was sheathed in the workman's belt around his waist. He drew it back over his shoulder and struck the brickwork as hard as he could. He continued until a chunk of rock fell from a corner. A sliver of light penetrated the gap, which grew larger by the strike.

After a few more bricks fell away, Skull stopped to catch his breath and ordered the women to clear the broken stones out of his way. Adhering to his commands, they pitched in and lumped the stones to one side.

Happy he had sufficient room, Skull continued. When there was another pile of shattered stonework at his feet, he again told the women to clear it.

After his third attack on the wall, massive cracks appeared in the barrier. Without wanting to destroy any more brickwork, he holstered his hammer and pushed at what was left of the weakened structure.

With a few shunts, the whole wall collapsed, and the late afternoon light filled the tunnel. To Skull's surprise, this end of the tunnel opened into a wood, too. However, it was not thick, meaning they wouldn't be able to stay long. They would be detected too easily.

Skull looked around and saw cars travelling along the mountain above them. This was fine, as they were far away. They wouldn't be seen, especially with the light fading. Ahead of them, and leading off into the bushes, an old, rusted train track jutted beneath overgrown shrubbery. In the distance, a train chugged.

"We're close to Treherbert train station," Paula said. "There's people close by."

Skull turned on her and slapped her across the face. He was displeased. He didn't want to be close to people.

They needed to move from here, but not until the sun rose again. They needed rest.

Skull spent the best part of an hour covering the tunnel's opening. He put back as many bricks as he could before concealing the damage with branches and greenery.

Satisfied, he moved them on. He kept them in the thickest parts of the covering, which was sparse. They had to snake their way through trees and overgrown bushes.

Then Skull stopped them dead in their tracks. The sound of children laughing filtered through the trees. "*Shh!*" he said, putting a finger to his mouth.

Eight-Ball looked at him, their babies sleeping in her arms, and licked her dry lips. "*Food!*" she uttered, putting her babies on the floor in a safe place.

Thinking Paula might be a hindrance or try warning the people, Skull again turned on her and punched her in the jaw. She crashed to the floor and didn't move. He took hold of the rope and lashed it to a nearby tree.

"I need you," he said, guiding his sister to a large boulder close by from where they could spy on the family of four. The young children, a boy and girl, played by the campfire. The mother and father sat in foldaway chairs beside their tent.

The father looks weak. Soft, Skull thought.

"Not too close to the fire, children," he heard the father say.

"They're only playing, love," the mother said.

Skull drew his knife. "Kill the children," he told Eight-Ball. "I have parents."

"Katie, give me my aeroplane!" the young boy grumbled to his nine-year-old sister, who he knew was more than capable of pummelling him. She'd beat him before in front of his friends – the memory always made him blush.

"*No!*" she said, turning on him. Her swift movements caused her pigtails to dance. "I'm the boss, not you!"

"Who made you boss?!"

"I'm nine and you're eight. I'm older, Robert," she said, poking her tongue out at him. "So that means I'm in charge." She shoved him hard in his chest.

He fell backwards – his glasses fell from his face. "Mam! Dad! Katie pushed me!" he whined, but they ignored him.

"Go on and play!" his mother said, locking arms with her husband.

Robert got to his feet and chased Katie into the trees and bushes.

They heard their children laughing and bantering, but couldn't see them.

"Don't wander too far!" their father yelled.

"Ha-ha, they'll soon come running back when they're hungry," the mother said. "Early night tonight?" she teased, putting a hand up the inside of her husband's leg.

"Once the children are asleep, yes." He leaned in and gave her a kiss on the lips. "I love you, Lucy," he said, pulling back.

"I love you too, Tim," she said, leaning over to give him a long, lingering kiss. "*Ugh*, Tim! You're getting loads of saliva in my mouth." She giggled, and then gasped. "You're shaking!" A large hand clamped over her mouth.

Frantically, she looked about her. Tim was slumped in his seat clutching an open wound at his throat that gushed blood. Stab wounds covered his body, his face ashen. Within seconds, he stopped moving.

She screamed but it was muffled.

The man who had his hand across her mouth was huge, his body filthy. He had a wild, crazed look in his eyes and his lips twitched with a half-smile. *"Pretty,"* he said, stroking her face with the tip of his bloodied knife. "Shame."

She moaned and shook violently. Tears formed at the corners of her eyes.

Skull stuck the tip of his knife into her eyeball, causing it to pop –metal scraped against bone. He pushed the blade in until the haft met with her face. He then twisted the steel and retracted it slowly. Effortlessly.

She flopped in her chair and remained still. To make sure she was dead, Skull took her other eye out and slashed her throat. Behind him he heard the children screaming.

He chuckled smiled and licked his knife clean.

He turned at the sound of rustling bushes to see his sister standing there. Under her arms, she held both children. They were lifeless.

She dropped them close to the fire and then fetched Paula, who had stirred and was staggering to her feet. Eight-Ball grabbed her and led her to the fire. Her mouth sagged when she was hauled past the wasted family. Her eyes fused briefly with Skull's, who stared at her as he stripped chunks of meat off the children with his knife.

She snapped her head in a different direction, much to Eight-Ball's sniggering amusement. "I can't be a part of this," Paula sobbed.

When they were standing close to Skull, he stopped prepping the children and addressed them. "We stay tonight, then up to hills tomorrow. When sun rises."

Eight-Ball grunted and walked off again. He presumed she was going to collect the babies, who cried hysterically in the distance.

Skull watched her as she returned and went into the family's tent. "You stay here," he told Paula, grinning. He then turned and looked to where they'd come from. He longed to go back. He wanted revenge on the people who'd killed his family. But now was not the time. He had to keep himself, his sister and his children safe.

"I *come* back for you. And I *kill* you," he whispered.

Chapter 15

Chester drove the Bentley into the street and wondered if the address was right. *Could Griff have got it wrong?* he thought. *That dumb fuck is prone to getting most things wrong. Hell, he can barely read, for fuck's sake.*

The street, Oxblood Grove, was situated on the outskirts of Swansea. It was located behind four other streets that were downtrodden in comparison.

Fucking Millionaire's Row, Chester thought. *Posh cunts.*

Every other drive had an expensive-looking car parked on it, with some boasting two or three vehicles. Chester also spotted a speedboat on one, which angered him.

"Toffee-nosed pricks!" he said, winding his window down and spitting onto the road.

The homes looked to be four-or-five-bedroom properties, with a bungalow here and there. All had neatly trimmed hedges and cut lawns. Not one had a For Rent or Sale board attached to it.

Why would they? Champagne and strawberries here, he thought. *I fucking hate rich bastards.* "Eat them, that's what I say," he blurted.

"Eat who?" Janice asked.

"The fucking rich!" he spat.

A man waved as they drove by. He was busy clipping a tree in his front garden.

Chester gave him the finger.

"Stop it!" Janice giggled. "We can't draw attention to ourselves."

"Ah, fuck 'em. I'll be heading back inside after this little rampage," he said. "All I ask is that we kill that fucker, Huw Davies!"

"We will, babe. We will, I promise."

"I know," he said, looking out of his window. "But first, we need to take care of this fucking faggot Thornebank. He'll probably have plenty on my good pal Huw."

"I thought the copper in the boot was for information?" Janice said.

"Well, I hope one of them can tell us something."

"Yeah, but I hope they keep quiet for a while… You know it turns me on seeing you get messy with fucks who get in your way, baby!"

"You're a sick little bitch, aren't you?" he said, turning to look at her. He put his hand between her legs and rubbed her pussy. "Is she wet and wanting?"

"You'll have to find out for yourself, big man! Maybe you can take me on a bloody floor?" she said.

Pulling his hand away, he thought about her words. "I'll see what I can do," he said, smiling, and then turned the volume up on the CD player. Chester sang along to the band playing.

"Who is this?"

"Disturbed. I love this song! It's called 'Sickness'."

"Nice."

As he drove further down the street, Chester couldn't help but be a tad envious – he would have liked living somewhere like this. Somewhere quiet and secluded. For a second, he imagined himself with a good job and a nice car. Possibly a Porche or a Ferrari. *If only life had turned out better,* he thought.

Right from the start he'd been tossed shit cards: a raping thief for a father and a junkie whore for a mother. If they weren't spending their days taking lumps out of each other with their fists, knives, broken bottles or anything else that came to hand, then they were out on the rob, kicking peoples' heads in and taking everything they could.

A modern day Bonnie and Clyde.

Until Chester had put a stop to them when he was twelve – cyanide in the tea.

Dad always kept such things lying around, he thought. After seeing someone get poisoned in a film, Chester had thought it a good idea to rid the world of scum. He'd be a hero. A crusader of crime like his favourite superhero, The Flash.

But it hadn't quite worked out that way.

People had come and taken him away. He hadn't understood why at the time. Chester had been passed from home to home, screwing with his head and causing him to run up against far more dangerous and deadly people than his parents.

A child should never experience being touched by an adult.

Thoughts of being a real-life Flash had faded. Evil seeped in – he started hurting animals, and then boys and girls of his own age.

Life was cruel. However, Chester was worse.

After running away from his last home at seventeen, Chester had found sanctuary on the streets, which became a haven for his crimes. The first woman he had raped and killed had been unplanned. Chester had stumbled out of a pub, drunk, and set upon the youngest after finding her on a deserted street. It had led to the slaughter of eight females in total – before being taken down, arrested and then sentenced to ten years for armed robbery and one count of rape.

He'd never been tried for the murders through lack of evidence.

"Maybe we could get ourselves a little place like this?" Janice said, breaking his chain of thought.

"I was just thinking that." Chester gulped the knot in his throat down. *It's too late for me,* he thought. *It will never happen, baby.* "One day, sexy. One day," he lied, facing her. "God, you're so damn pretty!"

"Aw! Thanks, babe."

"Just saying."

"What number are we looking for?"

"I'm pretty sure you brother said one-zero-five in his text. Hang on, I'll look," he said, digging her phone out of his pocket. He flipped through the messages and found Griff's. "Yeah, that's right."

"Okay, well there's one hundred..."

"*There*!" he blurted. "Park in that gap."

"Where?"

"Between the van and that BMW."

"Got it," she said, swinging the Bentley into the parking spot.

Chester jumped out before Janice had time to switch the engine off.

"Hey, Mr. Keen! Wait for me!"

"I am. I just want to get a scope of the place. It's so quiet around here."

"It is. Where the hell is Griff?"

"I'm not sure. Maybe he went inside?" Chester suggested.

"You think? You know how much of a pussy he is."

"True, but he may have wanted to prove a point."

"Maybe."

Janice's phone started to ring. Griff's name blinked on and off the screen. "Didn't know he was a mind-reader!" Chester quipped and answered the phone. "Yeah? Cool. We're outside. We have a friend with us. You'll see. Open the door for us."

Ending the call, he asked Janice to pop the boot. He then went around to the back of the gentleman's car and raised the door. Standing over Gregson, who was wide awake, he smiled. "One smart fucking move out of you, and I'll kill you, boy," he told the copper. "Nod if you understand."

Gregson did.

"Good. Now, I'm going to take your gag off and, again, if you make a daring move, I'll kill you. Understood?"

Another nod.

Chester ripped the duct tape from his prisoner's mouth. "If you're bright, you might make it out of this alive and get to tell plenty of stories." He grabbed the copper's arm and dragged him out of the boot.

Gregson's knees clicked as he stood straight and arched his back. He moaned as everything snapped into place. "Thanks," he whispered. "Do you have a drink? It was so dry in there!"

"Janice? Bring that bottle of water with you. The gun, too."

Gregson's eyes darted back and forth at the mention of the firearm. He'd been stripped of his radio, cuffs and baton.

"Don't worry, it's not for you. Yet," Chester said. "Fuck, it may not be used on you. Like I said, play it smart."

"*Anything*. I don't want to die," he rasped.

"Then you won't, if you give us what we want."

"Just tell me what you want and I'll provide."

"All in good time," Chester said as Janice thrust the bottle of water at Gregson's mouth.

"Drink!" she snapped.

After a few gulps, she pulled the water away from him, and Chester pulled him from the car over to the house.

"Get up the steps," Chester told the compliant officer. "Now, inside." Before Chester followed him in, he glanced around - the street was empty. He smiled, and then entered the home and shoved Gregson down the passageway. "Griff? Where are you?"

"In here, Chester. The kitchen," Griff yelled back.

"Cool." Chester gave Gregson another hard shove into the kitchen. "Well, if it isn't my old pal Thornebank!" he said with a raised voice on seeing the screw tied to one of his kitchen chairs. An apple corked his mouth.

Thornebank snorted with fear.

"Yeah, I'm happy to see you, too!" Chester continued and ruffled the man's hair. "Get some more chairs, Griff: one each for me, Janice and Pig-Boy here." He kicked Gregson, who had been pushed to the floor. Chester noticed Janice had her gun trained on him.

"*Hmmm-mmmm-hmmph*!" Thornebank groaned.

"I'm afraid you're going to have to speak up. I think I've gone a bit deaf in my old age," Chester said.

Thornebank's face turned a bright red-purple. The veins in his neck protruded and his eyes bulged. His nostrils flared. His writhing caused the chair to creak.

Chester gripped the apple and tore it from Thornebank's gob. He gave the warder a crack across his already crimson face. "*Shhh!*" he demanded.

"Y-Y-You fucking animals!" he stuttered and then savagely inhaled a lungful of needed air. "You're"—he stopped to draw another breath—"all going to pay for this. You mark my words!"

"Shh-shhh!" Chester said, stroking the man's hair.

At that point, Griff walked in from the dining room with more chairs. "Here you go," he said.

"Great. Bring one over here, Griff. I want this pair back-to-back," Chester said.

"*Up!*" Janice instructed Gregson, who obliged. "Get in that fucking chair!" The copper complied. "Tie him, Griff," she said.

Her half-witted brother giggled as he did so, making Chester smile.

"I don't think you'll need the gun now, Janice," Chester said, taking a straight razor out of his top pocket. Inscribed in the sharp blade was the name Eddie.

"Who's Eddie?" Griff asked.

"An old friend. Are they both tied tight?"

"Yes," Janice said. "Now what?"

"I want you two to make sure this place is locked down. Close all the curtains and bolt the doors. Janice, I think you need to move the Bentley. Get rid of it. I'm sure by now the bodies at the Kit-Kat Club will have been discovered."

"Got it," she said, heading out the door.

"I'll make a sweep of the house," Griff said.

"Before you go, Griff, tell me: how in the hell did you manage to take this son-of-a-bitch down on your own?"

"I pretended to be a double-glazing salesman," Griff said, snorting a laugh.

Before Chester could respond, Griff was off on his errand. "Well, fuck me," he said to himself, turning to Thornebank. "Fancy being outwitted by a fucking moron!"

"You filthy motherfucker!" Thornebank raged. "You're going back inside and you'll rot in that hell!"

"Actually, that's my plan. I miss the walls. I even miss the arseholes trying to grab my arse." He leant in and put the blade closer to the screw's eye. "One false move and I could half blind you."

Thornebank arched his back to pull away from the glinting blade. "You don't have to do this!"

"But I want to."

"They'll *never* release you!"

"Promises, promises."

"I'm not joking. They'll throw the key away. You'll die in Cardiff nick, *Nailfree*!"

Gently, so the pain would last longer, Chester drew the steel down Thornebank's cheek. The grooves in the word Eddie turned red.

"*Argh*!" the screw yelled. "*Bastard*!"

"Keep it up and I'll cut your tongue out!" Instantly, Thornebank closed his mouth. "You don't ever get to call me that again, *fucker*. My name's Chester, not Nailfree. Nobody calls me that on the outside."

"But it's your name!"

Chester got into the man's face. "My mam and dad were Nailfree, and I don't want to be associated with those dead fucks."

"You killed them, didn't you?!"

Chester punched the man in the face four, five, six times before he bridled his rage and stopped himself from killing him. He needed him, for now.

Thornebank groaned, his face streaming with blood. One eye was closing. Broken bits of teeth surfed out of his mouth on crimson saliva. "Untie me…*Please*!" he gasped. "I'm going to be…" Before he could finish his sentence, a stream of chunky spew erupted from him and mixed with the blood on the floor.

"You dirty bastard!" Chester said.

"Just kill me or fuck off!"

Chester clenched his fists. He wanted to pound the man until he stopped breathing, but he couldn't. "Tell me, how's my good friend Gary? Still pissing in his pants, no doubt."

Trying to pick his head up but failing, Thornebank answered, "He's dead. We found him hanging an hour after you were released."

"Oh no!" Chester mocked. "Not my dear friend Pissy-Pants Gary! Cardiff nick will never be the same!"

"Stop playing fucking games, Nail…*Chester!* Tell me what you want. *Please*," he begged. "I don't want to die like this. Whatever it is, I can help you."

"I can't promise you'll live, but if you give me what I want, then you might save the life of this man," Chester said, pointing at Gregson. "Also, I'll make your death quick and painless, and won't murder your family."

Thornebank sighed. "What do you need from me?"

Janice and Griff walked back into the room.

"Wait," he told Thornebank, facing his comrades. He noticed Janice had removed her scarf and shades. Her jacket, too. She wore only a thin T-shirt that depicted Sid and Nancy as rotting zombies. *It looks amazing on her! The tightness of it makes her small tits poke out more than they should!* "Well?"

Janice was the first to speak. "It's all clear out there. I parked the car a few streets away. Nobody saw me."

"*Excellent.*"

"I did all you asked, Chester," Griff said. "I even went around the back of the house and made sure everything was locked up tight." A nervous smile twitched across his face.

Chester put a hand to his shoulder. "Good boy," he whispered. "Now, as me and Janice try to get something out of this pair, I want you to ransack the place – we're going to make it look as though a burglary took place and went wrong." He winked at Thornebank.

"*Yeah*! I'll get on it, Chester," Griff said, leaving the room.

"Right, you!" Chester addressed Thornebank. "I'm looking for some information and if I don't get what I want, then I'm going to dice you both into tiny pieces. Your families will be next!"

"Just spit it out!" Gregson said.

"I want to know about a DI Huw Davies. He's not based in Cardiff or Swansea, but Bridgend."

"Huw Davies?" Thornebank said. "Name rings a bell…"

"How about you?" Chester asked Gregson, giving him a nudge.

"*Erm*, I'm thinking."

Chester didn't believe him. "Are you holding something back?" he asked, stepping around Thornebank so he could see Gregson's face. Sweat beaded the officer's forehead.

"I'm trying to think. The name sounds familiar. I used to work at Bridgend a few years back, but I was transferred to Swansea."

"*Hmm*, we're getting somewhere."

"I've got it!" Thornebank said. "He's the copper who was mixed up in those killings two years ago – his daughter was snatched."

"I see. Tell me more," Chester demanded.

Thornebank proceeded to tell Chester everything he knew about the incidents that occurred in Blaengarw, and how Huw's daughter was abducted and an unorthodox rescue mission had taken place.

"It's all online," Thornebank protested. "Have a look for yourself."

Chester slapped him across the face. "I need personal details, you *fuck*! Where does he live?"

"Don't hurt him any more!" Gregson butted in. "I can give you what you need. I know a few things about Huw's daughter…"

"*Quiet*, you fool!" Thornebank said. "He'll kill us!"

"Shhh," Chester told the screw, digging Eddie into the side of his neck and ripping it across his throat. A short spurt of blood found its way into his mouth as he stood and watched his victim slowly bleed out.

Before Thornebank succumbed, Chester got close to his ear. "I bet you didn't think it would end like this. I want you to know that I'm going to wipe out your whole family. Every last fucking one of them," he lied. "I'll rape the women first, even the young ones."

Thornebank gurgled and spluttered as his life drained away.

"What the fuck have you done?" Gregson screeched.

Janice walked up to the dying guard and stuck her fingers in the slash wound. She then sucked them clean. "Mmm, tastes like chicken." She laughed.

In the background, Griff could be heard smashing furniture and décor.

"Now, tell me every little fucking detail you know," Chester said, walking around the chairs to face Gregson.

"I-I'm trying to think. It's pretty hard to when you have a knife in your face!"

"It's not a knife but a razor. Start talking. *Now*!"

"Okay, okay. I only know about his daughter. Honestly! I didn't work with the DI, but I heard about what happened before I was moved."

"So, what about his daughter? Where does she live? With daddy?"

"I'm not sure. All I know is that she sees a shrink once a week. I know where, too!"

"Her name?"

"Storm."

"How do you know this?!"

"I know the shrink. She's a friend of my sister. People talk and information leaks," Gregson said. "I can give you the shrink's work address – I was once referred to her. That's part of the reason I was transferred."

"I don't want your life fucking story. Janice, get the man a piece of paper and a pen."

"Sure thing!"

"I hope you're not lying to me."

"I'm not."

"Good. Because if I set you free and I find out you've lied to me, I'll hunt you down."

"Are you *really* going to let me go?!" Gregson said.

"I'm a man of my word," Chester said, smiling.

"Here you go, boys!" Janice said, handing the pad and pencil to Chester.

"You'll have to untie me if you want me to write it down."

"Hmm, what do you think, Janice? Shall we?"

"Why not?"

"Okay, but don't make me have to kill you," Chester said.

"I'm not going to try anything. If you're planning on letting me go, then what's the harm in freeing me?"

"He's got a point," Chester said, slicing Gregson's restraints. "There, now write the fucking address down. The *real* one!"

Gregson scribbled the details down on the piece of paper. "Can I go now?" he asked.

At that moment, Griff walked in. "I think I may have found—" he started, but was stopped by a sudden outburst as Gregson charged at Chester and Janice.

Before they could stop him, the copper bowled into them full force, taking them to ground with him. The gun jumped out of Janice's hand and slid towards the TV.

Gregson and Chester tried to scramble to their feet, with Janice down and clutching her side. She was winded.

Beating Chester to his feet, Gregson rammed a knee into the jailbird's guts, sending him to ground.

"Get him!" he coughed out to Griff. "He's going for the *gun*!"

Gregson and Griff both crashed onto the handgun and rolled about the floor grunting.

"*Give*…!" Griff demanded. "…*Mine*!" he said with effort. A swift knee to his balls buckled his grip on the gun but he continued to fight. "Dirty bastard!" he raged, and then spat in the copper's eyes.

Though temporarily blinded, Gregson managed to get two more powerful knees to Griff's nuts, making him let go of the gun.

"*Argh*!" Griff said, gripping his privates and rolling away. "Fucking pig!"

Gregson turned on Chester, who ducked as a bullet whizzed over his head and shattered a lamp. He cocked the hammer as Chester peeked from behind the kitchen counter. He tried again, but Chester was too quick in ducking out of the way. The bullet drilled into brickwork.

Gregson turned the gun on Janice, who had regrouped on the floor. "Goodnight, bitch!"

Griff tackled him from behind and sent him staggering. The gun went off. A slug ploughed into Janice's leg below her knee cap.

Blood spurted.

She screamed.

Chester ran to her, noticing Griff had the situation under control: he was on top of Gregson and punching away at the man's face. The gun had crashed to the floor.

"Are you okay, baby?!" Chester asked. "*Shit*. There's lots of blood." He took his shirt off and pressed it to her knee. "We need to get you to a hospital!"

"No, babe!" she said. "Just get this done and go on without me. I'll call an ambulance from here. I'll make up some bullshit story…."

A bang from behind startled them. They snapped their heads in its direction.

Griff whimpered.

The gun was nowhere to be seen.

"Get off me!" Gregson said, rolling the wounded man off him. His face was spattered with blood. The room stank of gun smoke and oil.

Getting to his feet, Gregson turned the weapon on Janice and Chester. "Don't fucking move."

"Chester!" Griff said, getting to his knees. He held his oozing guts together with bloodied fingers. "Am I dying?" he asked, his voice warbled.

"Griff!" Janice cried.

Gregson cocked the gun and put a bullet in Griff's head.

Janice screamed.

"You *motherfucker*!" Chester bellowed, attempting to get to his feet.

"I don't think so," Gregson said, cocking the gun. "Don't make me shoot you, too."

"You're an officer of the law – you *have* to take us in!" Janice said.

"Did it look as though I was taking him in?!" he said, nodding at Griff. "No. But we are going to sit here and wait for the cavalry to arrive." Gregson picked the home phone up and dialled.

He only took his eyes off his prisoners for a second, but it was long enough for Chester to make his move. He pounced like a jungle cat.

Gregson's mouth sagged in surprise.

The gun's hammer fell.
Another loud crack of gunfire tore the room apart.
Janice shrieked

Chapter 16

Once she'd got back from her walk with Stevie, Storm had put the TV on. There had been no new developments in Swansea, and the police still hadn't made a full statement.

Storm knew what had happened. Who was involved.

She'd also hoped her dad would have been home when she got back, but there was no sign of him. Only a note from Skye, which had been pushed through the letterbox.

'Tried calling but couldn't get an answer. I understand if you don't want to see me, but I would like to try and resolve the issues we have. I'll call again later. Love, Skye. X X'

Storm had crumpled it up.

Now, as seven o'clock approached, Storm started to get worried. Where were they? They'd been gone all day. Telling herself not to stress, she pushed on with what she had to do.

"Come on, madam," she told Stevie. "Time for bed. Would you like a story?" Stevie looked at her mother with wide eyes and cooed as she was carried upstairs to her bedroom – Huw had transformed the spare room into a nursery, giving it a princess theme.

Storm placed her daughter into her warm cot and pulled the covers about her. "There," she said, taking to the chair by the side of the bed. "Which story?" She looked at her daughter through the oak-coloured bars. "How about *The Hungry Caterpillar*?"

When the story was done, Stevie's eyes were closed and she was breathing rhythmically. Storm put the book back on the shelf and gave her daughter a kiss on the head. She smiled as she turned the night light and baby monitor on, and left the bedroom, leaving the door ajar.

Storm exhaled. She was rattled. Had been since seeing the news earlier. It was all she'd thought about, but she hadn't let the anxiety build inside her – she'd called Dr. Veech, who'd played the news story off as something completely different.

"There's nothing to worry about," she'd said.

It had helped calm her, slightly.

"Where are you, Dad?" she muttered. Digging her mobile out of her pocket, she decided against calling him. "I'm not his mother!" *No, but I am his daughter*, she thought, *and I'm entitled to worry*. "Fuck it." She dialled his number. "*Dad?*" she blurted, thinking he'd picked up, but it was his answer phone. "Shit," she said, trying his number again but getting the machine.

She didn't leave a message. Instead, she hung up and kept the phone in her hand as she trotted downstairs to the living room.

Should I start food for them? Is Mr. Gibson coming back? I wonder where his goons are?

She heard a key in the front door. The sound of her dad's jovial voice filled the hallway.

"…Aye, I knew there was no point in going out there," he said, chuckling.

"I guess you were right, Huw. I just wanted to see it for myself," Mr. Gibson said.

"Well, I'm glad you've satisfied yourself. I can't say I was happy in digging up the past, but there you have it."

"I'm sorry about that, truly. I just needed to see. You know, for peace of mind. I too have lost people."

"It's fine, I understand. First thing tomorrow, I'll take you to where I hid Lawrence's possessions. He was renting a small place not far from here."

"He asked you to?"

"Yes," Huw said. "He…"

"He what?"

Huw sighed. "Look, I haven't been totally honest with you. I never intended to tell you this because I thought I'd never see you or that you'd find out… Lawrence never gave me the money. I found it and kept it. I thought after everything we'd been through, we deserved a little silver lining."

"And that's the reason why you've been trying to stop me from coming down?" Mr. Gibson asked.

"Yes. Also, I couldn't stomach going through things with you face-to-face. I was hoping I'd never have to."

Storm didn't make a sound. She didn't want them to know she was close by as she eavesdropped.

"Will you be heading back tomorrow?" Huw asked.

"Yes, after I take care of a bit of business in Swansea."

"Nothing to do with the murders at the Kit-Kat Club?" Huw asked. Mr. Gibson said nothing. "I'll take the silence as a yes."

"If you will," Mr. Gibson said. "May I use your house phone? I don't appear to have any signal on my mobile. My boys must be wondering where the hell I am."

"They must be good if they've been waiting for you all this time," Huw said.

"They're well rewarded!" the gang boss said.

"I'm sure they are—Hiya, love!" Huw said, catching sight of Storm. "I didn't hear you moving around. I thought you were upstairs."

"I was. I just put Stevie down. I was going to put tea on but I wasn't sure what time you'd be home. I wish you had called – I've been worried sick!"

"I'm just going to go and use the phone," Mr. Gibson said.

"Yes, you go ahead," Huw said. "I tried, but there was no signal in the woods."

"Well, you could have tried harder!" she scolded him, tears welling at the corners of her eyes. Crossing her arms, she gave him a hard stare.

"Hey, what's this about?" he asked, moving closer.

Tears spilled down her cheeks. "They're back, Dad."

"Who, love?" He put his arms around her.

"Those sick, man-eating fucks, that's who!"

"Hey, calm down. How do you know?"

"The news. There's people gone missing in Swansea. Four or five. The police haven't released many details."

"Right, okay? People go missing all the time, Storm. You know that. I worked many a missing person's case."

"In the woods, though? And we're not talking one person, but a handful! It's weird, Dad. You have to admit that, surely?!"

"Nothing to fly off the handle about, love."

"I'm not so sure."

"Well, we'll see what's said on the news later. Let's not get carried away—"

"They never found *his* body!"

"*Shh!*" he said. "Maybe we shouldn't go to this re-opening on Saturday night. I think it'll be too traumatic for you."

"*No!* I want to go. Dr. Veech thinks it will help me. We have to go. Besides, this has nothing to do with that!"

"Okay, fine, but, if anything else upsets you then it's off. I'm not having you distraught over things, Storm."

"Okay. Oh, shit! I almost forgot – a DI called for you today."

"*Oh*? From Bridgend station, I take it? Not Watson, was it? God, will that man ever get used to my role?! It's been two years and still he comes running—"

"No. He was from the Swansea department. *Erm*, Cope. Yeah, that's right. Cope. Dylan Cope," she said, pulling away from him.

"Oh, I see. What did he want?"

Storm looked around and saw Mr. Gibson had re-entered the room. The dapper fella stood behind her, his hands crossed in front of him. He wasn't much shorter than her father, but he was a lot older. He unnerved her.

"He didn't say. He seemed to know us, though," she said. "It was creepy, but he assured me that he was a copper. He told me he would come and see you first thing."

Baffled, Huw looked at Mr. Gibson, who shrugged his shoulders.

"Did he leave a number? Contact information?"

"No, nothing."

"Right, okay. I'll give the station a ring," he told them, leaving for the phone.

Not wanting to stand in silence, Storm turned the volume up on the TV. She flicked it to the news channel.

"Mind if I put the kettle on, young lady?" Mr. Gibson asked.

"No, go ahead," she told him, not taking her eyes off the screen in front of her although there was no mention of what had happened in Swansea.

After a few minutes, Huw re-entered the living room. "Well," he said, "I managed to get a number for our friend Cope, but I can't seem to get an answer at his place."

"He could be eating or sleeping," Storm suggested.

"Yeah, or he may have been called out. They offered to try and get a hold of him for me, but I refused. He could be busy. I'm sure it'll keep," Huw said, and then turned his attention to Mr. Gibson, who was sat in front of the TV opposite Storm. "Anything from your boys?"

"No, *nothing*. They should be answering their phone. It's a golden rule."

"Do you want me to take you out there?" Huw asked.

"No, no, not now. You're here with your daughter, and I wouldn't want to worry her further."

"It's fine," Storm said. "If you want Dad to pop you over there, it's cool. Just ring to let me know you're safe if you're not rushing back."

"No, honestly, it won't be needed. If they think it's funny to ignore the boss, then they can stay where they are. We can go to them tomorrow?" he asked Huw.

"Yeah, that's fine be me."

"And you don't mind me staying another evening?"
Huw shook his head.

"It's cool," Storm chipped in. "Will you both be gone early in the morning?"

"Possibly, why?"

"I was wondering if you'd give me a lift to Dr. Veech's office?"

"We can drop you on the way," Huw said, taking a seat on the sofa next to Mr. Gibson. "Did Skye call?"

"Yeah, but I wasn't here. There's a note on the table from her which says she'd try again, but I must have missed her second attempt, too. I took Stevie to the park so we could feed the ducks."

"That's nice, love. So, Skye may come back and try tomorrow. Have you decided whether or not you're going to build bridges?"

"*Dad!*"

"I'm only asking, love. You know what I think." Huffing, Storm got up to leave the room. "Running away from your problems is not going to help," he said, stopping her in her tracks.

But it wasn't his words which gripped her, but the ones coming from the newsreader on TV. Information had been leaked to the media – not only were there civilians among the missing, but also police officers. Blood, flesh and body parts had been found at the scene, along with fragments of clothing and bone.

Storm started shaking. "I told you, Dad!" she said, pointing at the TV.

"No, *impossible*," Huw muttered. "It's been *two* years!"

"We need to find out what's going on," Mr. Gibson said.

At that moment, the phone rang. Storm picked it up. "Hello? Yes, he's right here," she said. "Dad, it's for you."

"Who is it?"

"I think it's the DI who was looking for you earlier."

"Hello, this is Davies. Yes, as a matter-of-fact I do have the news on. Yes, that's right. Look, what's this got—Do I what? No, I don't think this is related...You're crazy if you think I'm going on some wild bloody goose chase!" Huw said. "Look, *mate*, I'm not dragging my family through all that shit again. I've already lost too much. I don't even think this has the same…You've found *what* exactly? No, tell me now…Look, I really don't think you coming here is going…*What*? Oh, God!" Huw sighed and then conceded. "Fine, come tomorrow morning. Bright and early? I'll be waiting," he said, putting the phone down.

"What was that all about?" Mr Gibson asked, turning the TV off. The news had concluded.

"Dad?" Storm asked, watching her father place his hands to his face.

"It's happening again," he said, his voice cracking.

"You're scaring me, Dad. What did that man want? What's going on?"

"He reckons it's all linked, and that some of the lunatics we encountered *did* survive and have been living out in the woods close to Swansea. It's more than likely, according to Cope, that they were found by railroad workers."

"Railroad workers?" Mr. Gibson said. "What the hell would rail workers be doing out in the middle of the flipping woods?"

"Apparently, there's an old tunnel there that's to Treherbert in the Rhondda Valleys. There were plans to re-open it. It's been closed for decades."

"The woods must have claimed it," Mr Gibson said. "Swallowed it in green. They were probably out there to survey it."

"Yes, there was a council worker with them. All three have disappeared, along with the rail workers' supervisor and two coppers," Huw said.

"*Shit*!" Storm said. "I don't want you going out there, Dad!"

"Look, I may have to. Detective Cope and Mr. Gibson will both be with me."

"*No!*" she said, putting her arms around him. "What if they come for me and Stevie?"

"That's not going to happen. I promise."

"How can you be sure?"

"Because Cope seems to think they're moving away."

"And what brings him to that conclusion?" Mr. Gibson asked.

"He thinks something has been overlooked at the scene."

"Which is?"

"The tunnel itself. He told me that the brickwork didn't look right. The bricks had been disturbed. Maybe knocked down and replaced. He's not sure, and that's why he is coming here first thing tomorrow. He wants me to go with him to the tunnel and see if anything can be found."

"Well, my boys and I will come with you. We have hardware, if you know what I mean," Mr. Gibson said, winking. "I have a little payback to dish out."

"*Fuck*!" Huw said. "I can't believe this shit is happening again. Why now? *Shit*!"

"Why can't Cope do this on his own, Dad? Why does he want you?"

"Because he thinks I have knowledge on how to track those maniacs, and that I know what we'll be up against. What a joke!"

"We need to see this thing through, Huw," Mr. Gibson said. "I'm heading to bed. We're going to need our rest and I have a few phone calls to make. We could finish this thing, Huw!"

He knew the heavy was right. It would bring to end a shitload of grief.

"He's right, beaut. You know that, don't you?"

Storm wiped the tears from her eyes. "Yep," she said. "I'm off to see Veech tomorrow, so I'll have that to occupy my mind. I won't tell her about this."

"Good. And tell her we're on for Saturday night."

Storm smiled. "I'm off to bed," she said, trying to sound cheerful.

Chapter 17

As soon as the alarm on her phone buzzed, Dr. Veech rolled over and slammed her hand down on top of it. It was too early to face the world, but she had to get up. She had to be in her office at seven.

"*Fuck!*" she mouthed, rolling off the sofa in her attic office. The place was a mess. Even though she'd spent yesterday holed up in the den, she hadn't bothered cleaning her destruction. In fact, she'd created more.

She'd taken a pair of scissors to the sofa – bits of fabric littered the room. Most of her pictures had been smashed, their contents ripped or stabbed.

I don't give a fuck! she thought, walking across the scattered glass and other bits of debris. Some of it broke and crunched as she stepped over it barefoot.

In the past, she'd taken to her own body by scratching her face and yanking her hair. She'd even punched herself and head-butted walls and tables to try and calm down. She couldn't do that now. Every day she had to face the public. She didn't want people at her clinic asking questions.

When she reached her cracked mirror, Dr. Veech examined her naked body. Bruises dotted her breasts, stomach, upper arms, and abs. Most of them, a result of pinching herself.

This had fuelled rage to destroy more things.

It was a vicious circle.

She ploughed her fist into the weakened glass. What was left rained onto her feet and exposed the panelling. "*Fuck!*" She inspected her hand – the knuckles were bruised, cut and had dried blood on them. "Nothing a good scrub won't cure," she said, an intact photo of Huw catching her attention. "It's entirely your fault!" she screamed, picking up a large shard of glass and hurling it at the picture.

She climbed down the ladder to the ground floor, which stank, especially the kitchen. She hadn't bothered throwing the Chinese food she hadn't eaten away – the foil packets still lined the kitchen work top. The curtains remained closed, making the bungalow resemble a tomb. Dust motes floated in the stale air.

"I'll sort it out later," she said, waving a dismissive hand at the mess.

After a hot, brisk shower, Dr. Veech poured herself a mug of black coffee. "Time to make myself look decent," she said, sitting on the sofa to apply her make-up with the aid of a small flip mirror.

Afterwards, she dressed and finished her coffee. She took some toast to eat on the way, along with a flask of coffee and a sandwich for her lunch. She was minus her laptop, so all she had to carry was her work bag.

When she reached her car, it was gone six-thirty. Her office was little over a twenty-minute journey. *Even less at this hour of the day*, she thought. Her first client wasn't due until eight, but she liked getting there to be set up and waiting; she hated being flustered.

In the rear-view mirror, she gave herself a hard stare. "Time to get professional, Samantha," she said, taking a few deep breaths and then reversing the car down her drive.

She looked at her hands on the steering wheel. She'd managed to scrub the dried blood from under her nails, which she'd glossed with a deep purple varnish. Some bruising remained, along with minor cuts and scrapes. Nobody would notice. *Not unless they stare,* she thought, humming along to the music on the radio.

With little traffic on the road, Dr. Veech reached her office by ten-to-seven. Unlocking the door, she put the main lights on, along with a few more as she went. The receptionists were due in by seven-thirty, which was another reason why Veech liked to get there early – she wanted to make sure the staff got there on time.

She'd fired a few in the past for poor time-keeping.

The heating had already kicked in, and off, which was on timer. Walking into her office, she could feel the benefit of having the heat click on at six-thirty, as a cosy feel rippled through the air, taking the chill out of the room. Closing her door, she unloaded everything onto her desk before pouring herself a mug of coffee from her flask. There were no new messages waiting on her answer phone.

"Good," she said.

She went back to the inner office, closed the door and sat at her desk. She could now hear movement and voices beyond her door. Gloria and Stephanie, the receptionists, had arrived.

"I'm glad I'm not the only one who can make it here on time," she said, flipping through her diary. "Ah, Mr. East is first up this morning. That should be fun." She took a sip of coffee. "It's bad enough he's a pervert, let alone a chronic masturbator. I do hope he can refrain from touching his dick – I could do without seeing that walnut whip of his this morning!"

Patient number two on the list, she thought, taking a look, *is Morgan Quest.* Quest, a teenager, had been abused physically and mentally by his father, leaving his mind a scarred and ruined mess. She'd worked with him for four years, trying to untangle his knotted wiring, which she was slowly achieving. His story had caused her to cry when alone at night with his file; she'd grown to feel motherly towards him.

Not dwelling on his name too long, Veech moved on to the next name written in her electronic booking system: Storm. Her blood started to boil. She wanted nothing more than to slap the girl, but knew she had to remain professional. *Besides, she will probably want me to go to that event with her and Huw on Saturday night, which will be my cue to try and get my claws into him,* she thought.

Dr. Veech smiled and closed her appointment book. *That's enough looking ahead. The pervert will be here soon.*

She got to her feet and walked to the office door. Opening it, she saw Gloria at the reception desk – the older woman had bleached blonde hair, making her look like a canary, Veech thought, fighting back a laugh. Gloria also wore tacky jewellery and skirts of inappropriate length, which she'd been warned about before.

I'll have to pick her up on it again, Veech thought. "Gloria?" she called.

The woman pulled at her skirt before turning to face her. "Yes, Dr. Veech?" She smiled, revealing crooked, tobacco-stained teeth.

There's that 'tombstone' smile, Veech thought. "When Mr. East arrives, send him in immediately. I'll be waiting for him."

"Yes, of course."

"Thanks," Dr. Veech said, closing and standing behind her door. She placed her ear to the cool wood, knowing Gloria and the young, perky-titted Stephanie spoke behind her back. For seconds, nothing but filing cabinet drawers could be heard opening and closing. Keyboards were typed on; clocks ticked.

Then, trying to keep her voice low, Stephanie said, "What did the old crow want this time?"

"Nothing really," Gloria answered in a hushed tone. "She told me to send her first patient straight in. She's got William Wanker this morning!" She stifled a cackle.

"Oh, God!" Stephanie snorted a laugh. "She should let him have his way with her – it might loosen her up!"

"Ha-ha!" Gloria cackled, which was followed by a smacking sound. "You're awful!"

"He-he! I'm surprised she didn't send you home to change, Gloria. She's done it before."

"I know. And that's what I thought she wanted. I'd love to tell her to piss off, aye, but I need the job."

Dr. Veech wanted to storm out of her office and tear a strip off the women. *Maybe fire one as an example?* she thought. *No. No matter how annoying they are, I need them. I'll hold on to the bitches for now. Christmas is coming. Getting rid of the fucks before the holiday period will be most satisfying. Especially Stephanie, who has two young children to think of. Doesn't Gloria have grandchildren? Yes, and she loves spoiling them.* "Yes, it's going to be a cold old Christmas for that pair," she said, tittering.

Going back behind her desk, Dr. Veech heard a new voice in the reception area. It was Mr. East, or William Wanker, as he was known by Gloria and Stephanie. *Charming,* she thought, settling into her chair and turning it to face the window.

There was a knock at her door. "Come in, please." She didn't turn her chair to face him as he entered. "Take a seat, William."

"Th-th-thanks, Doctor."

He sounded nervous and she knew why.

The first time William East had walked into her office, she had been greeted by the man's cock. A couple of times after that, he'd exposed himself to her, hence why she kept her back to him to begin with.

She heard his zipper slide down, followed by the sound of his hand fumbling around inside his trousers. His breathing became ragged. She'd told him to try and control it in her presence, but he couldn't.

Or wouldn't?

It seemed she couldn't get him to control his masturbating no matter how hard she tried.

She allowed him to continue.

"How are you feeling today, William?" He answered with a grunt. "William, you must learn to control your urges! We've spoken about this in great depth over the past few months. Are you continuing with the exercises I gave you?"

"Yes, Doc. I am. I just... I can't help it!" His breathing sounded torturous.

"William, we cannot go on like this! It's been almost a year and still you haven't shown any signs of improvement. I may have to refer you to someone else."

"*No*, don't do that!" The shuffling sound stopped.

Veech felt it was now safe to turn and face him.

His eyes were on her exposed legs.

Had I remembered he was first on my list this morning, I would have worn a longer skirt and not one that covered me to the knee, she thought. "William, my eyes are up here."

"*Huh*?!" he gasped.

"Take your hand out of your trousers, William. *Good*. That's better."

"Sorry."

"Right, maybe we can talk like adults?" she said, picking her pen up in readiness to take notes.

When William left, Morgan Quest was fast through the door, not allowing Veech time to finish her notes regarding her session with East. Not that it bothered her. *I'll keep Storm waiting whilst I catch up after Quest has gone*. The thought brought a smile to her face.

Before settling with Quest, she informed Gloria to make Storm Davies wait in reception until she was ready.

In her chair again, she considered Quest. He looked solemn, his eyes heavy and his face a little sunken from the last time she'd seen him. He'd left their previous session with a smile on his face and a giggle in his voice.

"How are you feeling today, Morgan?"

He didn't respond.

The poor thing is only seventeen - so young and brittle, she thought.

The abuse had started when he was four years old and continued until he was ten. Somehow, he'd managed to find the courage to blow the whistle on his father, who'd been found guilty of sexual assault, battery and physical abuse – they gave him fourteen years. The maximum he would serve would be seven to eight, depending on behaviour.

The system's awful, Veech thought. *Castration would have been better!*

Once his father had been taken away, Quest's mother had been deemed unfit to care for her son, and Morgan was sent to live with his aunt – his mother's sister.

A year later, his mother had been found dead in her home. Suicide. Her body had been discovered swinging from a support beam in the attic. The woman's neck hadn't snapped on impact. Instead, she'd choked herself to death, a pool of dried piss beneath her – the report had been hard to digest.

After those events, Morgan had receded into a shell and wore a metaphorical mask. Nobody but Veech had managed to get through to him. It had taken two years before he'd spoken a single word.

The moment had been beautiful.

A proud moment in my career.

"Don't you feel like talking today, Morgan? You know you're safe here with me," Veech coaxed, getting up and going to the boy's side. She put a hand to his shoulder.

"Yes, I want to talk," he said, his chin touching his chest.

"Good," she said, patting his shoulder. She went to her seat, clicked her pen to attention, and put his file on her lap. "And what would you like to talk about, Morgan?"

"My mother."

Veech looked up at him. "Okay. Tell me what's on your mind."

Storm arrived at Dr. Veech's office five minutes late. The morning had been hectic, what with her dad and Mr. Gibson going out and Storm having to make breakfast and prepare Stevie for their trip. In between, she'd also tried watching the news for more information on the incident in the woods. However, the reporters had been quiet about it, instead focusing on a drug related incident which had taken place in Swansea.

Before she'd left the house, DI Cope still hadn't arrived. He'd called Huw to say he was running late, and that he would be with them in an hour or so. Storm had told her dad not to fret about the lift into town, that it was early enough to catch the bus. Making him promise to stay in contact, she'd left.

Pushing Stevie's pram into the building, Storm felt lethargic. She hadn't slept well due to worry. She was scared she was going to lose her dad, her daughter and her own life. She wasn't sure she wanted to bring this up with Veech, but thought it may be good to have someone to talk to about it, even though she'd promised her dad she wouldn't.

"I'm here to see Dr. Veech," Storm told Gloria.

"The doctor is with someone at the moment. If you'd like to take a seat, she'll call when she's ready." A synthetic smile wrinkled her face.

"Oh, okay." She pushed Stevie over to a row of seats. She sat and turned the pram around so she could see her daughter. "How's my girl? Maybe you'll have a sleep for Mammy whilst she talks with Dr. Veech?" she said as Stevie fought to stay awake.

Stevie didn't make a sound, and gave in to sleep. Small bubbles of spit popped and splattered as her breathing became rhythmic. Storm smiled and pulled her phone out of her pocket. There was a new message. She opened it. It was from her father.

'Hiya love, just to let you know we're still at home. No sign of Cope. Skye has put in an appearance, and was disappointed in having missed you. I told her you'd be here later today, so she said she'd call back and take you for a coffee, if you were up for it. I told her to ask you. I didn't ring in case you were with Veech. Speak later.'

Storm sighed and replaced her phone. Not feeling like replying, she sat and waited. Her mind reeled with what her dad might discover. *Are they really back, or is it coincidence?*

After a further ten minutes passed, Storm considered asking the reception staff if she should book another appointment, but then Veech's door opened and out walked a teenage lad. He had a huge smile on his face and the good doctor had her arm around his shoulders.

"Just remember, Morgan," she said to him, "I'm always here if you need a chat. I gave you my mobile and home number, didn't I?"

"Yes, thanks," he said. "I'll see you Monday."

"Stay positive! I don't want to see you again like you were earlier – work on the exercise I gave you."

"I will." He left and gave Dr. Veech a wave.

She waved back, and then looked at Storm. Their eyes locked. "Could you give me a few more minutes, Storm? I just need to finish writing up some notes. Okay? Good," she said, turning and heading back into her office, giving Storm no chance to object.

What the hell was that all about? Weird.

A few minutes later, a buzzer sounded behind the reception desk. The blonde woman called her. "Miss Davies, the doctor will see you now."

"Thanks," Storm said, getting up and taking the brake off the pram. She pushed it over to the doctor's door and entered without knocking.

"Ah, Storm. Come in, dear," Dr. Veech said. "Close the door behind you, please. Come, take a seat."

She pushed the pram close to the desk and then slumped into the soft seat opposite her doctor.

"*Aw!* And this must be little Stevie," Dr. Veech cooed, getting up and walking around her desk. "How adorable! She looks just like you!"

Storm smiled at that. She liked being told her daughter resembled her.

Dr. Veech smoothed her skirt out before sitting down again. "How are you feeling today?"

"Not too good, if I'm being totally honest with you."

"Oh? What's the problem?"

"Apart from the obvious?" Storm said with a sneer.

"Of course," Dr. Veech said. "How silly of me!"

"That's okay, seriously. You're not to know what's going on."

"What's happened?"

"Have you been watching the news?"

"Yes, that gangland incident is awful! They think it has something to do with the disappearances in the woods," Dr. Veech said.

"It's now connected with the story in the woods?" Storm asked.

"Yes. It was in this morning's paper. Hang on." Dr. Veech went over to her sofa and picked the paper up. Unfolding it, she looked at the front page. "Here," she told Storm, pointing at the article. "It says there may be a possible link between the two."

"Let me see." Storm took the paper. "It doesn't say there's a *definite* link between them; it says there's a 'strong chance both events are linked.'"

"I see. And what exactly does this have to do with how you are feeling, Storm? Have these stories brought back bad thoughts? Have they triggered more daydreams?"

"No, not really. Although I did have a waking terror last night," she admitted.

"Do you want to talk about it? Is it related to this?" Veech asked, holding the paper up.

"It is, yes."

"Right, okay. Do you want to firstly tell me why it's related and then move on to the dream you had?"

"On the news last night, there were reports of bones, chunks of flesh and bits of clothing found at the scene in the woods, and six people had gone missing, two of which were police officers. They're back, Dr. Veech."

"That's impossible."

"*Nothing* is impossible, Doctor."

"You and your dad killed them, Storm. They're *dead*. This," she said, holding up the paper, "is gang and drug related."

"Two of those killers were *never* found. I know they had lethal wounds, but who's to say they didn't survive? Many people walk away from bad injuries on a daily basis," Storm argued.

"That's a possibility, I suppose," Veech confessed, writing **'*STORM IS A DAYDREAMING CUNT!!!!*'** in her note pad.

"I hardly think this is funny," Storm said on seeing a thin smile spread across her doctor's face.

"I don't find it amusing, Storm."

"Then why the smiles? My dad has gone looking for those fuckers and I'm just about keeping my shit together here, *bitch*!" she snapped.

"Storm, calm down, *please*. I was not smiling at you or your problems. Something just popped into my head, I'm sorry. It was unprofessional of… Your *dad*?"

"*Yes*! He's going into the woods today with some DI who contacted him last night. This DI, Cope, also thinks the disappearances are linked to my past. He thinks he may have found something, possibly where they're hiding. I'm scared."

Tears spilled down her face as she twiddled a loose strand of hair. "What if he *never* comes back?"

Dr. Veech could do little. *My Huw,* she thought, g*one into the woods looking for demons who no longer exist? Jesus, what a fucked-up family. However, he's still my precious Huw and no harm will come to him. No, not my manly man. Never. Why? Because there's no fucking monsters in the woods!*

"When did he go?" she asked.

"This morning. Why?"

"Maybe we can talk him out of it?"

"Could we?" Storm asked. "He may listen to you!"

"Let me try calling him first. Do you have his number?"

"Of course." Storm dug her phone out of her pocket. She saw a message on the screen from her father. "He's sent me a message."

"What does it say?"

"'DI Cope has turned up! We're heading off to check on Mr. Gibson's men before going to the crime scene. I'll be back later this evening, maybe tomorrow morning. I'll keep you posted!'"

"We might be able to catch him before he leaves," Dr. Veech said, picking her office phone up.

"There's no point. The text was sent almost an hour ago," Storm said. "Besides, I think it's a good thing. If my dad and the rest do find those things in the woods, then they will kill them and end this!"

"Okay," Dr. Veech said, putting her phone down. *My Huw will be fine – there's nothing out there.* "I'm worried for you," she lied. "Why don't we finish our session and I'll take you home?"

"That would be great, thanks."

"Let's not dwell on things with your dad. Tell me about your dream last night. What happened?" she asked, plucking tissues from out of a box on her desk and handing them to Storm.

The girl turned them down. Instead, she used the back of her hand to dry her face. Before speaking, she glanced at her daughter to see if she was still sleeping. "I was at the new murder scene…"

"Go on."

"I saw *him* and a woman, but he didn't attack me like he normally does. I was getting a view of what they were up to: eating human flesh and feeding it to babies. It was sickening. It was as though I was getting a glimpse into the present, or possibly their future! I know it sounds stupid, but that's how it felt."

"I see. Please, continue."

"After they had fed, my dad turned up, along with Mr. Gibson."

"Mr. Gibson?"

"Yeah, he's one of my dad's friends who's been staying with us, the one I mentioned the other night on the phone."

"Okay, so what happened?"

"They were both killed, and I could smell their blood. My dad's blood especially! It was awful. I woke up shortly after that."

"It must have been traumatizing for you. With this newest dream, are you sure you're up to going to the re-opening tomorrow night?"

"Yes. I feel I have to. What you said makes sense. I need to face my demons. Dad said he's going, too. Are you still coming?"

"If you'd like me to, yes."

"*Please*. I think I'll need you there to help me through it. They're putting a couple of bands on which is going to be hard, what with Scuzz…"

"I know, but I'll be there to support you."

"I think it's time I got going," Storm said. "Time's pitching on and I need to feed Stevie. Do you mind?"

"Not at all! I have a free two hours now, so I'll probably head for lunch after dropping you off. Come on, let's get you home."

Once the pram was packed into the boot of the doctor's car and Stevie was in place, they drove off.

"Thanks for this. I really appreciate it," Storm said.

"Think nothing of it! I have your best interests at heart, Storm."

"Thanks, and I am sorry for blowing up on you earlier."

"Think nothing of it," the doctor said, putting the radio on.

"*…And in other news, three bodies were found at the home of a prison warder in Cardiff earlier today. The warder, a Mr. James Thornebank, aged fifty-four, was found brutally murdered along with a young police officer by the name of Daniel Gregson. The third man, who has not yet been identified, may be connected to the crimes at the Kit-Kat Club in Swansea. He may have also been involved with the disappearances of the people in the woods. The chief of police will make a statement later today…*"

"Jesus!" Storm said. "What the hell is going on?!"

Chapter 18

After Storm left, Huw and Mr. Gibson had settled down with a mug of coffee whilst they'd waited for Cope to turn up.

Thirty minutes later, there was a knock at the door.

Huw answered and was met by an average-sized man who looked dapper in a shirt, tie and clichéd trench coat.

Where does this guy think he is? 1940s Chicago?! Huw thought. "DI Cope?" he asked.

"Yes," Dylan said. "May I?"

A few more pleasantries were exchanged, and Huw let the man into his home. Not that he was happy to do so, or for being dragged into a crime investigation he had no business being involved in.

He led Cope into the living room and introduced him to Mr. Gibson. Huw informed him that Mr. Gibson was Lawrence's employer, and that Lawrence was the mysterious third party that all the papers had referred to.

This caused Mr. Gibson to open up. He proceeded to tell Cope why he and Lawrence were involved in the first place. He told him about the death of his wife and girls, and that the killers were the same ones who'd tangled with Huw.

"I see. So, you think what happened in Swansea is linked to your events?" Cope asked Huw.

"Yes, I do, and I think all the evidence points to it, as much as I don't want it to be true."

"Agreed." Cope sighed. "The information was leaked to the media yesterday afternoon."

"We thought as much. So, what's the plan?"

"I'd like to venture out to there. I think I know where the killers may be hiding," Cope said.

"*Where*?!" Huw demanded.

"I'm not entirely sure, but I think they may have made their escape down the tunnel, which comes out in Treherbert."

"We need to stop them!" Mr. Gibson said.

"We do, and fast," Cope said.

"What's the rush? We can't go up against an unknown number," Huw said. "There could be a whole fucking clan of them like last time."

"If we let them go now, they will be lost to us. Have you seen the surrounding woodlands of the Valleys? They'll be able to disappear without a trace. Lay low and never come to the surface again," Cope said. "This could be our only chance."

"He's right," Mr. Gibson said. "We need to act, Huw, like we discussed last night. And fast, by the sounds of things. It took Lawrence long enough to trace them."

"Just the three of us?"

"We need to keep it low profile," Cope said. "I don't want to cause widespread panic."

"I have a friend or two who could help us," Mr. Gibson said. "Also, the boys I came with."

"Heavies?" Cope asked. Mr. Gibson nodded. "I'm not sure that's a good—"

"They're coming!" Huw said. "I'm not going on a fucking killer hunt without some hefty backup. Now, you either deal them in or deal me out."

"*Christ!*" Cope said. "Fine. But it stays between us. Deal?"

Huw nodded and shook Cope's hand.

"I'm in," Mr. Gibson said.

"Good, then maybe we should get cracking?"

"Yes," Huw said.

They piled into Cope's Ford Fiesta Zetec, with Huw taking the passenger seat. When he was buckled in, he sent Storm a message.

"Where to first?" Cope asked.

"We need to pick my boys up," Mr. Gibson said.

"Fine. Where are they?"

"I left them stationed at the Kit-Kat Club."

"That place is a mess!" Cope said. "Nobody there is breathing."

"My guys are highly skilled. They won't be dead, but hidden. Out of sight."

"I don't care how good they are. I'm telling you, everyone there is dead. Were they suited fellas?" Cope asked, watching Mr. Gibson's face turn sour in the rear-view mirror.

"Yes. *Why?*"

"I found them dead yesterday, along with one of my PCs. I'm not going to bother wasting my time taking you there for you to see. We need to get cracking!"

"Fucking *time*?!" Mr. Gibson spat from the backseat. "They're my boys, you jumped-up little prick!"

"*Hey!*" Cope said. "They were trash, just like you, as far as I'm concerned. You live by the sword, you die by it. End of. Besides, I've lost one of mine own."

Huw watched as Mr. Gibson undid his belt and leaned in close to try and get his hands around Cope's neck.

"Leave it out!" Huw said, grabbing Mr. Gibson's arms. "Arguing and fighting among ourselves is not going to bloody help, is it? *Jesus*!"

"I could do without that shithead's quips!" Mr. Gibson said, sitting back in his seat.

"You're lucky you're involved," Cope said. "I suggest you belt up."

"Fucking wise arse! And where's my Bentley?"

"It was found this morning. Didn't either of you hear about the bodies found?"

"No," Huw said. "Any ideas who could be running around offing druggies, Cope? No offence, Mr Gibson."

"None taken, my boy."

"There was a local goon released from prison early this week. A Chester Nailfree…"

"Nailfree? I know that man!" Huw said.

"Me, too," Mr. Gibson butted in. "How do you know him?"

"I'm the man who put him away," Huw said.

"That was *you*?" Mr. Gibson said. "Why didn't you tell me? Nailfree was part of my organisation for years. I employed him as an enforcer."

"Jesus! This gets better all the time," Cope said.

"The man is a sicko," Huw said. "We wanted to get him tried for murder, but couldn't find enough evidence to make it stick. In the end, we had him on dealing, rape and GBH."

"I could have given you concrete proof!" Mr. Gibson said. "After I caught him skimming, I wanted nothing more to do with him. I wanted him killed, but he managed to escape my clutches. This is another reason why I came down here."

"Did you know a Carl Hendry?" Cope asked.

"Yes," Mr. Gibson said.

"He's also been found dead, along with a couple of his dogs."

"Do you have any *good* news for me?!"

"No, I don't. Apart from knowing where your car is," Cope said, looking in the rear-view once again.

"Oh, marvellous," Mr. Gibson said, rolling his eyes.

Huw said nothing and dug his mobile out of his jacket pocket. There was nothing from Storm. "Where are we heading now?" he asked.

"Ask the Godfather," Cope said.

Mr. Gibson didn't bite. "Well, if we're heading Swansea way, we could swing by the docks. I have some businesses down there and some men I could lay my hands on to help us. We may also be able to get some guns."

"Jesus Christ," Cope said. "What have I mixed myself up in?!"

"Look, if you want to take them down," Huw said, "then you'd better start getting used to your hands being dirty, pal, because we can't play by rules when our opponent doesn't understand them!"

"We might not be up against that much of a challenge. Hell, we could be looking at a drug and gang thing and nothing more."

"You don't really believe that though, do you?" Huw said. "Otherwise, why drag me into this?"

"No, I don't. And for what it's worth, I'm sorry about what happened to you and your daughter. I spent most of last night reading up on it all, which I found pretty grim."

"You could say that," Huw said.

Cope took the turn he needed for Swansea docks on the murkier side of the city. At night, he had three teams of two-man patrols doing a beat.

Most cities were glum and had their rough spots like Swansea: homeless, football hooligans, drug dealers, pushers, mules, pimps and prostitutes. Most of life's unwanted used the dock area for their unhealthy activities, Cope thought, looking at how abused the area was.

His men did their best to keep the place safe by moving the filth on and by stopping the women from toting their business. It wasn't safe for the scantily clad ladies of the night. Over the years, some had been killed, with multiple others being raped and/or beaten.

Cope knew some of the women and classed them as friends. If they were unwilling to move on, he made sure they were safe. He didn't like what they did, but got *why* they did it. Besides, it wasn't just the women getting attacked in the area, but also dock workers, people who were trying to earn an honest wage.

"God, what an eyesore!" Huw said. "And I thought Cardiff docks were bad."

"Aye, what a *shithole*!" Mr. Gibson said.

"It gets worse by the month down here. I've lost count of the men I've had hospitalised from doing beats at the docks and surrounding areas."

"I could probably help you with that, Detective," Mr. Gibson said.

"No thanks. I don't want to be a part of any illegal activity. No blood money will cross my palm," he said, looking in the rear-view mirror.

"Ha-ha!" the gangster chuckled. "I'm not asking for *anything* – no money, no favours. I'm offering to keep your boys and gals in blue safe, not to mention the docks free of trouble."

"Go on," Dylan said.

Mr. Gibson smiled. "This chap we're about to meet, Kirk – he *runs* this dock, along with Cardiff's and Newport's. He knows everything and everyone, so if you want things under control, he can help. He'll keep the place clean and your patrolling coppers safe. Guaranteed."

"And why would you want to do that for me?"

"Because I respect the law, Cope. I may sit on the other side of the fence, but I still respect you. I'd do anything to help."

How warm-hearted of you! Cope thought. "One of my men is dead because of you!" he blurted.

"Nailfree was, and is, a renegade. I want him dealt with myself! Have for years. But please, I urge you to speak with Kirk."

"Well, thanks for the advice. I'll think about it."

"You do that," Mr. Gibson said.

He looked at his watch. It was time to get ready. They would arrive soon.

He didn't like mixing work with coppers, even though one of them was retired. Still, this couldn't be helped. The order had come from the top: Mr. Gibson. The money man; the guy who'd helped him many times and got him back on his feet after he'd been released from prison. If it hadn't been for Mr. Gibson, Kirk wouldn't have had the job as dock enforcer.

Kirk lifted his bulk off the sofa and crossed to his carryall. *Mr. Gibson had been looking for a big strong man to guard his docks, and had come to me first,* he recalled, rifling through his bag filled with handguns, a machine gun, grenades, radios, and more.

Kirk had accepted the job, which involved guarding shipments of drugs and guns that left the docks. He'd also been given the responsibility to pick his own team. People he trusted. And, if any of them stepped out of line, it was up to him to deal with them and their mistake.

The men Kirk had enlisted were ex-cons, but in all the years he'd been running the area, no shipments had gone missing. Also, there'd been no stealing, double-dealing or backstabbing.

Satisfied everything was in his bag, Kirk zipped it up.

"We're going to need guns, bullets and plenty of both," Mr. Gibson had told him. *"And not just for us, but also for the cops."*

"Who are we fighting?" Kirk had asked.

"'A dangerous enemy, Kirk.'"

He stood and pulled his drooping cargo trousers up. He placed the loaded bag by the door and caught a glimpse of himself in the mirror.

"What an Adonis!" he told himself. Kirk stood at six-foot-seven with impressive muscles: his arms, shoulders and back rippled. His head was shaved. His nose was flat and his eyes were sunken but quick. Kirk didn't miss a trick, especially when it came to guarding his boss' money and investments.

He wore a white, washed-out vest with an open check shirt. The bulge of a gun could be seen under his armpit. He turned from his mirror image and stepped outside. He removed the shades he had in his top pocket and put them on. The sun was brilliant. It was hard to believe he would be killing people on a day like this.

"Needs must," he uttered, locking the door to his boat. It wasn't clear to him how long they would be gone, but it didn't matter – he'd put his number two in charge, a man by the name of Ralph "Teeth-Pulling" Jones.

The nickname said it all.

Ralph and Kirk had grown up and gone to prison together. He was a man Kirk trusted more than his own mother, God rest her soul.

Getting off his boat, *The Great White*, Kirk looked about him. None of his boys were around. He knew most of them were doing patrols, whilst others were inside the warehouses going about their business. Some were probably drinking and playing cards.

He didn't mind that at all.

The boys were hard workers in and out of drink. They respected and feared Kirk. They knew heads would roll if shit didn't get done, and that was why he gave them plenty of leeway to booze and gamble.

He heard a car approaching.

Dylan rounded the corner into the dockyard, and hit the brakes when he saw a giant of a man standing in the road. "Bloody hell!"

"Nothing to worry about," Mr. Gibson said, putting his hand on Dylan's shoulder. "That's my man, Kirk."

"Is that *one* man?!" Huw asked.

"You wouldn't think it, would you!" Mr. Gibson said.

Dylan stayed quiet as he drove close to the giant. *What the fuck am I doing? Getting involved with shitheads, that's what. Fuck, a drug dealer and his muscle. I should be heading off on my own – there's no saying there's man-eating monsters in the woods!* he thought, but deep down he knew something awful was awaiting them in the tunnel.

The passenger door opened. "Pop the boot," Kirk said. "I'll toss my gear in there."

Without a word, Dylan put his thumb to the boot button on the dash and pushed. It made a low *thump* sound in return. "There you go."

"Cheers!"

"Why does he sound as if he's been up all night drinking whiskey and smoking cigars?" Huw asked.

186

"The voice is an act," Dylan said. "I've seen it a million times. The likes of him thinks it puts the shits up people."

"You're wrong," Mr. Gibson said. "He had an accident as a child – he was kicked in the throat by a ram."

Dylan raised his eyebrows, then looked in the rear-view. He could see the top of Kirk's head. "What's he doing back there? Is he okay?"

"Kirk?" Mr. Gibson asked.

"Coming," the man said, his voice but a rough whisper. "Just giving the gear the once-over – I thought I'd forgotten torches."

"Have you?"

"No, boss. I have plenty. Batteries, too."

The boot slammed shut, making Dylan cringe.

The man folded himself into the back. "Couldn't you have got a smaller car?!" he asked Dylan, a chuckle escaping him.

"Ha-fucking-ha," Dylan said.

"Oo," Kirk said, raising his hands in front of him as though he was holding a handbag. "Sorry, missus!"

Mr. Gibson laughed and clapped a hand to Kirk's shoulder. "I apologise for my associate's humour – it's an acquired taste."

The DI eyed him in the mirror. "Is that right?" He clenched his teeth. "Get your belt on, Kirk. I know you hate us 'pigs', but this is my show. Any bullshit and I'll run you and your boss in, make no fucking mistake about that. I'll also crush this little dock business you have going on. Understand?"

But he wasn't finished. He turned in his seat so he could tear into them more, spittle flying from his mouth as he became irate. "You pair are only here because of the ex-DI. I wanted to go it alone, but it would seem we are up against something worse than the likes of you two."

"I didn't want anything to do with this shit in the first place. I would have been quite happy for you to have gone it alone and kept my past buried. *Thanks*!" Huw said.

"Look, we need to work together to achieve what we all want," Mr. Gibson said. "I'm not here to step on toes. I just want to get this done."

"That's fine by me," Dylan said. "But before we go, I need to know I have your full co-operation?"

"You have ours," Mr. Gibson said.

"Mine, too," Huw confirmed. "But if we don't find anything by tonight, I'm heading home. I have a thing with my daughter to attend tomorrow night. I can't and *won't* let her down."

"We'll be done and dusted by then, I'm sure," Dylan said, starting the car.

Dylan parked his car half-a-mile from the crime scene and they walked the rest of the way.

When they got closer, Dylan had Mr. Gibson and Kirk hang back, thinking there may be officers still posted at the scene. He'd told them at the station not to bother, that the forensic team had got what they needed.

Surely there will be nobody here now?

A smile crept across his face as he led Huw towards the tunnel – the area was deserted. All that remained were a few police tape. Before calling Huw last night, Dylan had stopped off at the station to inform his superiors that he wouldn't be around for a few days.

"I've had a tip from a snitch about the killings at the Kit-Kat Club," he'd told his commanding officer.

He'd been excused and wouldn't be bothered until he returned. If they knew what type of stunt he was pulling, they would fire his arse. *I have to get this right*, he thought, going up to the bricks blocking the tunnel entrance.

He put his hands to the stone. They were ice cold. A chill whistled through the cracks and brushed his face. The faint sounds of dripping water and squawking rats could be heard beyond.

He put his ear closer. A brick was disturbed and fell inwards. "I knew it!" he mouthed. Backing up, he gave the structure a hard kick, sending bricks tumbling. They crashed to the disused tracks behind.

"Bloody hell!" Huw said. "You were right. Not hard to see why the forensics missed it – someone did a good job in covering it back over."

"Up here," Dylan called Kirk and Mr. Gibson. "*Quick*!" He heard their rushing footfalls and pushed himself away from the wall.

"So, it's true," Mr. Gibson blurted.

"We need to go now," Dylan said, "whilst we have a lead. It's only already been a day."

"They could still be in there. Lost in the darkness," Mr Gibson offered.

"I doubt very much that they're lost," Huw said. "If it *is* them, then they will be able to see perfectly fine in there."

"Give me a hand," Dylan said, removing more bricks.

Without another word, all four men pitched in and uncovered the opening to the tunnel - it was a wide-open, toothless mouth, ready to swallow them alive.

Kirk opened his bag and gave them each a flashlight and handgun. "I'll go first," he said, pointing the weapon and torch out in front of him.

A howl of wind cut against them as they entered the tunnel and disappeared into the blackness.

Chapter 19

Paula woke for the second time. Her jaw had stopped stinging but the memory of the family and the pain she'd felt for them remained. She had intended to warn them, but darkness had taken her.

"He knocked me out," she muttered, lying dazed beneath a night sky – her ankle was roped to a tree, the knots impossible.

Still, no further harm had come to her, and food and water had been left by her side. Paula calmed herself and devoured the feast to stop her stomach from aching and rumbling.

They only knocked me out so I wouldn't be able to help the family, and not because they were being mean, she told herself. *He wouldn't hurt me intentionally, not now – he thinks I'm obeying.*

But you are…

No! I'm only making it look good.

After filling her belly, Paula spent the next few minutes picking at her restraints, but they were too tight. She gave up. *This is hopeless! I'll just keep playing ball for now. There will be better opportunities for escape. In time, he'll trust me enough so he won't have to rope me,* she thought, drifting back to sleep.

Birdsong and the smell of cooking food stirred her. Paula felt wonderful as she sat up and stretched – she was engulfed by nature. *There's nothing to think about: work, family, friends… All ties are severed! No stress, worries or boss riding my arse!*

Wow, hang on - what am I thinking? Don't I care if I don't go back?

"What's wrong with me?!" she uttered.

"Look how liberated we are!" the voice inside her head said.

*"No…*I want to go back!" she whispered.

Paula arched her back and rolled about the floor – the rope at her ankle bit into her flesh but she didn't care. She giggled, thrashed and tossed about the fallen leaves, twigs and loose grass. *"Freeeee,"* she squealed. "I'm free, free, *free!"*

She laughed some more, which sounded insane.

Paula thought she heard and felt something crack inside her head.

Someone is flipping the switch inside my brain! Nah, it's just we haven't been taking the antidepressants…

A large shadow fell over her.

Paula turned onto her back and looked up. It was Skull. He had a lopsided grin on his face as he stared down at her. Loose bits of flesh clung to his lower lip. "We go soon," he told her.

"Okay," she said, her heart galloping. Blood rushed to her ears and her chest pumped up and down rapidly. Her nipples stood erect – she didn't bother to cover them.

She followed his gaze to her tits.

She was starting to feel captivated by his primitive ways. It excited her.

He's going to take me at some point whether I like it or not, she thought. *And if I fight, he'll probably beat me. Make it hurt more than it has to.*

Paula looked to her side and saw the woman busying herself with her children. She looked back at him and slowly parted her legs. Coyly, she bit her bottom lip.

A quiver of excitement shot through her.

I'm close to orgasm! her mind screamed, watching as his dick hardened.

She welcomed him with open arms, inviting him on top of her.

He was rough. He bit and scratched her flesh, but it heightened her pleasure. He nuzzled into the side of her neck.

As he rammed into her, she let out a sharp, shrill yelp. Paula had not expected him to be so forceful and brutal, considering she had invited him. Yet he grabbed her shoulders and shoved against her as hard as he could.

She felt a trickle between her legs.

Blood!

Paula didn't try to stop him.

His blackened nails tore at her skin. Paula gasped and moaned with every bolt of excitement that coursed through her – she couldn't remember the last time she'd felt so alive and exhilarated.

It seemed to go on and on as he pumped and pumped – each rough thrust felt as though he pushed deeper into her. Like she was being rammed into the earth.

More fluid dribbled from between her legs and she wasn't sure if it was a mixture of their juices, or more blood.

She grabbed tufts of grass either side of her as she climaxed. His whimpers were minimal. "Oh, *shit!*" she gasped, another wave of pleasure washing over her.

Then he grunted and gestured that he was coming. Skull grabbed her sides tightly and thrust his dick deep inside her. She felt his cock pulsate as it shot its load. He then collapsed onto her chest.

They lay together for a few moments before he finally moved.

She smiled at him.

He was emotionless.

"I untie you. We move," he said, cutting her ropes and allowing her to stand.

"You don't have to keep holding that," she said, indicating the rope. "I'm not going anywhere. I promise."

"*Move!*" He grabbed her arm and led her in Eight-Ball's direction.

Skull wanted them deeper in the forest by sunset, because he knew people would come. It was only a matter of time.

Skull held Paula's leash as he led her into the woods. Eight-Ball, carrying the babies, had the rear. They had tried concealing their presence by hiding the family tent and what was left of the bodies.

"Faster!" he told Paula, who was being dragged along.

"There's no need to be rough! I could go faster if you weren't holding me."

"*Umph!*" Skull threw the leash to one side. "Stay close," he told her. "I trust."

"Hey! That almost whipped me in the face, Skull. There's no need to be so physical," she snapped at him. "You don't have to hurt or abuse me anymore. I *am* trustworthy. I *want* to stay! I like it…"

What am I saying? Paula wondered. *This can't be right, can it?! I'm a professional woman. I have a job, house, and family and friends who love me…They must be worried sick. I-I... I also have a shrink and happy pills – tablets that help make life bearable.*

What? Have to go back? No, I don't. I don't have to be a slave to the coin or to my husband and children. A drone to the machine that's killing me slowly through drink and depression. I could get used to the killing! And the shock of having to eat people and wildlife is already wearing off on me.

Her mask was slipping.

At first, the fear of being caught trying to escape had made her stay, but as the days and nights had drawn on, Paula had backtracked. She no longer wanted to run. She'd been kidding herself.

I had a chance to try and escape this morning. I could have found something to cut the restraints or had a better attempt at picking at the knots. Was this the reason why I let him close so easily? Do I enjoy being controlled?

Yes, I do! I've just never had the chance to explore it until now!

Being put in her place was a buried urge. Most men in her life had been scared off by her need to control, thinking she was a little weird.

Well, not this one! she thought, looking at Skull. *He may not understand my needs but that's okay.*

As they continued through the woods, they heard a noise ahead. It sounded like thickets being thrashed.

Paula felt his hand on her shoulder as he brought her and Eight-Ball to a stop.

Skull grabbed Paula by the neck. "Behave!"

"You don't have to worry about me."

Skull scoffed at Paula and moved closer to the bushes in front of him. He kept low as he parted the greenery. Before him were two men with horses. This pleased him, but he didn't know if he would be able to kill both on his own. They were big men, possibly farmers.

Skull looked back and saw Eight-Ball had her arms full, what with the babies and some of their equipment. "*Ugh!*" he grumbled, facing the men again. He knew he had to give this kill up, because attacking them alone was out of the question.

"We can't go!" Paula told Skull. "Those men have horses and supplies. I will help you. *Please!*"

Skull didn't trust her. He didn't know if she was trying to use the situation as a means of escape, or if she genuinely wanted to help and be a part of them.

She show progress, he thought. *I test her.* "You go stand out there. I go around," he told her, indicating circular movement with his hand.

Paula was about to step out of hiding when Skull pulled her back. "You wait. I go first. When you can't see me, you go," he said.

She nodded. She knew what he meant.

Now that Skull had disappeared, she pushed through the bushes and exposed herself to the men. They didn't notice or hear her, and continued with their work.

Annoyed, she yelled, "*Help!*" Her sudden outburst startled the men and they looked her way - they seemed younger than her thirty-four-year-old self. "Will you *please* help me?!"

At first, they gawped at her, her nakedness a thrill. But then they looked horrified. She was filthy – her body was caked in dry blood and forest.

"I've been attacked," she said. "They tore my clothes off!" She started sobbing.

"Who...*who* did this?" the biggest of the two asked. He'd been wearing a kerchief around his mouth, but lowered it to talk.

"*Men*. Down there!" she wailed, pointing in the direction they had come from. "*Five* of them. They held me down and ripped my clothes off. They took turns raping me! You have to help! *Please*!"

"Jesus, Christ!" the second man said. "We should call the police!"

Paula fell to her knees. "*Please*! You must help. *Help*!"

"Come on, Eric!" the big man said. He pulled the kerchief free from his neck and removed a flask from his saddlebag.

"Okay, Ted," the other said, walking towards Paula.

"Are they still looking for you?" Ted asked, unscrewing the cap from his canteen.

"I-I..." Paula gasped. "I'm not sure. Can I have some, please?" she asked. "My mouth is so dry!"

"Of course," Ted said, handing her the water. "Drink as much as you need. I'll get you my coat to use."

"No need, just call the police!" As she took the bottle, Paula glanced at the hunting knives sheathed at Eric's and Ted's sides. She could also see an axe embedded in a stump close to where the men's horses were tethered to trees.

There was no sign of Skull. Not yet.

"*Thanks*," Paula said, taking large gulps of water.

"I'll call the police," Eric said.

"Thank God!" she said.

A slight rustle behind the two men got her attention. Paula looked up and saw Skull stalking out of the bushes. He grabbed the axe and crept towards Ted.

Paula sobbed as loud as she could to cover Skull's noise.

Skull thudded the axe into Ted's face. He folded like a deckchair. Blood escaped his wound like a ruptured dam.

Skull dived for Eric, but was too slow – the bigger man sidestepped and elbowed him at the base of his neck. He fell, sprawling headlong into nearby thickets.

"*Jesus*!" Eric yelled when Paula went for the knife at his side, but he managed to swat her thieving hand away before putting his bear-like paw to her face and shoving her backwards, hard.

Paula slammed into a tree, knocking the breath from her. As she slipped down the bark, she coughed up blood. She curled into a wheezing ball. All the while she kept one watery eye on Skull.

"Come on!" Eric screamed. "Let's have you!" He drew his knife.

Skull got to his feet and winced. His left side was beaded with blood from his skid along the ground. He grunted when he poked his injury and then licked his blood-stained fingers clean. "I'll cut your throat!" he said, walking forward.

Eric also advanced, his knife at arm's length.

Paula tried to get back to her feet but collapsed under her own weight.

The men circled each other, with Eric whipping his knife back and forth in Skull's face. "Come on, make your move!" he taunted. "Not so tough without the element of surprise, are you?!"

Then Eight-Ball emerged from the trees. Skull stood still and smiled.

"What are you waiting for?" Eric said. "Come and get—*Argh*!" he screamed as a thick branch slammed down on his outstretched arm. He dropped his blade.

Skull took his chance and advanced on the man.

"You've broken my fucking arm, you ugly *bitch*!" Eric yelled.

Eight-Ball lunged at him and clamped her broken, bent teeth down on his face. She squeezed so hard, bone broke. Some of her rotten teeth fell apart and surfed away on the blood pumping from his nose, but it did not stop her.

"Get off!" he screamed, going to his knees.

Finally managing to get to her feet, Paula watched Skull approach with Eric's large hunting knife.

"I want to do it! Give me the knife!" she demanded and walked towards Skull.

Eric whimpered. Blood and tears streamed down his face. Eight-Ball wrapped her man-like hands around his throat, pinning him to his knees.

Skull hesitated at first, but turned the knife and offered her the haft. Paula smiled and took it. Skull joined his sister.

"Pull his head back," Paula demanded. "By his hair."

"*Arrgh*!" Eric screamed, his neck exposed.

"Let's see you push me now?!" she said. She put the blade to the man's throat and slowly sawed through his neck.

His eyes crossed as he choked on his blood. Hot squirts of it splashed her face, mouth and eyes. Some managed to find its way up her nostrils.

She giggled when Eric's head came off in Skull's hands.

After their run-in with the farmers, Skull, Eight-Ball and Paula took a few hours to explore the area. At first, it seemed that they had bumped into two men out for a horse ride. However, on further inspection, the three found they'd stumbled onto private land. A log cabin stood among the foliage, set back out of the way. Smoke had been billowing from the chimney when they'd approached, but they found nobody inside, which suggested they were alone.

They found more horses in a small stable at the back, along with a pigpen and chicken coop. Skull located hunting rifles and spare ammo in the cabin, along with food, water, beds and a roaring fire with plenty of wood.

Skull told them they would be staying for a few days. It was a good place, and the horses would come in handy for when they were ready to leave.

"Nobody look for us here. We safe," he said.

Nevertheless, Skull didn't want to get too cosy. He was sure people would be on their tail. Even if there weren't, he didn't want to play things too safe. In a few days, they would leave.

As night descended, they sat around the fire in the living room. Skull made constant checks at the front and rear of the cabin.

Instead of using the food they'd brought with them, they'd carved and cooked the farmers – there was enough meat left over to last them a few more days.

"Are we moving on in the morning?" Paula asked. "People will be looking for me by now. I don't want to go back!"

"Stay tomorrow," he said. "We rest."

Paula nodded.

Eight-Ball cradled her babies and said nothing.

Paula got to her feet and rooted through cupboard drawers. She found a couple of bottles of wine and took them to the kitchen, where she uncorked them.

"Drink?" she asked Skull, who took the bottle and sniffed the contents. Grunting, he gave it back to her. "Please yourself!" Paula took a few greedy swallows and wiped her mouth with the back of her hand. "It's lovely."

"You two. Sleep now!" Skull told her and his sister.

"I'm going to shower first," Paula said. "I want to freshen up."

"*Rest!*" he snapped.

"I will, but I want a shower first!" she bit back, holding her ground and then stomping off with the bottle of wine.

Eight-Ball didn't say a word as Paula huffed past her. Instead, she tucked beneath the blanket she'd placed by the fire after making sure her babies were sleeping safe and sound.

When Eight-Ball started snoring, Skull got up and went to the front door to make sure there was nobody outside. Satisfied, he stepped out, and checked on the horses and livestock. He was happy in thinking they were safe for the night.

We kill chickens and pigs if we stay. 'Nough food to last days, he thought.

He gave the area another scan – even though it was dark, he could see well enough, having grown up in caves and dark places. He also had excellent hearing and smelling abilities – he could track like a sniffer dog if need be.

People looking for us, we move deeper into woods. Have to hide! He slammed his fist against a tree in annoyance. He didn't know how far he would have to take his family, but knew it would be a great distance. This angered him. His plan had been to get strong and hunt down the girl.

It wait, he thought. "Family first."

When he opened the cabin door, Skull was greeted by the sound of running water. His hand instinctively went for his knife and then he realised it was Paula.

He made his way over to the bathroom and opened the door to a sliver. He spied on Paula as she washed herself and marvelled at how her body glistened under the spray and soap.

His animal instinct took over.

Skull threw the door wide with force, causing it to bounce off the wall. Paula shrieked. He tore the shower curtain off its flimsy hooks and Paula yelped once more. Before he could grab her, she caught a hold of his hand and led him into the shower.

"I knew you'd come. I lingered on purpose."

The hot spray caught him off-kilter but he liked it.

Her lips met his.

He grabbed her sides and pulled her close. Their bodies smashed together, splashing water everywhere. All the mud and debris sluiced off him, running down their bodies and legs. His cock pressed against her.

She swapped position and placed herself under the spray and bent forward. Paula then placed her hands flat against the tiles and spread her legs, exposing her arse and pussy to him.

Skull didn't need coaxing. He grabbed her hair and yanked her head back. Her squeal made him smile, but she didn't complain when he pulled again. He let go of her hair and grasped her small tits as he rammed his cock inside her.

Skull thrust hard and fast, keeping his hands on her breasts. The spray of water bounced off her back and splashed his face, but he didn't lose concentration.

After climaxing, Skull got out of the shower and left Paula pressed against the wall. She slid down the tiles into a crumpled, sitting position. Her body quivered.

She said nothing, staring at him until he turned and left the room.

Skull entered the living room and checked on his sister and babies before lying next to the fire. In the darkness, he heard Paula get out of the bath and enter the room – he saw her nakedness in the shadows cast by the flames.

He was unsure what to do. *Do I get rope? Tie her?* Even though she'd killed for him and given him her body willingly, Skull still didn't completely trust her. He had to be vigilant – he had little ones to think about.

Then she did something unexpected.

Paula lay by his side and pressed her wet body against him. She tangled her legs with his. The fire crackled in the background. She didn't say or do anything except cuddle him.

Within a few minutes, Skull heard her soft snores. Normally he would have shoved her away but didn't. He couldn't understand why as he drifted off to sleep.

Chapter 20

After the fight had broken out in the warder's home, Chester had managed to wrestle the gun off Gregson – he'd emptied the gun into the copper's face and chest. He had then dragged Janice out of the house and down the street to their car.

Some of the neighbours had heard the gunshots and had been peeking from behind curtains as the blood-soaked duo fled.

Pictures were being shared.

The police had their man in their sights. It was only a matter of time before they found him and took him back to his box-sized home.

Once he'd got Janice into the car, Chester had jumped behind the wheel and sped from the scene. As they fled, Chester had knocked two people down before ploughing into a parked vehicle.

His head had bounded off the windshield, breaking his nose. A few teeth were knocked free. He'd scrambled out of the car and had been forced to draw his empty gun on people who had gathered. To his amazement, he'd managed to get Janice into another vehicle and out of there.

It hadn't been safe to take Janice to the hospital, so he'd taken her to a friend who'd failed medical school. The wannabe doctor had managed to remove the bullet and patch her up successfully. But, she could barely walk.

She would slow Chester down.

Chester's friend had homed them for the night so they could hunker down and catch their breath. Chester had suggested they go to a remote house he had close to Bridgend. High on drugs and weak from blood loss, Janice had agreed, even though she'd stated earlier in the day that she wanted to go to her own home.

"The pigs will be crawling all over your home by now! That wouldn't be a wise move," he told her. Chester had other plans that needed seeing through. He'd waited too long for things to fuck it up now.

The following day, Chester stole another car and drove them to the secluded home he'd told her about. When they arrived, Chester parked around back. But he needn't have worried: there was nobody around and the home was flanked by woods and fields.

He got out of the car and went around to the passenger side to pick Janice up. He cradled her in his arms like a baby and carried her to the front door.

"You never told me about this place?"

"I've not told anyone, babe."

"Can we live here?"

"Not until all this shit is sorted."

"Stay with me!" she pleaded. "Forget that pig. Stay. *Please*!"

"Janice, you know I can't do that."

"I'm in agony, Chester. *Please*!"

"*No!* Besides, it's your own stupid fault for getting shot in the first place."

"Don't say *that*! I couldn't fucking help it that Griff let that pig get the better of him."

Not responding, he took her into the living room and dumped her onto the sofa. "I'll get you a pillow and blanket," he told her. "I want you to stay here."

"Okay," she sobbed. "Can I use the TV?"

"Yes, but make sure the curtains are closed and the lights remain off. I'll get you some food."

"Thanks, but I'm going to get blood on your sofa!"

"I wouldn't worry about that. I'll have it taken care of. I'll be right back." Chester disappeared upstairs and fetched some bedding. On returning, he propped a pillow under her head and threw the duvet over her.

"Thanks, babe!" She snuggled under the duvet. "I don't think your mate did a good enough job, you know."

He ignored her. "I'll get you some water and tablets to keep you going."

She smiled at him.

When he got to the kitchen, he punched through a cabinet, and wrenched doors off cupboards. Plates and cups exploded across the room as he hurled them in his fury. She wasn't going to make it, he could tell. She was still losing blood – all his mate had managed to do was slow things down.

Janice would either bleed out or go to prison by calling the cops and turning herself in.

There was only one thing he could do to make sure she was safe.

Chester drew a butcher knife from a drawer.

He went back to Janice with a glass of water and a box of pain killers. "Here you go, baby."

"What was all that noise?"

"Oh, I was rooting around looking for the pills," he said, handing her the tablets and placing the water on the table.

She popped two pills into her mouth and washed them down with a swig of water.

He sat by her side and smiled. "I love you, Janice, and we're going to be together forever. Prison won't come between us," he said, brushing her hair out of her face with the back of his hand.

"They have to catch us first!" She smiled back at him.

"That's true. But when—*if* they do, it won't keep us apart."

"You're acting weird."

"I'm sad, baby. Sad I have to go on alone when I thought you and Griff would be here to help me take care of that fucking pig."

"I know. I wanted that, too. I never intended to fail you."

"Nah, you haven't. Don't even think that." Chester put his hand behind his back and removed the knife from his waistband. "Just know that I love you more than anything." He bent down to kiss her on her lips.

He let his kiss linger before punching the knife through the duvet and into her guts. She gasped and tried to pull back, but he ripped the knife up her stomach and into her chest.

Blood squirted up Chester's face and turned the white duvet red. Janice tried to hold her ruined guts together but failed. Blood trickled from her nose and erupted out of her mouth. Tears spilled down her cheeks. She tried to speak, but only gargles came. Bloody saliva popped and bubbled as she attempted to form words.

Chester bent over and stroked her forehead. "*Shh*, baby. I love you. I could never forgive myself if you had to spend time behind bars. I'd rather see you dead," he told her. "I'll be with you soon." He took a hold of her hand and squeezed it.

"*I…ugh…argh…love…*" she gargled. Blood spattered Chester's face.

He smiled at her. "Goodnight, my love." He gave her a kiss on her forehead. When he pulled back, she was dead.

Chester stood and pummelled everything in sight: chairs flew through windows, curtains were ripped down and his booted foot shattered the TV.

After twenty minutes of destruction, Chester flopped into a chair and sobbed. Close by was a bottle of whiskey, which he grabbed. He needed to stay focused. To think about his next move now that Griff and Janice were dead.

He wiped his eyes and looked at the greying Janice. Most of the blood on her face had dried. She looked peaceful.

Did I have to kill her? I could have kept her out of it! he thought. *No, that wouldn't have worked. Her prints, along with Griff's, are all over that house. There were eyewitnesses, too. They'd have thrown the book at her. You can't kill two coppers and hope to get off! Besides, if they hadn't have charged her with murder, they would have tagged her with aiding and abetting. Fucking pigs!* He swigged the fire water.

"I couldn't have seen you go to jail!" he told Janice, getting to his hands and knees to crawl to her.

He took her hand in his. "This is all my fault. I should be lying there, not you…" He kissed the back of her hand and then got to his feet, crashing back into the chair.

He gulped more whiskey and wondered what he was going to do – in all the confusion his plan had slipped his mind.

Where were we meant to be heading after the screw's?

"The *doctor!*" he yelled, jumping to his feet.

That bitch completely slipped my mind. Yes, that's right, he thought. *We were going to pay that fucker a visit. Huw's headshrinker. No, not Huw's – his daughter's. The little fucker must be messed up. If I can locate the doctor, then I can force her to take me straight to her patient's house. Huw's house.* This made him smile. "Hang on, how are we going to find the doctor?" he asked Janice. "We don't even know her name, baby?!

"Wait, wait, what the fuck's wrong with me? I have the information! That pig cop gave it to me," he said, rooting through his pockets for the piece of paper. He found it in his back-right and pulled it free. Unfolding it, he looked at the address for the doctor's surgery. "Doctor Samantha Veech."

He slugged more whiskey as he walked over to the large sideboard adorning the room. On top of it were various trinkets: plates, vases, glassware and ornaments that had belonged to his family – along with the home.

Opening one of the drawers, he rifled through it in search of the phonebook. Not finding it, he moved on without closing the drawer and opened the next. Nothing. Chester kept going.

"Got you, you fucker!" he said, grabbing the book and pulling it from a drawer. He ignored the mess he'd made and sat back down. Chester opened the directory and found his eyes needing to adjust to the words. "I have to lay off the fucking booze!"

His eyes momentarily flickered to Janice.

Her lips are blue…She's so cold!

Chester tore his eyes off her and focused on the directory. "Doctors, that's what I need to look under," he said, thumbing his way down the index. "Veech, Veech…" he mouthed, scanning the *V* section.

Not finding it, he almost threw the book across the room but came to his senses. "Hang on. Not doctor, but psychologist!"

He flipped through the *P*'s and found what he was looking for. Again, he mouthed to himself as he searched. "Got you!" Keeping the page open, Chester used Janice's mobile to make the call.

It rang four times before a receptionist answered. "Dr. Veech's office, how can I help?"

He hung up. He didn't know what to say. His mind felt clouded by the whiskey. "*Shit!*" he said, looking at the clock. It was a little before midday. He tried again.

The same woman answered.

"I'd like to make an appointment to see Dr…erm, Veech. Dr. Veech," he said, trying not to slur. He couldn't tell if he was doing a good job though.

The woman told him that the doctor was full until next week, and that there were no slots available. After taking some details, which Chester lied about, he asked for directions to the office and their hours of operation.

After she told him what he wanted to know, Chester hung up on her mid-sentence. "Fuck you, bitch!" He felt happy looking at the address. "Nothing's going to stop me now!" he said, relaxing in his chair and closing his eyes.

Within minutes, Chester was out cold.

His dreams were invaded by Janice. She loathed him and wanted him dead. As much as he struggled and cried in his booze-induced slumber he continued to sleep until three in the afternoon.

Waking with a start, he threw the whiskey bottle that had been resting against his side. "Where? What? Fuck! *Jesus!*"

He checked Janice. She was dead. Unmoving.

He got to his feet and walked around the room. Sweat poured from his forehead. His head thumped. Chester went to the kitchen and searched the cupboards for more pain killers. Downing four, he filled a glass with water and pissed in the kitchen sink.

Feeling relieved, he went back to the living room and retrieved the doctor's information – it was time to hit the road. From where he was, it would take him close to forty minutes to reach her office, which would be closing at five.

"Shit, I hadn't meant to sleep for so long! Still, I must have needed it," he said, checking himself in the mirror. "*Fuck,* I better put some fresh clothes on. I can't walk around in blood-soaked gear!"

Chester headed upstairs to change into clothes he knew he had hanging around in his old wardrobe. Once dressed, he kissed Janice goodbye.

Fucking hate leaving her here like this. Not much choice – I have to take care of business. She would understand, he thought, covering her with the duvet.

When he got into the car, he took one last look at the house. He would never see it, Janice or Griff again. He felt sad. Life had taken a sharp U-turn.

"Janice," he whispered, starting the car and turning it around. Chester headed onto the main road.

As he drove, he pushed all thoughts of Janice from his mind and concentrated on the job at hand. How would he play this? Was he going to barge in and take the bitch hostage?

It's pretty clear there's staff there, he thought. *Well, a receptionist. Taking her from her workplace by force might be hard.*

"I'll hang around outside for the bitch. Follow her home," he told himself in the rear-view mirror. "Or, I wait until I think the building is empty?"

Not a bad plan, he thought. *I could park-up and wait. Stake the building out and find what this bitch looks like.*

Yeah, that's what I'll do. I'll wait the bitch out.

It was closing in on four o'clock when Chester reached Dr. Veech's office. The place seemed quiet. Deserted, almost. Chester found the perfect parking space opposite the small building.

Nobody went in, nobody came out.

He sat in silence. Few cars passed by, which was good. Nobody was paying attention.

After waiting patiently for thirty minutes, Chester decided it was time to get out of his car and investigate the window at the side of the building. He could see a light shining behind it.

Could that be the good doctor's office? Let's find out!

Chester crossed the road and sneaked around to the window. It was ajar. Soft voices came from within. He moved closer, enabling him to see through the well-polished glass.

A woman, who sat with her back to him, was taking notes. A young lad of around twenty was laid on a sofa, talking to the ceiling.

That's got to be my woman! Chester thought.

Instead of heading back to his car, he loitered a little longer. He needed to make sure she *was* Dr. Veech.

When her patient confirmed it by speaking her name, Chester ran back to his car.

As five-past-five approached, lights within the building switched off. When two women came out of the office, one much older than the other, Chester ducked out of view until he thought it was safe. He watched them walk towards a car and get in.

A few seconds later, the lad who'd been with the doctor appeared – his hasty tracks made Chester smile. "That's it, fuck off!" he said.

To his delight, the light in the consulting room switched off. "She's coming, thank fuck! I was beginning to think I'd be here all fucking night."

Chester watched as Dr. Veech closed and locked the main door.

He kicked his car to life and watched her approach hers. When she pulled out of her parking space, he followed.

"She can take me home with her," he said. "All those files she was carrying. Poor thing! Maybe I can give her a back rub!"

Ten minutes later he followed the doctor onto a quiet street. When she pulled into her drive, he parked his car opposite.

Chester watched as she entered her house, oblivious to his presence. He decided to give it a couple of minutes before knocking on her door.

Chester sprinted across the street and up to the bungalow. Nothing stirred. He pushed the bell and heard it chime within. "How pleasant!" he muttered.

He heard the sound of approaching footfalls, followed by deadbolts clacking. Chester turned his back to the door as it opened, not allowing the doctor to see his face.

"Yes, can I help you?" she asked.

He turned and punched her in the jaw.

Chapter 21

The dark was consuming.

Even his flashlight and good intentions did nothing to drive the fear from Huw – never had he experienced such impenetrable darkness. He felt as though the walls around him were closing in and crushing the breath from him like an anaconda.

Not only that, but the journey was endless. They hadn't come across anything to suggest others had passed through anytime recently. Then again, it was pitch black – spotting something out of the ordinary would be difficult.

Huw had meant to contact Storm prior to entering the tunnel, but had forgotten. And now, with limited light and probably no signal, he risked dropping and losing his phone.

I'll ring as soon as I get out of here! His thought spurred him on. Huw needed to get to the other side as soon as possible, because he knew his little girl would be worried. *Can't stop.* Won't *stop!* *Not that I want to sit in the darkness and feel its weight on my shoulders.* He quickened his pace.

"How much further do you think, chaps?" Mr. Gibson said, breaking the silence.

"Not much, I hope," Kirk said. "These fucking rats are trying to get up my trouser legs. Little bastards!"

Huw sniggered, finding a reprieve from the anxiety.

"Put bicycle clips on," Dylan said. "That'll stop 'em!"

"Oh, ha-fucking-ha," Kirk said. "I really need you, don't I?!"

"Get moving," Mr. Gibson said. "Don't keep stopping to talk. *God*, I'll be glad to be out of this tomb!"

"Let's just hope it's not a wild goose chase," Huw said.

"Let's not start that again! We all know they're out there, Huw. That they've resurfaced," Dylan said.

"I want those fuckers dead!" Mr. Gibson said.

"When we get to the other side, I'm sure we'll find more clues."

"Ten-to-one, we run into some whack job who likes to hurt animals." Kirk slipped on a wet piece of railway line. "*Fuck*!"

"What the hell?!" Huw cocked his gun.

"Easy, Sundance! I slipped, that's all. It's wet around here."

"Can't you hear the water dripping?" Dylan asked.

"*Shit*!" Kirk blurted. "I think we might have to turn back."

"What is it?" Mr. Gibson asked.

"*Look!*" Huw said, raising his torch. Ahead, in the thin beam of light, the track couldn't be seen due to it being submerged.

"How deep do you think it is?" Dylan asked.

"Well, it's up to my calves already," Kirk said.

"Mind walking a bit further?" Huw asked.

Without another word, the big man took a few tentative steps. The water rose to his knees, and then his waist, where it stopped. "It doesn't appear to be any deeper than this. Come on," Kirk called.

Huw went second, followed by Mr. Gibson. Dylan took up the rear.

"Bloody hell, my nuts have shrivelled!" Mr. Gibson said.

"I can't feel mine!" Dylan admitted. "But I believe they're halfway up my back."

"It's getting shallow," Kirk informed them. He had stopped and appeared to be waiting for them.

"You're sure someone would have come this way?" Mr. Gibson asked. "It doesn't seem likely – not with all that water."

"Don't be so sure," Huw said. "We made it without a struggle, didn't we? Besides, a little water isn't going to stop or slow those murdering, man-eating fucks."

The group trudged on for a few more hours and found little trouble. No water. No dangers. No obstacles.

Then, when they rounded a bend, Huw was first to spot a new problem – a section tunnel. Its roof or wall had collapsed, blocking their path. *Bollocks!* It looks like we'll have to turn back after all. There's no way anyone got through this. You must be wrong, Cope," he stated.

"We can't!" Dylan said. "We'll lose a day trekking back."

They huddled around Huw and raised their lights.

"Hang on. I think I see a pathway," Huw said. "Look. By there – someone or something has disturbed the rubble."

"He's right," Dylan said, walking to the area Huw was referring to. "Rubble has been cleared to create a slender passageway. I can see the other side. Come on, lads."

Kirk followed Dylan, with Huw on his heel. "God, this is madness!" the big man said. "We should have driven to the other side!"

"This will be quicker," Dylan said. "Trust me."

"How could this be quicker?" Kirk asked.

"It's a direct route. It could take us hours, days even, to find the end of the tunnel in the valleys."

"I thought you said it came out in Treherbert?" Huw asked.

"It does, but I'm unsure where. And I'm not going around asking – if my superior knew what I was doing, he'd string me up by my balls!"

"And if this little mission of yours goes wrong, *I'll* have you strung up by the balls," Mr. Gibson said.

Dylan stopped and turned to face the crime boss. "You and what army, pal? Fucking Lurch over there?!" Dylan hooked a thumb over his shoulder.

Kirk grunted at this.

In the light of his torch, Huw could see Dylan's face turn red.

"It's okay, lad," Mr. Gibson told his gorilla, then turned to Dylan. "I'm not accustomed to being spoken to in such a manner, DI."

"No, I don't suppose you are." Dylan got in the older man's face. "You know how I feel about your kind. You're filth."

"Yes, but you know you need me. Huw certainly does."

"Guys, guys, come on. We haven't got time for this, for fuck's sake. My daughter's probably going out of her mind with worry," Huw said, getting between the pair.

"A punch-up isn't going to solve anything," Kirk said.

"Agreed," Huw said, pushing on.

"I think we should be moving?" Mr. Gibson said.

"Yes, I do too. If you make any more threats, I'll take you down, *mate*!"

"Fucking pig," Mr. Gibson uttered.

Huw shook his head. *This is total madness. All of it!*

Up ahead, cracks of light filtered through a wall.

"That's got to be the exit, guys," Huw exclaimed. "I can feel fresh air." He picked his pace up. Freedom was a breath away.

"Thank God for that!" Mr. Gibson said.

"What time do you think it is?" Huw asked. "My watch is broken."

"It's seven," Dylan piped in.

"*Seven*?! Jesus! We've been in here hours! I need to get home to Storm."

"Calm down," Dylan said. "It took slightly longer than I thought. As soon as we get outside, you can call her and let her know you're safe and that you might not be home until the morning."

"I can't stay out here all night, man!"

Kirk started pushing at the wall, distracting Huw – bricks toppled and more light spilled in.

"We haven't come all this way to go home," Mr. Gibson said, siding with Dylan.

"He's right. We can't say 'fuck it' after all this. By the time we convince the cavalry to come out here, the trail will be cold."

Huw conceded. "Fine, okay."

"Good," Dylan said.

"Do you guys mind giving me a hand?!" Kirk grunted.

Dylan and Huw joined Kirk's side and helped push the rest of the structure down. When the dust settled, Huw saw the sun was starting to fade, but the heat that remained warmed their cold bodies.

"Jesus, I'm glad to be out of there!" Huw said, taking deep breaths. "All I can taste is dust." He dug his mobile out of his pocket and noticed there were no missed calls or texts. "Odd." He realised there was no signal on his phone. "*Fuck!*"

Looking up, he saw Mr. Gibson and Kirk standing together. They were looking at the ground and saying something. *What have they found?* he wondered.

His phone made a series of silly jingles as the signal returned. Huw saw three missed calls, a voice message and a text message, which he opened first: '*Tried calling you several times but couldn't get an answer. Please call me when you get this. Storm. X'*

He dialled her number and let it ring until it was finally answered. "Hey, love…Yeah, we're fine. Sorry I've not been in touch…Yeah, bloody signal. We've been in the woods," he lied. "Listen, I don't think I'm going to be home this evening. I know, but—*No*, I'll be around for tomorrow night. *Promise*. No, *definitely*. I'll be there! Look, I'd better go. I'll keep in touch…I love you, too. Bye," he said, ending the call.

"Huw, over here!" Dylan called. He had joined Kirk and Mr. Gibson. "I think we may have found something."

He pocketed his phone and walked over to them. "What is it?"

"Look!" Dylan pointed at the ground.

Huw pushed his way between them and looked in the mud. There* were three sets of footprints, two of which were exceptionally large and appeared abnormal. Deformed, even.

"Well, I guess that certainly proves they came through here," Huw stated.

"Come on, let's get after them," Mr. Gibson said. "Follow them."

Huw didn't wait for an invitation as he forged through the foliage in pursuit of his prey.

As the sun began to set, Skull decided it was time to leave the cabin. After telling the women to prepare for their travel, Skull set about laying traps in the surrounding area. It took him close to an hour to do.

Finished, Skull mounted one of the horses with Paula at his back. Eight-Ball, who had her babies strapped to her chest, mounted a beast of her own. They set off through the woods at a gentle pace. Skull hoped to cover as much ground as possible before nightfall, with plans of finding a good place to set up camp for the evening.

"The forest sounds are nice at night. Don't you think so?" Paula asked him, breaking his chain of thought.

He didn't answer.

"Look at all those stars! Such beauty. I've missed out on so much. Thank *you*!" she told Skull, giving him a squeeze.

He grunted and shook her off.

"No need to be like that!" She put her arms around his stomach once again. He didn't resist. "See, you do like it."

Soon the moon was high in the sky. Its milky rays slashed through the trees, lighting up the ground ahead of them.

"Good," he muttered. "We have path."

Skull stopped when they came to a small lake. Sufficient distance had been covered and the light was lost. "We stay," he said, jumping off his horse and tethering it close to the water so it could drink.

He went to his sister and helped her off her horse and tied her animal close to his.

"Set up camp," he told them. "I get wood for fire."

He watched the women go about their duties and then headed off into the forest.

When he returned, Skull saw a circle of stones had been laid to accommodate a fire, into which he placed his collected kindling. He lit the fire and sat beside it.

Paula joined him.

Eight-Ball, who had taken up shelter under a massive oak, was feeding her babies.

"We should be safe here," Paula said.

Skull nodded. "We go when sun up."

"Do you really think there are people coming?"

He grunted. "They look for you."

"They may have thought I was killed, and haven't bothered?"

"They still come. They know about me."

"Yes, I know about you, *too*!" He glared at her. "You were behind those killings in Bridgend a couple of years ago," she said.

"Bridgend?"

"Yes, the town where you killed all those people and set fire to a building."

"Yes. My family help."

"Your sister, too?"

"And more. We were bigger family," he said, proceeding to explain to Paula what had happened and how much he wanted revenge on Storm.

"You know where she is?"

"Yes. But I was weak. Couldn't get her. Now I strong!"

"I will help you." Paula took his hand in hers.

"Good. But first, we need to be safe. My *babies* need to be safe."

"Agreed! I need to get some sleep," she said, yawning and stretching. Paula settled down by his side and rested her head on his lap.

He looked over at Eight-Ball and saw she had settled the babies and was sleeping herself. Content, Skull sat for a while and stared into the flames.

He hoped the traps at the cabin worked. He was adamant people were coming. He could sense it.

Maybe I hang back? Let the women go. If traps don't work, I can kill people. Babies be safe, he thought. The idea made sense. *I set a trap here. Make them think Paula dead!* Did he even need her? Was she that much of an asset? *I could kill her now. Let people find her. That work too! More women where she came from.*

His hand went to his knife.

No. She good woman. Listen and like me. I make babies with her and Eight-Ball.

If he was to hang back, then Skull knew exactly what he needed to do. It may waste time, but it would be worth it. Also, if it worked, it would mean they could disappear for good. Then *I go back and kill her*, he thought.

For his plan to work, he would need to find others to kill. He smiled as he stared at the fire. Skull rocked back and forth. *Shouldn't be too hard. Always people in woods!* His smile grew bigger, exposing his teeth and gums. Shadowy flames danced across his face. *Yes, a good plan.*

He lay down and drifted off to sleep.

The footprints had taken them a few miles in a northerly direction, before ending abruptly in the middle of nowhere. They were left with a cold, dead trail. Night had settled in.

"Now what?" Kirk asked. "I can't see fuck all!"

"There must be more tracks around here somewhere. They couldn't have been *that* careful in concealing their movements," Dylan said.

"You don't think so?" Huw chipped in. "They did well in covering their tracks at the tunnel in Swansea. They fooled your men, didn't they? If it hadn't have been for your quick thinking, they *would* have gone undetected. These are hill people. They know how to hunt, track and be sneaky. Don't underestimate them. I did, and it got a lot of people killed."

"He's right. They have the advantage out here," Mr. Gibson said. "They're crafty sons-of-bitches!"

"What if we can't get a trace?" Huw asked.

"We keep looking. No matter how long it takes," Dylan said.

"This is fucking madness!" Kirk threw his bag onto the ground. "I'm not moving until daybreak."

"I agree with Kirk," Mr. Gibson said. "The last thing we should do is stumble around in the dark on their territory. They'll pick us off."

"Christ, they could be watching us now," Huw said. "We should lay low and keep our voices down. We need to wait for daybreak."

"*Fuck!*" Dylan said, throwing his hands up. "You're probably right. What a bloody mess."

"What time is it?" Kirk asked.

"*Erm…*" Huw struggled to read his watch. "It's a lick after gone eleven-thirty."

"The sun will be up in a few hours – let's just wait it out," Kirk said.

"Then what?" Huw asked.

"We pick up the trail again – I'm sure they've left other signs behind."

"Have you got any food or water in your bag, Kirk?" Mr. Gibson asked.

"I've got enough to go around. I expected us to be out here the night, possibly two."

"Good, then we rest until sunup. Our targets aren't going to travel in the dark," Mr. Gibson said matter-of-factly.

"You don't know for sure," Dylan said.

"They could even be in the area!" Kirk pointed out.

"Well, *whatever*. We can't stand around here yapping," Dylan said.

"We could head back to the tunnel? That would offer us shelter, at least," Mr. Gibson offered.

"No, that's a bad idea – it's a few hours' walk," Dylan said.

"Agreed," said Huw. "If we're going to do this, I say we stay here, as much as I don't like it."

"I'm unsure," Mr. Gibson said. "What do you think, Kirk?"

When Kirk didn't answer, Mr. Gibson walked to where the man had been standing. "*Kirk*?! Where did he go?"

"He was standing there a second ago," Dylan said, turning and aiming his torch into the bushes. "*Kirk*?!" he called, keeping his voice as low as possible.

Not wanting Dylan to go alone, Huw pointed his light at the bushes in front of him and pursued the DI, leaving Mr. Gibson to stand guard.

"Where the hell did he go?" Dylan asked Huw.

"I'm not sure…"

"*Shh*, I see him!"

"*Where*?" Huw asked.

"Right in front of us!"

"Is he hurt?"

"Not by the looks—*Psst!* Kirk!"

"Will you two keep it down?" Kirk said. "I've found something."

Dylan and Huw quickened their pace.

"What is it?" Dylan asked.

Kirk pointed his flashlight at his find.

"What the *hell*?" Huw gasped.

Before Kirk could answer, they were startled by Mr. Gibson bursting through the bushes.

"Bloody hell!" Huw said. "You almost gave me a fucking heart-attack, man!"

"What is it?" Mr. Gibson asked, ignoring Huw.

"The foliage has been trampled here," Dylan said.

"But what *is* it?!"

Kirk bent for a closer look. "Flesh and dried blood."

Huw gave the area a sweep with his light and noticed more tracks and specks of hardened blood behind them. "*More*!"

Their torches illuminated Huw and the section of ground he was looking at. There was more than gore: clothes, toys, body parts, strips of fabric, flesh, teeth…

"I guess this is the final bit of proof we needed, gentlemen," Dylan said.

"The same as what was found the other side of the tunnel," Huw balked, looking at the fatty mess and blood-spattered toys. His stomach had grown weak since leaving the force. "Your suspicions were correct, Dylan. Not that I doubted it. I just didn't want to believe."

"Let's follow the tracks," Dylan suggested.

"Fucking right," Kirk agreed. "Let's get those child-murdering cunts!"

Chapter 22

She'd forgotten to tell her dad about Skye coming around earlier in the day to see her and Stevie. It had not started well.

Begrudgingly, Storm had let the woman in. The conversation had been one-way traffic. Storm hadn't wanted to see Skye again and had told her so. But Skye was persistent. It aggravated Storm and made her bite.

"It's a shame you weren't so clingy years ago!" she'd said.

"I deserve that," Skye retorted. "But it's not how you think it is. We were young, foolish and clueless. I didn't know how to bring a child—"

"And what about Dad?! Do you think he did? He managed. Still does. We don't *need* you, so why don't you fuck off?! Leave us alone. You're dead to me. To Dad, too!"

Storm cracked her across the face again.

However, Skye hadn't let it lay. She'd slapped back, forcefully, causing Storm to dish out another smack across Skye's face, which was much harder.

"You don't *ever* get to touch me again!" she'd told Skye, who had leaned out of Storm's way. She'd looked, her eyes wide. Her lip bled.

But still Skye had tried to win over Storm. "I love you. Always have!"

"That's rich! And why are you repeating the same old nonsense as the other day? You've already told me this BS! You've seen your grandchild, which I have to say is very lucky. If it was up to me, you'd get nothing." Storm had picked Stevie up and cradled her to her chest.

"Then why are you being so kind?" Skye had said, wiping the blood from her lip.

"Because of Dad. He's the only reason. Like I said, you're nothing to me. *Never* will be!"

"Please give me another chance. I'm begging you! That's all I'm asking, Storm. We all make mistakes!"

"Why? Why now? You've had years to try and make a difference."

"I know, and I'm truly sorry!" Tears streamed down her face. "I'm a bad person, and I don't need you or your father to tell me that. I'm just looking for a second chance – to be forgiven. *Please*!"

"I need to put Stevie down. Why don't you make us a cuppa?" Storm had huffed. She'd been too tired and worried about her father to argue. "We can chat a little longer. It doesn't look as though Dad's coming home anytime soon…"

"I'd like that. But why don't you let me put Stevie to bed?"

"I'm not sure that's a good idea. I like to read her a bedtime story—"

"That's okay, I can do it. I used to read to you when you were growing inside me…" Skye had said, letting her words trail off. A poignant expression washed over her face.

Storm had felt a lump develop in her throat and relented, handing her daughter to Skye. "Okay, you take her. Her nappy will need changing."

"Where's her book and things to change her?"

"She likes *The Hungry Caterpillar* – it should be on her nightstand. She has a changing table in her room. You'll find everything you need in there."

"Oh! *The Hungry Caterpillar*, is it?!" Skye cooed. "That's a new one to me."

"Dad and I normally take this part in turns," she'd confessed. "I think he likes the book more than Stevie."

"Well, he used to be an avid reader."

"I'll get the kettle on," Storm had said, wiping the tears from her eyes

"Great. I'll be down shortly."

As Storm waited for the kettle to boil, she listened to Skye on the baby monitor reading the bedtime tale to Stevie with a funny voice. It brought a smile to her face and a fresh tear to her eye.

Could she find it in her heart to forgive?

She poured hot water into waiting mugs with coffee at their bottoms. Storm thought about it. *Could* she forgive? It was something that would take time. You couldn't forgive someone that easy. There was no trust. Skye would need to earn that.

And what about Dad? she thought, stirring the coffees. *What will he think about me making peace with her? I don't think he'll care, as long as I'm happy. It's not like she'll be my mother, but a friend. Maybe. But only with time. Many visits and conversations…I hardly know the woman!*

Storm took the drinks and the baby monitor into the living room. She heard Skye wishing Stevie a pleasant night's sleep, followed by, "Gran loves you, Stevie."

As she placed the mugs down on coasters, Storm heard Skye coming down the stairs. "Did she go down okay? She can get cranky at times."

"She went down a dream, bless her. She's gorgeous. I can see you and your dad in her."

"Poor lamb!"

Skye chuckled. "Is that one for me?" she asked, pointing at the mug closest to her.

"Yes."

"Thanks."

"I only put milk in. Do you take sugar?"

"Yes, but only one."

"I'll—"

"No, sit yourself down. I could do without the sugar," Skye said, tapping her almost flat stomach.

Storm, for the first time, realised she looked nothing like her mother. "Do you really see me and Dad in Stevie?"

"Of course. I wouldn't have said it otherwise. Why?"

Storm looked down at her coffee. "Nothing, I guess. I'm just being silly."

"Hey, I may not have been around the last so many years but I can tell something is bothering you. *Spill.*"

Looking at Skye, Storm smiled. This was something she thought she would never do with her mother – share a chat over a coffee. She gave Skye all the lurid little details about what had happened in the woods, and how she became reckless and loose after it. "I can't help but worry she'll think bad of me for not knowing who her father is."

"Aw, baby!" Skye said, setting her coffee to one side and grabbing her daughter's knee. "Stevie won't think any less of you. She'll understand that you went through a stressful time."

"That's what Dad and my doctor told me…I don't want her thinking I'm a bad mother!"

"You can't think things like that. Besides, she's just a baby now – you haven't got any explaining to do right this second. She'll understand, trust me."

"I guess," Storm said, wiping tears from her eyes.

"Hey, come on. You have Dad. And me. If you want me, that is. We're all here for you, Storm. We'll help you through it all."

"Thanks. I'm sorry for being so fucking horrible to you!"

"You had every right to be. I did you an injustice, love. I gave up on you. Walked away."

"I may have thought I hated you, but I don't. I don't think I ever have or will. I just wanted my mam," Storm said.

"That's good to know. I've lost count of the amount of times I wanted to pick up the phone or come running to you, Storm."

"I'm glad you finally found the courage to come running."

"When I heard about what had happened, I knew I had to get to you. Or at least a message," Skye said, taking a gulp of coffee.

"Where are you staying tonight?"

"At a local hotel."

"Stay here. I'd like the company." Storm looked up at the clock and saw it was getting late. She removed her phone from her pocket, hoping she'd missed a call or text from her dad. Nothing.

"I'd like that," Skye said. "Do you mind if I take a shower? I need to get settled for the night if I'm staying."

"Of course," Storm said.

Skye got up and headed for the bathroom.

Storm switched the TV on just as her mobile rang. 'Dad' flashed on and off its screen.

After a short conversation with him, she felt a lot better – she could relax now she knew he was fine, and that he wouldn't be home until the morning.

That's cool, as long as he's safe, she thought. *It'll give me and Skye some time to ourselves.*

"Did I hear you on the phone, love?" Skye asked, coming out of the bathroom with a towel wrapped around her head.

"Yeah, it was Dad. He called to say he wouldn't be home tonight."

"Still caught up in his work, I see, even though he's not with the force anymore?!" Skye said. "I remember those late-night calls from him to say I wouldn't be seeing him."

Storm felt slightly wounded by her comment, but let it go. After all, she was right. "I guess some things never change, right?"

"True. What's he doing, anyway?"

"He thinks he's found a lead on the people who attacked us," Storm said. "I think he has too, and I'm worried about him."

"He'll be fine! Your father will put a stop to them, trust me," Skye said. "He won't let anyone or anything get the better of him."

"Yeah," she sighed. "I just don't want the past to destroy us."

"That's not going to happen, love. Let's try and stay positive, okay?"

Storm nodded. "Let's watch something?"

"What do you fancy? Something funny? Is there anything good on the box?"

Storm flicked through the channels in hopes of finding something that would help keep her mind occupied.

"Did I just see *Brewster's Millions*? *God*! I haven't seen that film in years," Skye said.

"Yeah, okay. I don't mind watching that," Storm said. *It's one of Dad's favourites*, she thought.

"I'll make us a fresh cuppa," Skye said, picking her and Storm's mugs up. "Try not to worry. Your dad's as tough as nails!"

"I know. The way he handled it last time was incredible. He was there for me…" she said, looking at Skye. Storm could see the hurt and shame in the woman's eyes. "I didn't mean for it to come out like *that*! I wasn't trying—"

"Storm, it's fine. I know what you meant. He's always been there for you, love. Your father has cherished you from the moment I told him you were growing inside me," she said, wiping tears away. "I'm so, *so* sorry I left…"

"Skye, it's okay, honestly. You had your reasons, and we can make up for lost time."

"There's no excuse, really – I ought to have been there for my daughter! A mother should *always* be there for their child. *Always*!"

Storm said nothing.

"Your silence says it all. But it's fine. As I said, I've learned to accept. I guess I had to, knowing I'd never be close to you like a mother should. That's my punishment. The guilt, too."

"I'm sure we'll get closer over time, Skye."

"I hope so. If it's okay with you I'm going to hit the sack? I'm pretty worn out."

"Don't you want to watch the end of the film with me first? There's only twenty minutes left."

"No, I'm off up," she said. "What are you doing tomorrow? Maybe we could go shopping?"

"Nothing in the day, but in the evening Dad and I are going to a 'gig' of sorts."

"The grand re-opening?"

"Yeah, that's right. Did Dad tell you about it?"

"Yes, plus I've been around town. I was going to ask if we could all go together…But I didn't know how things would work out between us."

"Well, I certainly don't mind you coming, but you may find it a bit awkward. My doctor will be with us. Not only that, but Dad's girlfriend may grace us with her company. Although, I'm not too sure what's going on there."

"Is this the woman he works with?"

"Yes. Well, *used* to work with. He told you about her?"

"Yeah, the other day. Look, I don't want to intrude—"

"No, no, you *should* come. It'll give us a chance to talk further," Storm said. "I'd like it. It may even help me through the night. You do know that's where *it* happened?"

Skye nodded.

"Shall we have a girlie day out?"

"That could be fun!" Skye smiled. "We could hit a few shops in town and maybe get something nice to wear for the evening?"

"Sounds awesome. I know a few nice places for food too."

"Right, it's a deal!" Skye stuck her hand out for Storm to shake. "Best I get myself to bed, then."

"As soon as Stevie is fed and ready to rock'n'roll, we'll head off."

"Fine by me."

"Cool! I'll see you in the morning. Goodnight."

"Night, love," Sky said, leaving the room.

Storm picked the TV remote up and switched the set off, having lost interest in the film. She then put her head back against her chair. She had mixed emotions about everything.

Skye's clearly in bits over what she did, she thought. *Can this really work? Two days ago, I hated her guts! Imagine if it was me, though, and Stevie didn't want to see me after I told her about my past? I'd be crushed! Dad certainly seems to have forgiven her, and I don't think there's anything wrong with giving out second chances. Life's too short to hold grudges, right?*

Storm yawned, stretched and then checked her phone. No calls. No texts. *God, I hope he's okay!*

She put her thoughts to one side and texted him. When it was sent, she got up and proceeded to switch the lights off as she made her way upstairs. On the landing, she could see light coming from under Skye's door. She was still awake. Crossing to her bedroom, she tapped on the door.

Storm could hear her sobbing.

"Are you awake, Skye?" Storm asked, not wanting to show she'd heard her crying.

"Yep, I was just about to turn the light off. Goodnight!"

"Nighty-night," Storm said, and then walked over to Stevie's room. She pushed the partly open door wide and checked in on her daughter, who was sleeping soundly. "Aw, love her. Goodnight, Stevie. Mammy loves you!" she said, blowing a kiss.

When she entered her room and flicked the light on, *he* was there.

Skull stood on her bed.

He slowly turned to face her.

She wanted to scream, but it caught in her throat. Storm collapsed against the door, closing it tight. A wheezed "*Huuuuh!*" escaped her flapping mouth.

There was no head in his hand this time, just a knife, which was covered in blood from haft to tip. More crimson adorned his chest, arms and legs, along with mud and bits of foliage. His mouth twitched into a half-smile on seeing her. Slowly, he lowered one leg to the floor and got off her bed.

The mattress springs crunched.

"Mine," he growled.

Storm shook her head frantically as he closed the space between them. "No, *please*!" she whispered.

He raised his knife in readiness – blood dripped from its serrated edge. She pushed back against the door as far as she could and then cowered into a ball. "This can't be real! Wake up. Wake up! One, two, three, four…"

He was still coming when she opened her eyes. She could smell him and his natural surroundings: wet earth and bark.

"…Five, six, seven, eight…"

His image started to fade.

"…Nine, ten…"

He disappeared into thin air.

"Fuck, fuck, fuck…" she uttered, trying to catch her breath.

Stevie started crying but she couldn't get up – fear kept her welded to the floor. "He's gone. He's *gone*!" she repeated, rocking back and forth. "Breathe, Storm. Breathe. My daughter needs me…"

She got to her knees and crawled to her bed, which she used as support to stand. Her mobile then alerted her to a text message. With a shaking hand, she opened it.

"*Dad*!" she mouthed.

'I'm proud of you for forgiving her, Storm! Still tracking our targets – will keep you posted and speak in the morning. Love you. X'

Storm sighed, put her phone down and went to her daughter.

Chapter 23

Although he'd hit her square on the nose and it pissed blood, it had remained intact. Chester had then closed and locked the front door before dragging the unconscious, semi-naked doctor to her bedroom. He'd then thrown her onto her bed and tied her spread-eagled.

He was in.

Now, looking at her, Chester wondered why she'd answered the door in a robe, which had been open. He couldn't see a belt on it.

Maybe she's kinky? he thought, smiling.

He intended asking her when she woke up.

As he waited, he made sure all curtains, windows and doors were closed before rifling through her fridge and finding beer.

Happy he was secure inside the tiny property, Chester opened a can and sat in front of the TV. The news was broadcasting his story and face – the manhunt was in full swing. All known addresses and associates were being investigated. Beer spurted from his lips as the newsreader reported that Janice's body had been found. A nosy jogger had spotted him leaving the house.

"*Fuck*!" he said, slamming his can down on the coffee table. "But it's not a problem. At least Janice won't be lying there for weeks to rot into the sofa."

Thankfully, the jogger had not been able to identify the car in which Chester had sped off. The trail was cold.

Chester scoffed. "They haven't got the first idea where I am. Dozy pig cunts!"

He flicked through the channels and found his mug was being broadcasted on most stations – there was no getting away from it, until he found a *Family Guy* marathon being aired on a backwater site. "Sweet! Looks like it's on until two-thirty. Hopefully that bitch will have woken up by then – I haven't got all fucking night. Still, who gives a fuck."

Chester threw his empty can against the wall and got another. Whilst at the fridge, he spotted packets of meat and cheese. "Nothing like a midnight snack!"

He tore through the sandwich and took gulps of ice-cold lager between mouthfuls. "That's the fucking ticket," he said, burping. Once finished, he raided the fridge again – his hunger had now been sparked.

When did I eat last?!

He made more sandwiches and took them, along with beers and crisps, over to the sofas. He tucked in as he watched the adult cartoon. "A growing lad needs his energy!" he quipped, almost choking as he laughed.

A few moans from the other room made him turn the volume down on the TV.

"Who...who's out there?!" Dr. Veech said, her words slurred. "Please, I have money! Take what you want!"

Chester smiled. "Oh, I will – don't you worry about that!" he said from the living room.

She started sobbing.

He chuckled.

"Weeping is not going to do you any good, bitch. Tell me, do you always answer your door with your tits and bush hanging out? *Well*?!" he pressed.

"*No!*" she choked.

"Are you sure? You seemed pretty comfortable with it."

"Let me go, *bastard*!"

"*Wow*! Quite the mouth on you, Doctor. I was expecting you to be reserved – a lady. A professional. Not a foul-mouthed bitch who swears worse than a gin-soaked sailor," he said, getting up off the sofa. "I may have to take my belt off to you, woman!" Chester undid the buckle and slipped it through the hoops of his jeans as he walked.

"I'll cut your nuts off if you come near me!" she screamed, thrashing against her restraints. Her body thundered against the mattress.

Chester ran into the bedroom and shoved the first thing that came to hand into her mouth, which happened to be a pair of her panties. She tried to force them out with her tongue, but he rammed them further down until she started to gag on the stale garments.

"Shut. The. Fuck. Up! Or I'll slice your fucking throat open, cunt!" He brandished a knife he'd taken from the kitchen in her face.

Her eyes darted from side to side – her body quivered beneath his weight.

"If you keep up the noise, I will! Right now, I don't want to harm you. Chances are, I'm not going to either. All I want is information on a patient of yours. That's it. Give me that, and I'm gone. Okay?"

She nodded frantically and muffled something through her gag.

He removed her sodden knickers from her mouth and told her to repeat it.

"I-I…" she said, snorting and gasping for air.

"Don't scream, or I'll put this knife through your fucking eyeball!"

"I-I'll give you anything you want! Money, info…Don't hurt me. *Please*!"

"*Good*!" He traced the knife down to her chest and flipped her robe open completely, revealing her tits and hard nipples. "Not bad for an older woman," he sneered.

"*Bastard.*"

"Feisty as fuck, too. You should have better manners for a person holding a big knife to your tits!" He giggled and traced the blade down to her pussy. "I'm going to untie you. And, when I do, I want you to follow me into the living room. That's where I'm going to tell you what I want. Okay? If I don't get—"

"You'll slice my throat open and probably rape my cooling body," she cut in. A wry smile appeared on her face.

Taken aback, Chester didn't know how to answer. "Yeah, something like that." *Fucking weirdo*, he thought. *Crazier than a shithouse rat!* He used the knife to cut her binds. "Make yourself decent before coming out."

"Thanks," she said, rubbing her wrists and ankles. "My nose hurts."

"Yeah, sorry about that, but I had to shut you up." He laughed, looking at the blood on her face and in her hair. "What a fucking mess."

"Was there any need to hit me so hard?"

"Of course," he said. "I get off on hurting people."

"That explains a lot."

"What's that supposed to mean?"

"Nothing."

"Look," he said, turning on her sharply, "I don't need a fucking voodoo witch doctor to tell me I'm fucked in the head. Earlier today, I gutted my girlfriend like she

238

was a fish. I also killed my mammy and daddy, along with a whole host of other people. But I'm in control. I know when, and when not, to act."

She nodded. "Can you please remove the knife from my face? I've agreed to help and keep quiet."

He did as she asked. "I'll be in the other room. Hurry up!"

"Yes, *sir*!" She saluted.

"Weird bitch," he uttered.

Chester slugged some beer as he sat on the sofa and waited for her. *I hope she gives me what the fuck I want. I don't want to have to spill more blood, but I will if I have to.*

"*Hey!* Get your fucking arse in gear!" he yelled. "I haven't got all week."

"I'm coming, I'm *coming*!" she huffed, walking into the living room as she fastened her robe and wiped at the crusty blood on her face.

"You look better. Decent, even. Get on this sofa!"

Without argument, she took a seat next to Chester. "Before we start, I have one question—"

"I ask the fucking questions, not you!"

"I just want reassurance, that's all."

"For what?"

"That you *won't* kill me after I give you what you want."

"You should be worried about *not* giving me the information!" he said, pointing the tip of the knife at her chin. "Don't you think so?"

"No, because I'm willing to give you *anything*. I don't really give a shit about my patients!"

What the fuck? Is she serious? She looks it. She doesn't seem to have a sense of fear about her, either. What's her game? he wondered. "Okay. You have my word."

"Your word means fuck all, dickhead."

"You're starting to test my patience, bitch!" he said, digging the knife into her flesh. A trickle of blood escaped the puncture.

"Go ahead. Slice my neck open, you fucking maniac. See if I care. You'll never get what you want then, tough guy."

"I could always ransack this place – I'm sure I'd get what I wanted!"

"Yeah, you could, but I don't keep anything on paper at the house. Everything is on my laptop, which is upstairs."

"Let me guess: it's pass-worded."

"Yes, and your tiny mind will never figure it out."

"You know, I could beat it out of you!"

"And I'm sure you'd enjoy that. But I'd never tell."

Chester huffed. He could tell he wasn't going to get anywhere by threatening her. "I wholeheartedly promise that I won't harm a hair on your head after I get what I want."

"And *why* should I believe you?"

"What choice do you have?" he asked, putting the blade to her chin.

"Okay, fine. But put the knife down. You won't need it."

He did what was asked of him. "Happy?"

"Extremely," she said dryly. "I know you won't hurt me – I've dealt with enough whack jobs to know if you're lying or not."

"*Huh!*"

"So, what is it you're after?"

"I need info on a patient by the name of Storm Davies. Her dad Huw, too."

Her heart sank. "I'm not sure I can give them up. Then again…"

"*Well*?!"

"I'm thinking! It's not an easy one for me."

Chester grabbed her hair and snapped her head back. She screamed, but he cut it dead with a chop to her throat. She wheezed and gasped for air.

"I'm giving you *one* more chance, slut! You either give me what I want, or they're going to find pieces of you for months!" he roared. "Tell me!"

Tears ran down her face as she tried to regain control over her breathing. "You…you bastard!" she choked.

"I never said I was an angel," he whispered in her ear. "Now, fucking give me what I want, or so help me, God!"

"I-I…Let…let me…get my breath back!"

He yanked her hair again. "Stop stalling!"

"I'm…I'm *not*!"

"I want their address!"

"It's on my laptop. I'll get it! Please, let my hair go!" She was finally able to talk and breathe normally. "*Ah*," she said, putting her hands to her scalp when he let go. "There was no need for that. I was going to give them up."

"You're not doing very well, Doc. You're going the right way about getting sliced and diced!"

"Follow me," she told him, leading him to a hatch in the hallway ceiling. She popped the trapdoor and then clicked the ladder into place and climbed.

"There's a room up there?"

"*Yes.*"

"Fair enough." He followed her into the cramped space and had to duck slightly. "Holy *fuck*!" he gasped, seeing the photos of Huw she'd pieced back together on her wall. "What the fuck is this?!"

"We *used* to be lovers," she said, blasé.

"*Lovers*?!" His astonishment made her titter. "What the fuck's so funny?"

"Ha-ha! Your *face*!" she said. "You look shocked *and* pissed off."

"I'm having a hard time seeing the funny side."

"So what? I fucked him. What does it matter to you? Are you going to kill me because of it?"

"No. You have my word. You know that. The only reason I'd kill you is if you made a stupid move or withheld information."

"Then you won't be killing me."

"But...But—"

"But *what*? Spit it out."

"You had feelings for him. Still do by the looks of things!"

"Nah, not any longer. I thought I did, but I'm over him. His bitch of a daughter has turned me off."

"Not because he gave you the push?"

"Who says he gave *me* the push?" She got in his face. "Don't think I'm scared of you, *shithead!* I've dealt with worse."

Her defiance turned him on. "You should be fucking terrified of me, because I'll do things to you your mind cannot comprehend, Doc."

"Whatever. Mammy or daddy issues? Were you caught fucking your sister? Is that it?"

He backhanded her. "Keep your trap shut!"

"*Huh*," she giggled, wiping blood from the corner of her mouth. "You were, weren't you?!"

"Were what?!"

"Caught screwing your sister. That's why you're so angry," she said, laughing absurdly loudly.

"You're crazy!"

"You're a fine one to talk! Pass me my laptop so I can get you the fuck out of my life."

"Here," he told her, picking her PC up off the bed and shoving it in her chest. "Be fucking quick!"

"It'll take as long as I like, thanks."

As he waited, he looked around her room and drank in the images of Huw and the newspaper articles. "Is it true?"

"Is *what* true?"

"That cannibals ate her friends?"

"So I'm told, yes."

"*Fuck*. Really?!"

"Yes, *really*. I'm a doctor and don't lie."

"No need to be a *cunt*! I was only asking a question."

"I'm sorry. You're right – I should be polite to a vile pig that forced its way into my home, assaulted me, and threatened to slit my throat."

"Tell me it didn't make you wet!"

A smile flashed across her face. "You dirty bastard!"

He took the laptop from her and threw it onto the sofa.

She flinched but didn't back off. "I thought you wanted the information?"

"It can wait," he said, undoing his belt. "Get your gown off."

Hesitantly, she complied. "You're a naughty fucker indeed! I'd love to get into that mind of yours," she admitted, slipping her robe off. "Where do you want me?"

"Sofa." When she went to stretch out, he stopped her. "I didn't tell you to lie down. Kneel on it!"

"Like this?" she asked, putting her knees on the arm and bending over. She thrust her pussy into the air.

"Exactly like that."

She was completely shaved bald. He probed her with his tongue and placed his hands on her arse. It wasn't long before she was shoving herself against his face.

"Don't stop!" she begged, her breathing ragged.

He slapped her arse, making her yelp. Once he'd had enough of eating her cunt, he shoved his cock into her anus after using her pussy juices to lube it. He then grabbed her hair. He then yanked her head back and rode her like a National winner to a sweaty, finishing-line climax.

"You dirty bitch!" he panted. "Do you always let strange men fuck your guts out?!"

"Depends on the man," she said, casually slipping her robe back on. Her face and neck were flushed. "Now, where were we?"

"The information on Huw and Storm…" He continued to pant. Chester wiped sweat from his brow.

"Ah, that's right. I'll…*Wait*! I have a better idea!"

Chester grabbed her arm and pulled her close. "I want that address!" he snapped, shoving her onto the sofa. "No funny business, remember?!"

"I wasn't going to, idiot."

He stepped towards her, his fist clenched.

"Sorry," she said, "but there's no need to be so bloody rough."

"What were you going to say?"

"You don't *need* the address. I know where Huw and his daughter are going to be tomorrow night. With my help, you could snuff them out in one go. No fuss, no hunting."

"And why should I trust you?"

"I let you screw me in the arse! What more do you want? Do you see me fighting you? No. I want to see that little shit suffer. *Him*, too!"

"Because he chucked you?"

"That, among other reasons. I may even join in with you…" she said, a smile appearing on her face. "*What*? Can't a girl get a little bit of action in her boring life?!"

"Well, that's fine by me. However, don't cross me. I would hate to have to terminate our friendship."

"As I said, I'm on your side."

"Fine. What's the plan?"

"Tomorrow night, father and daughter are going to the grand re-opening of the recreational centre – it's where they were attacked by the cannibals two years ago."

"Why the hell would they do that?!"

"I suggested it. A little bit of therapy for the poor girl."

They both laughed.

"And she went for it?!" he asked.

"Yes. Not that it's a bad idea, but I don't think she's mentally ready for it. I was looking forward to seeing her break down and cry like a bitch."

"Well, well," he said, shaking his head. "Okay, where is it?"

"Firstly, we need to know if she's *definitely* going. I'll ring her in the morning."

"And I'm supposed to trust you?"

"Yes, you are. Now, why don't you come down to my bedroom? The bed is much softer…"

He didn't argue and followed her down the ladder.

Chapter 24

The men had pushed on until tiredness had finally finished them off and they stopped to rest by a brook with a little over four hours until sunrise.

Whilst three slept, one took guard.

First up was Huw. He'd insisted on taking first watch, giving him time with his thoughts. Sitting with his back to a tree, he dug his phone out of his pocket. There was a message from Storm, which had been sent hours ago.

"So, Skye's staying the night?" he said, chuckling. *I never thought I'd see the day,* he thought. *I'm glad Storm found it within her to forgive.*

He reread the text and replied. Even though she would be sleeping, he knew she would like to see a text from him when she woke up. He responded by telling her how happy he was that Skye was there with her. He also promised to be home in time for the grand opening, and that it was fine that Skye wanted to tag along.

After the message was sent, he replaced his phone. *What the hell am I doing out here?* he asked himself. *Chasing monsters, my friend, that's what! Madness. I wonder what Pitman would say?* The thought brought a smile to his face.

A chill settled in him – not much could be seen in the dim moon glow. The group had decided to keep their lights off while they rested. It made sense. If someone was out there and watching, then their whereabouts would be obvious. And with three out of four men sleeping, whoever was guarding would be a sitting duck.

In a way, he hoped the cannibals were long gone. He didn't *want* a confrontation. The past belonged where it was. Why rake it up?

I have too much to lose…Giving up the badge was the best thing I ever did, he thought, looking down at the gun in his hand. *When this adventure's over, we're moving. Cutting all ties. There's nothing here for us. I don't care what Storm says. It'll be for the best. We should have gone when it first happened. Then we wouldn't have this shit right now. But who was to know?*

"I should have known," he muttered, smacking his fist on the tree he rested against. *When that fucker's body wasn't found, I should have known. Alarm bells should have been screaming, 'Get out!'*

"*Huw*?!" a voice whispered in the dark, startling him.

"Who's there?!" he asked, cocking his gun.

"Don't shoot! It's me, Mr. Gibson. I thought I'd relieve you, old boy. I can't sleep, so I may as well make myself useful."

"But I've only been guarding for thirty-odd minutes. I like the peace and quiet."

"Yes, I can understand that. It's nice being away from the hustle-and-bustle of built-up areas."

"Something like that, yes. This is the first time I've been alone with my thoughts in a couple of days. It's been pretty hectic of late."

"That can be a dangerous thing, you know?!" Mr. Gibson said.

"What makes you say that?"

"It can drive you to drink, madness and despair."

"I can understand that form of thinking. How did you deal with it?" Huw asked.

"With the loss of my family?"

"Yes."

Mr. Gibson settled by Huw's side. "I made friends with Jack Daniels."

"Storm and I lost our friends. I blame myself. My little girl was taken from me. They beat and r-raped her!"

Mr. Gibson put his arm around Huw. "These things are sent to test us. They're also things we can recover from. When I lost my family, I wanted revenge. Blood. The first few weeks, however, were spent inside a bottle. My business suffered. I lost men, money and ground."

"How did you find the strength to crawl out of that bottle?" Huw asked, keeping his voice at a whisper.

"Rage and revenge replaced the sorrow and self-pity after I sobered up. It pushed me to start caring again, and that's when I went to Lawrence."

"How did you feel when you knew most of them had been killed? That it was over?"

"I didn't feel as happy as I thought I would. I still don't. Even if we find the rest of them and kill them tomorrow, I still won't," he said. "Revenge won't bring my girls and my wife back."

"You're right. First light, I may head home."

"But we need you! Wouldn't you like to know it's over? Bring a close to it?"

"Yes, but at what cost? I want to see my daughter and granddaughter grow up."

"I can understand that, but as long as the threat is out there, you will be constantly looking over your shoulder. We could save others from the same fate."

"I guess you have a point – I'd never have peace of mind. Those bastards keep taking from me: my job, my sanity, my friends and possibly my future!"

"All good reasons to see it through, Huw."

"I know you're right."

"And don't worry, you'll be there tomorrow evening for your girl, even if I have to drag you there myself! I know that's playing on your mind too. Get some rest."

"It's fine, I'll wait with you," Huw said. "I don't feel sleepy, to be honest."

"Horrible, isn't it?"

"Yes. Why can't *you* sleep?" Huw asked.

"Like you, I have too much on my mind."

"That bad?"

Mr. Gibson nodded. "I can't get those monsters out of my head, Huw. And my girls – they're always with me in here and here," he said, pointing at his heart and head.

"Understandable."

"We're honourable men, Huw. That's why it hurts so much."

"I can't argue with that."

Huw and Mr. Gibson decided to leave Dylan and Kirk sleep until daybreak. As light seeped through the trees, filling the surrounding area with morning sun, birds and other wildlife stirred in the forest. Dawn had come.

It was time to push on.

"Think we should wake Kirk and Cope?" Huw asked. "There's plenty of light to work with now."

"I'll get our gear together if you wake them?"

"Yeah, no problem," Huw said, getting up and checking his gun. His flashlight was no longer required, so he tucked it down the back of his trousers and went to

Dylan and shook his shoulder. "Dylan," he said. "It's time to get moving."

"What time is it?" he asked groggily.

"A little after six." Huw heard Mr. Gibson potter at his back as he moved on to rouse Kirk.

Shortly after six-thirty, Huw was leading them through the trees, following the tracks in the dirt. Kirk, Dylan and Mr. Gibson followed close behind. They moved fast but low, not caring if their activity was heard.

"Can you still see tracks?" Mr. Gibson asked.

"Yes," Huw answered. "They're starting to thin out, mind."

"Can you see anything ahead?" Dylan asked.

"Nothing but dense forest. There's a lot of disturbed branches and trampled green however, which is a good thing. It gives us something to work with."

"Anyone could have disturbed the foliage, Huw – I'm sure lots of hikers and campers come through here," Dylan said.

"No, they wouldn't – there's a trail for them. I saw it after we left camp." Huw removed his mobile. All signal was lost beneath the crushing green. "Shit!" he uttered. When he looked up, he noticed Mr. Gibson had overtaken him and was disappearing into the shrubbery. "Hey! *Wait*!"

Huw went to put his mobile back in his pocket but dropped it. "*Damn*!" he muttered, getting to his hands and knees. "Where the hell is it?!" He ran his hands through the loose grass, gravel, twigs and pine. "Oh, fuck. Come on, come on! *Wait*!" he called after Mr. Gibson. By now, Cope and Kirk had also gone around him.

Didn't they notice me down here?

"I've lost my—"

A scream froze him in place. His grip on his gun tightened, and he checked to make sure the safety was off.

Huw cocked it and moved in the direction he'd last seen Mr. Gibson. He eased branches out of his way with the muzzle of his gun. Nothing flew at him, which he'd been expecting.

Dylan and Kirk came into view – they had their backs to each other as they swept the area with their guns held high. Mr. Gibson was nowhere to be seen.

"What's going on?" Huw whispered.

Dylan turned to him and put a finger to his lips.

Then Huw heard Mr. Gibson, who sounded pained, and rushed through the foliage ahead of him.

"Oh, *fuck*!" Huw gasped.

Mr. Gibson was pinned in a bear trap. The steel jaws had cut through his leg below the knee. His lower leg was hanging by threads of sinew. Blood pumped and pooled about him – the colour had drained from his face.

"*Help*!" Mr. Gibson rasped.

Huw rushed to him and tried to pull the steel jaws apart. "Jesus Christ! Give me a hand! The man's bleeding to death!" he yelled.

Dylan got to his knees next to Huw and placed his hands on the trap. The snare was slippery with blood.

"It's no good!" Dylan grunted.

"H-h-help…" Mr. Gibson panted. "It hurts!"

Huw gagged when he glanced at Mr. Gibson's ruined leg and saw the splintered bone and flesh. "Kirk! *Help*!"

"You…must get…*Arggh*!" Mr. Gibson tried to speak, but his life drained from him.

"It's no good," Dylan said. "He's dead."

Huw continued to struggle with the device. "No, no, no! *Fuck*! Fuck this shit!"

"Boss?" Dylan said.

"Why didn't you help him sooner?!"

"There was nothing we could do," Dylan said. "We thought they were here. It could have been a fucking ambush, Huw!"

"But it wasn't! Fuck! *Fuck*!" Huw yelled. "We need to get back and call this in!"

"We can't! We have to keep moving."

"You can fuck off, Dylan! I'm not getting myself killed!"

Dylan grabbed Huw's shirt and pulled him close to his face. "Look, unless you fucking help—"

"Get your hands off me!"

"Not until you listen."

"Guys, we have to do something. We can't stay here – we're sitting ducks!"

Dylan let go of Huw. "I thought you said you'd seen a log cabin, Kirk?"

"It's over there," he said, pointing.

"Huw, help me drag Mr. Gibson over there, yeah? Kirk, pull the trap's peg out of the ground."

"Got it," Kirk said.

"Let's get him over there, Huw. We can decide what to do then, okay?"

"*Fine*!" Huw said, gritting his teeth. "But you and Kirk can bring him. I'm going ahead to see if I can find any more traps. I think this was put here on purpose."

"Okay," Dylan said.

Huw took the lead and walked towards the cabin. He kept his guard up and looked about the ground to make sure there were no more steel snares or trip wires. *Why the hell would anyone want such an ugly device?* he thought. *There are more humane ways. Bastards!*

As he moved closer to the building, his guts knotted. *What if they're inside waiting for us? No, they would have come out on hearing the noise and taken us head on.*

When he saw hoofprints on the ground, two sets of them, his guts relaxed. He now had a strong feeling that the cabin was empty. *Someone's ridden out of here in a westerly direction*, he thought, spying snapped branches and trampled foliage. *There can't be many of them. Four at most.*

Huw climbed the porch steps and looked through the window. He couldn't see anyone moving inside.

He placed his hand to the doorknob and was about to turn when he heard rustling from behind. He looked over his shoulder and saw Kirk and Dylan dragging Mr. Gibson's body out of the covering. He put his finger to his mouth to silence them. They stopped, let go of the body, and readied their guns.

"*Hello*?! Anyone home?" Huw said, pushing the door wide.

Silence greeted him.

He moved forward, his gun leading the way. "*Hello*?! Anyone?"

Once he'd swept the building, Huw called the others from the porch. "It's clear!"

Knowing the place was safe, Huw gave it a virtuous search. He wanted clues. The lock on the door hadn't been disturbed, and neither had the windows. *If they came this way, they wouldn't have let people live*, he thought.

"Do you think there's a phone here?" Dylan gasped.

"Want us to look around?" Kirk asked.

"Yes," Huw said. "Try and turn up some clues."

"I'll search around the back, see if anything appears to be missing or broken," Dylan said.

"I think some horses have been taken. I saw hoof marks leading into the trees."

"You think *they* took 'em?" Kirk asked.

"Definitely. I've known them to use horses before."

"I'll have a look," Dylan said.

"What are we looking for, exactly?" Kirk asked.

"Something that will tell us they've been here. Check the bathroom, Kirk."

"Sure, no problem."

Huw went to the fireplace and got on his hands and knees. There were flecks of blood on the carpet, along with strands of hair. *Could be anything,* he thought.

"Bathroom looks as though it's been used recently, Huw. It's filthy. It looks as though a miner has used it!"

"Sounds about right," Huw said. "Strange for one of them to shower, mind. That's out of character."

"Could have been the woman they have hostage? The councilwoman?" Kirk offered.

"*If* she's still alive."

"There does appear to be horses missing," Dylan said, re-entering the cabin. "And it looks as though livestock has been slaughtered – there's blood everywhere!"

"We need to keep going before we lose them," Huw said.

"If they're on horseback, we'll never catch up. They could be a day's ride away," Kirk said.

"And they could be around the corner," Dylan answered. "Come on, let's go."

"What about my boss?"

"We'll have to leave him here," Huw said. "We'll send people for him once this is over."

They headed out the door and followed the hoof tracks into the woods.

Bird cry woke him. The sun was high in the sky, which chilled him. *How long I sleep? Where women? They should have called me!* he thought, sitting bolt upright.

Skull scanned the surrounding area – the camp's fire was still burning, but his sister and Paula were nowhere to be seen. The babies had been left by a nearby tree

He couldn't move his arms.

Nor his legs.

He'd been tied, his knife gone.

Skull squirmed and fought against his restraints until a nearby scream made him stop. He listened.

Another scream. It sounded like his sister, but he couldn't be sure.

He looked down at his body and saw the ropes had been tied well. There was no breaking them. Plus, he couldn't get his mouth near a knot.

Who done this?! his mind raged. *How I not hear? I hear everything. Nobody sneak up on me before. Never! People who followed us? They found us? No, someone else. Someone who wants to hurt us.*

Skull needed something, *any*thing that had an edge to it. Time was short – the women sounded as though they were in pain. Then he heard a new voice and a giggle from behind foliage close by. A few words were exchanged.

More than one! he thought, listening. *Voices belong to men.*

This made him thrash like a wild animal, but it was useless. He frantically looked about him, trying to seek out something to use.

Nothing.

Then his eyes fell on the fire.

He rolled towards the dwindling flames and put the knot at his feet to the fire. The rope smoked and he smiled. *It working!*

When the cord blackened, Skull pulled away and thrashed his legs. The binding frayed and unravelled. Eventually, it snapped, freeing his legs. He got to his knees and guided the knot at his back towards the fire the best he could without burning himself.

It proved difficult and dangerous, as Skull scorched his wrists. He bit down on a scream and pulled away from the heat. He squirmed on the floor and tried not to make a sound.

When the pain subsided, he tried again. However, this time the flames licked his wrists. The heat seared his skin as he edged closer, and he fought the pain with grunts and smiles.

"What the *fuck* do you think you're doing, shithead?!" a voice yelled. "Get the hell away from there!"

Skull didn't move. Instead, he let the fire do its worst before a club struck the back of his head with a sickening crack.

Crashing to the ground, Skull growled and spat.

"Tough fucking son-of-a-bitch, aren't you?" the man said, throwing a piece of timber to the floor. "We know who you are. You're the freaks the police are looking for, ain't ya?" he asked, kicking Skull in his ribs. "*Well*? Don't understand English, you big, dumb bastard?!"

Skull flipped onto his back and strained his arms against the ropes.

"No, you don't. Ignorant fucking hillbilly!" He wore dirty jeans with a matching T-shirt. His fat, sweaty face was unshaven, and his eyes reminded Skull of a weasel's. He held Skull's knife in his hand. "You want a taste?" he asked, putting the blade's tip to Skull's chin. "Don't fucking move, prick. You and the ugly woman over there are going to prison, but not before we have some fun!"

Skull lay still. The knife was pressed tight to his flesh. He felt blood bead, and then trickle.

"You stay right there, handsome," he told Skull, then called on his goon. "Kev! *Kevin*! This one's awake!"

Skull took his chance while the man was distracted.

"Where the fuck is he?! Kev—*Oof*!" he gasped, clutching his nuts and collapsing to his knees. The knife fell. "You...*fuck*!"

Skull forced his arms against the ropes as the man searched for the blade among fallen leaves and grass. After what seemed like a lifetime, the binds broke. He rose to his knees.

The man wheezed as his hand fell on the steel. He brought it up and brandished it in Skull's face. "Stay the fuck back! Kev?! *Help*!"

The cannibal charged at the man. His solid shoulder crashed into the guy's flabby gut, pushing the air from him. He was propelled backwards and rammed against a tree – the knife leapt from his grip and landed in a thicket.

Skull opened his mouth and lunged at the fallen man. He sank his teeth into the side of his fleshy neck and bit down.

"*Argggh*!" he screamed, managing to get a thumb to Skull's face and poking him in the eye.

The feral monster pulled back, taking with him chunks of flesh. He couldn't see, putting him at a massive disadvantage. Then it was his turn to be shoulder-charged and taken to ground.

They rolled about the floor, neither able to get the better of the other. Then, the man managed to get on top of Skull and head-butted him.

This had little effect on the tribe leader, who summoned all his strength and flipped the man off him.

The man catapulted into the dwindling fire, screaming when his body ignited. He sprang from the flames and tried in vain to dampen the blaze, but too much damage had been done.

Skull watched the man die before checking his babies and then heading off in search of his women, his knife in hand.

"You leave her alone, you filthy bastard!" Paula said.

"Shut up, bitch," Kevin said. "Or I'm going to hurt *you* instead." He got off Eight-Ball, who was tied like Paula, and listened. He was sure he'd heard Colin.

He's been gone a long time...

"Col?!" he called. "Did you call me? *Col*?!" No reply. "I must be hearing things."

"What the *fuck* do you want?" Paula snarled.

Eight-Ball writhed on the floor – her mouth snapped open and closed like a hungry gator.

"Keep still!" he ordered Eight-Ball, kicking her in her side. "Or I'll beat you more!"

Paula believed him. Even though he was skinny and looked like a weakling, he was the opposite. He'd been the one to pin Eight-Ball down and tie her, before knocking her out cold with one punch.

"Who the fuck are you, and what do you want?" Paula asked. "I want fucking answers."

"Sheesh. What a mouth. Maybe I should show you how to use it?" He started to lower his zip.

"I'll bite it off, pig."

He laughed. "We're not going to hurt *you*. *You're* our golden ticket. Hell, we're here to *rescue* you," he said and smiled, exposing yellowed teeth.

"What are you talking about? *Rescue* me?"

"Your name is Paula Harris, right?" Kevin pulled a piece of paper from his pocket. "This is you, right?" he asked, holding the sheet of A4 in front of her.

"Yeah, that's me. Where did you get that?!"

"What's wrong with you? Taken a hard thump to the head, or what? You're all over the news, radio, TV and internet. Everyone's looking for you. That rich daddy of yours put a big, fat juicy reward out."

"You won't see a penny of it! I'll see to that."

"*Bitch,*" he said, placing his knife to her throat. "Best you cooperate, *love*, or Colin and I are going to cut you up, just like we're going to do to her and him out there. We'll tell the police we found you hacked up. Either that, or Colin and I will take you back to ours…After all, you *have* vanished." He winked at her.

"*Bastard.* I don't want to go back, so you may as well kill me."

"You actually like being with these freaks?"

"They're my family, fuckhead."

"Ha-ha!" he gaffed. "That's fucking rich. Hey, Col, you've got to listen to what this bitch is saying. I think she's been in these woods too long."

"I wouldn't expect a retard like you to understand," she baited. "Fucking spastic."

He put the knife to her eye. "Maybe I'll pop it."

She whimpered. "*Don't.*"

"Not so tough now, are ya? Enough with your smart gob, sweetheart. I aim to take you back in one piece."

"How did you find us?"

"We didn't. You found us."

"What do you mean?"

"We saw you coming through here last night."

"You followed us?"

"Yep, we did. You can thank Colin, wherever he is, for noticing you."

"Great, I'll buy him a drink when we get back," she mocked.

"No need to be like that."

"Just let us go, *please*."

"You must be kidding. The reward is massive. Not only that, but these mutants are major news, Paula."

"What are you talking about?"

"They're the ones responsible for all those killings in Bridgend."

"I know," Paula said. "But I don't care – I belong out here and to them. I'm free—"

"You're going back, and that's that."

"*Noooo!*" she screeched. "*Skull!*"

"Fucking—"

A violent rustle of bushes from behind made him turn – his mouth sagged open in surprise. A blood-soaked Skull leapt out of the foliage with a knife raised high.

"*No!*" Kevin screeched. The knife plunged into his face, and his body folded like a deckchair.

Skull retracted the blade and stabbed time and again.

Paula called him, and he got off the ruined Kevin. Skull went to his women and freed them.

"We go. *Now,*" he said.

"I think they've either killed or let our horses go."

Skull grunted. "Get babies and go."

"What about you?" Paula asked.

"Go. *Now,*" Skull ordered. "Go high into mountains. Look after babies."

"But—"

He pulled her off the floor. "*Go.*"

Tears flooded out of her. "I don't want to leave you!"

"Take babies. *Now,*" he demanded, cutting a few of her locks. "*Go.*"

When Paula started walking away with the infants, Skull turned to his sister.

"Babies," Eight-Ball said. "*Babies.*" Her eyes were as wild as she was frantic.

"Safe," he told her. "We stop others."

Reluctantly, she nodded.

He couldn't believe Mr. Gibson was dead. *Another victim of those psychotic cave-dwellers*, Huw thought.

Losing Mr. Gibson had not been part of the plan. They came in as a team, and were meant to leave as one.

The cannibals were running scared. He could feel it. Two years ago, they would have come at them with everything. This time, it was different. They were weak.

It would end this time, once and for all. He wasn't going back without knowing it. Not now. The death of Mr. Gibson had been the final straw.

Why didn't we go straight back into the woods last time? We probably could have found and finished them off easily, he thought.

"What's up?" Dylan asked.

"I was just thinking."

"Anything I can help with?"

"Not really. Us coppers always seem to mess things up, don't we?"

"Seems a bit harsh," Dylan said. "What's brought that on?"

"The events from two years ago – I was just turning it over in my mind and the mistakes which were made."

"There's no point in beating yourself up, Huw. All us cops make mistakes."

"If I'd gone looking for them immediately then none of this would be happening. Mr. Gibson wouldn't be—"

"You're being silly, Huw. Nobody could have possibly known this would happen. You said yourself: the injuries they sustained would have been enough to kill anyone."

"I thought the leader had crawled off to die."

"That could still be the case. We *could* be after someone else entirely."

"No, it's them – only savage fucks like those freaks would set such a trap," Huw said. "I'm going to make sure I kill the fucker this time."

"Do you think we'll find the woman alive?" Dylan asked.

"I'm not so sure we will," Huw said. "They've probably eaten her by now."

"Fuck, that's disgusting," Kirk said.

"That's what those bastards do," Huw said.

"They didn't harm your daughter, though?" Dylan said.

"No, just beat and raped her."

"Hey, you know what I mean. They never attempted to eat her."

"No," Huw said, keeping his tears back. "They…they were going to use her as a breeding machine."

"They might do the same to that woman. Katherine or something…" Kirk said, scratching his head.

"Paula," Dylan corrected him.

Ahead of them, the sound of snapping branches brought them to a halt.

"What was that?" Dylan whispered.

They crouched and listened.

More sounds: rustling foliage and crunched gravel.

"There's someone heading this way," Huw stated.

"It could be wildlife," Kirk suggested, cocking his gun.

Huw and Dylan did the same.

"Come on," Kirk said, edging forward.

Dylan took up the middle, leaving Huw to guard their backs. He did complete circles every so often, ensuring there was nobody creeping up on them.

"It's safe," Kirk called from the front.

Huw stepped into a clearing with a lake and felt relieved.

"Okay. Shall we take a five-minute pit stop?"

"Sounds good," Huw admitted. He took his phone out of his pocket and saw that Storm had sent him a text. He walked to a nearby boulder and sat on it as Kirk and Dylan headed to the lake.

'Morning! I hope everything is okay and that you are safe? Please text or ring as soon as you get this, as I'm so worried about you. XXXX'

Huw texted back: *'Everything is fine. We think we've found a new lead. Hoping to have it all wrapped up in a few hours.'*

He snapped his phone closed and put it back in his pocket. Something caught his eye. Getting up, he took a few steps closer to a nearby tree. "What the...?"

There was blood on the bark. When he put his fingers to it, he discovered it was wet. He raised his gun and walked forward. He could see something on the floor in front of him. Huw pushed branches out of his way and the 'something' became visible – a man's body.

In the dead man's left hand was a clump of blonde hair; in the other, a piece of paper. Huw bent over, all the while keeping his gun trained on the man, and plucked the paper from his grasp.

It was a picture of the missing councilwoman, and the hair the man held resembled hers in the photo.

Huw pushed the body over with his foot. His face looked as though someone had tried peeling it off with a knife. Puncture wounds graced his neck and chest – there was upward of sixty stab marks all over him.

"*Shit*! This was recent," he muttered.

He backed up to where Dylan and Kirk knelt by the lake, his eyes and gun still trained on the body.

"Everything okay?" Dylan asked.

"There's a body. Over there," Huw said calmly, keeping his back to Dylan and Kirk. "It's been cut up like a Sunday roast. I think it may be one of our perpetrators. Looks like we had it wrong after all."

"*What*?" Kirk bellowed.

"How can you tell that?" Dylan asked.

"He's holding a lump of what appears to be Paula's hair, along with a missing picture of her."

"I'll take a quick look," Kirk said. The big man walked off.

"Maybe it was a double-cross?" Dylan offered.

"Whatever it was, we're close to the truth. I can feel it. I just—what the *hell* is that?" Huw screeched.

"*Another* body?" Dylan blurted, moving closer to the motionless mass on the floor behind a few large rocks.

"Are they dead?" Huw asked, watching Dylan raise his gun. He did the same.

"I don't know." Dylan rounded the rocks and gagged. "Dead horses! The flies are at them. Jesus, what a fucking mess."

Huw walked over to Dylan and looked. The beasts' innards lay scattered across the leaf-covered floor. Among them was the body of a second male.

"What the hell happened here?" Huw muttered.

Huw and Dylan turned around at the sound of a yell behind them – Kirk came crashing out of the bushes with a woman on his back. Huw's guts sank. He knew her. In that instant, the situation from Blaengarw came flooding back to him.

"*Bitch.*" He raised his gun to fire, but couldn't get a clean shot. "Turn around!" he yelled at Kirk, who was trying to pull her off him by yanking her hair.

"I—She's *heavy*," he gasped. "I-I…"

"Come on," Dylan said. "Let's get—*oof*!"

Huw turned to see Dylan had been viciously shoved out of the way by Skull, who had dropped from a tree. As Dylan fell headlong, his feet tangled with a fallen branch, sending him into the lake.

"*You.*" Huw snarled, coming face-to-face with Skull. He wrapped his hands around Skull's throat and squeezed with all his might.

Skull head-butted the ex-copper, making him break his grip and stagger backwards. Huw tripped and fell onto his arse. He vigorously shook his head to try and clear his foggy vision.

Huw got to his feet and frantically searched for his gun. It was nowhere to be seen.

Skull approached.

"*Fuck.* Where is it?" Huw yelled, and then he spotted Dylan running out of the water.

The DI rammed his shoulder into Skull's back and both men went to ground.

Huw looked over at Kirk and saw he had the better of the woman, with his gun pressed against her forehead. Then her hand shot up and out of the leaves in one swift movement. She swiped the knife she was holding across Kirk's throat.

He groaned, clasping his free hand to his spurting wound. Blood jettisoned across her face and deformed tits. Before he collapsed onto her, he pulled the trigger of his gun.

The single shell blasted half her face away.

"*Jesus,*" Huw whispered, but didn't let the outburst of violence root him to the spot. Instead, he went to Dylan, who was losing his battle. Skull was straddling and strangling the DI.

Huw ripped the feral man off the copper and helped Dylan to his feet. "Are you okay?"

Dylan nodded.

"Let's *finish* this."

Huw turned to face Skull, who was hobbling away, giving him the chance to grab one of the many guns and unload it into Skull's back. The tribe leader fell to his knees and crashed into the lake face-first.

His body rocked and bobbed on the current, lifeless.

"*Now* it's over," Huw said.

"Did every bullet hit?"

"Yes."

"Go and get help, Huw. I'll stay here. I could do with a smoke."

"But—"

"It's fine, seriously. I have my gun."

"Hang on, I have my phone." He removed it from his pocket and cursed not having a signal, and how shitty the coverage in the area is. "Looks like I'm walking. It could take me a few hours to get to a nearby town," Huw said.

"Go back to the tunnel – the town of Treherbert isn't far from there."

"I'll be as fast as I can. Promise." Huw ran off in the direction of the tunnel.

Dylan collapsed to the floor. He was out of breath and hurting.

He didn't notice Skull rise out of the water.

Chapter 25

Whilst in Starbucks, she had a message from her dad. It made her smile, because she had lain awake all night fretting about him, wondering if he was alive or dead.

She responded immediately, hoping he would either text back or ring. Neither happened.

"Good news?" Skye asked.

"Yes. It was Dad. He's okay."

"Great. I told you he would be, didn't I?"

Storm smiled. "Yep, you did."

"What did he say?"

"That they are fine and close to getting the job done."

"Will he be joining us this evening?"

"So he says. But, knowing Dad, things will crop up at the last minute."

"Well, me and your doctor will be with you."

"Oh, that reminds me – I need to ring Dr. Veech. I had a missed call off her this morning."

"Oh?"

"I need to give her a time to be at mine. Give me five."

"That's fine. I'm going to go to the little girl's room," Skye said. "The coffee's gone straight through me."

"*Skye*! Way too much information."

"Ha-ha! Is Stevie okay?" she asked, looking at the child's pram by Storm's side.

"Sleeping like a…well, baby."

"Shut up." Skye laughed. "I'll be right back."

"Okay," Storm said, stifling a laugh and dialling Dr. Veech's number. It rang six times before it was answered. "Hey, what's up, Doc?" Storm mimicked Bugs Bunny. "Ha! I couldn't resist." The phone went silent the other end, forcing Storm to speak again. "What's wrong…You want to pick us up tonight? Are you sure? My mother will be coming with us. Is that okay? Great. It'll save us getting a taxi… Stevie? My neighbour will be looking after her. I'm not sure. Skye and I were thinking of going down for eight? You'll pick us up at ten-to? Sounds good. I'll make sure Stevie's with her sitter well before then. Yeah, Dad's coming. Okay, cool. Thanks for this, Dr. Veech. I really appreciate all you've done for me. I'm not sure I could have done it without you. Also, before you go—oh, you can't talk? Okay, I'll see you in a few—"

Before Storm could finish, Dr. Veech hung up.

"Weird," she uttered.

"What's weird?" Skye asked, sitting down.

"*You.*" Storm smirked.

"*Cheeky.*"

"Well, if the cap fits… No, my doctor – she sounded strange on the phone."

"How?"

"As though she was rushing to get me off it – like she didn't want to talk to me."

"She's probably busy."

"It didn't sound as if she was in her office. I could hear a TV in the background."

"Maybe she's taken the day off to help you through this evening?"

"True. She's good like that. Oh, Dr. Veech is picking us up this evening. Ten-to eight, okay?"

"Fine by me. Will your father be back by then?"

"He should be. If not, I can always text him to say we're going ahead of him."

Skye nodded, and then drained the last of her coffee. "Ready for more shopping?"

"Aye, why not?"

Both women got up and left the coffee shop. They headed into the street where the sea of people swallowed them.

"Why the *fuck* did you tell her we'd pick her up?!" Chester yelled.

Calmly, Dr. Veech turned to him. "We're not going to the grand re-opening."

"*Huh*?"

"Jesus! Do I need to spell it out for you?"

"No need to get your knickers in a twist. I only asked a simple question."

"Why yell and swear at me?"

"I'm sorry," he said.

"Good. We're not going to go to the grand re-opening. We're just making it *look* as though we are."

"Right, okay…" Chester said.

"Are you following me?"

"Yes, I think."

"When we 'pick them up', that's when you have your fun."

"What if they don't let us in?"

"Why on Earth wouldn't they let me in?"

"Because we're meant to be going, not staying."

Dr. Veech rolled her eyes. "My God. I know that, but I'll say I need to use the toilet. Besides, we can barge our way in. What does it matter?"

"Sounds good, I guess."

"You *guess*? It beats taking them hostage at a crowded concert hall."

He nodded. "Yeah, it's a solid idea."

"We'll leave here around seven-thirty."

"That gives us four hours."

She nodded. "Go and get the gun from by my bedside cabinet. I want to make sure it's loaded."

"Do you have spare bullets?"

"Yes, they're in the cabinet – fish them out."

"Cool," he said. "Maybe you should arm yourself with a knife?"

"I was going to carry the gun, but maybe it's better you have it."

"Definitely," he said, rolling his sleeves up.

For a moment, she stood and admired his tattoos – some of the ink looked like it had been done inside. "I love your art. It's a turn-on," she confessed.

"There's plenty of time for fun before we head out."

"I was hoping you'd say that," she said, and headed to the knife block. Dr. Veech drew the biggest blade. "This should fit nicely into my bag."

He ran through the woods, sweat pouring from him. Thirty minutes later, he burst out of the bushes and was greeted by the tunnel and a town in the distance. Mustering his energy, Huw ran down the small hill and jogged the rest of the way to the tunnel.

Once there, he removed his phone and saw there was still no signal on it. "*Fuck!*" he yelled, tightening his grip on the mobile.

He fought the urge to throw it and set off towards Treherbert. Huw picked up speed when he spotted the old railway tracks. He ran down the sleepers to Treherbert's train station, where he found a phone box, dialled the police and gave them the necessary information.

After hanging up, he rang Storm and told her what had happened. At first she cried, then yelled with happiness as she realised it was over and they were safe.

Once Storm had calmed down, he told her he needed to wait and guide the police to Dylan, but he would be home soon.

When the call ended, Huw sat on a nearby bench. His feet throbbed and blistered, but that was the least of his worries.

He heard sirens in the distance.

"Thank God," he muttered, gazing into the trees ahead of him. "Help's coming, Dylan. We did it."

When Storm and Skye got home, it was a little after six o'clock. Whilst Storm fed, bathed and changed Stevie into her nightwear, Skye showered and dressed for the evening.

Skye offered to take Stevie next door so Storm could get ready. She agreed, and headed upstairs to the bathroom. She locked the door and started the shower.

Once stripped, she faced the full-length mirror on the back of the door and gazed at her scars. *At one time, I couldn't even look at them*, she thought, running her fingers over them.

She was ready for tonight. Prepared for it, especially now she knew those fucks were dead.

Do I even need Dr. Veech now? she thought. *Dad and Skye will be enough – we can let loose and celebrate. Is it too late to call the doctor off? Maybe, maybe not. I could always try once I get out of the shower.*

With her dreadlocks tied up, Storm stepped beneath the warm spray – it battered her body as she lathered it with soap. *I hope Dad gets back in time for the lift. I'd hate for him to have to drive down. He'll want a beer, especially after what he's been through. That's if I can't cancel Dr. Veech, that is.*

She couldn't believe what had happened to him out there. That the bastard who'd raped her was officially dead. It brought a smile to her face. *Maybe I can start leading a normal life again?*

The warm water relaxed her as it washed the suds from her glistening body.

Once finished, she shut the water off and stepped out of the bath. She wrapped a fluffy towel around her.

"*Lush!*" She giggled, unbolted the door and left the bathroom. The house seemed darker. Had a light or two been turned off downstairs?

"Skye? Are you back?"

No answer.

Storm shrugged and crossed to her bedroom. *What's taking her so long? Surely it was a simple, 'Hello, here's Stevie, her bag of things for the night and some numbers, just in case you need us. Anything else? Okay. Great. Bye.' She's probably over there making a meal out of things. A right song and dance.* Storm smiled, taking her clean Cujo T-shirt out of her chest of drawers, along with a pair of knickers and a bra.

She draped the sodden towel over her radiator, grabbed a pair of black jeans out of her wardrobe and dressed. A thump from downstairs brought her out of her dream world.

"What the hell was that?" she uttered, moving to her door. "Skye? Was that you?"

Nothing.

She went to the stairs. "Skye?" she tried again. Storm bent and looked down the steps. The front door was ajar – the wind made it rock before slamming it closed.

Her skin crawled with ice-bugs. Her hairs stood on end.

"*Skye!*" she yelled, placing her foot on the top step.

Her mother's sudden appearance around the corner of the living room door made her jump. "Are you calling? I was running the taps in the kitchen."

"*Jesus*. You scared the shit out of me!"

"Sorry. I didn't mean to."

"The front door was open."

Skye turned and lifted the door's handle, which engaged the locks. "There. Are you going to be much longer? Your doctor's going to be here in less than ten minutes."

"I only need to do my hair," she said, turning to head back to her room.

"Anything off Dad?"

"Nothing."

"He can follow us, I guess," Skye said.

"Yeah," she agreed, closing her bedroom door.

Storm headed downstairs and found Skye in the kitchen – she was helping herself to some of her dad's Vodka. "Want one?" she asked.

"God no. I can't drink spirits."

"Cider?"

"Yep."

"*Huh*, I was the same at your age."

"How was Stevie?"

"Aw, the little darling was fine. She was sleeping by the time I got her over there."

"You took her toys and food?" Storm asked.

"Of course."

"Great. So, we're ready to rock-n-roll."

"We sure are. Hey, do you smoke?" Skye asked.

"Sorry?"

"You know – *green*. You look like the type," Skye said, winking.

Storm couldn't help but laugh. "Yeah, I smoke, but don't tell Dad – he likes to give me hell about it."

"I'm no snitch."

"I'll get us some – I have a small stash in my room," Storm said. She was about to run upstairs when there was a knock at the door. "Well, that was good timing."

Storm opened the door and greeted her doctor. "*Hey.* Would you like to come in for five?"

"That would be lovely, yes," Dr. Veech said. Her attire didn't speak 'night out', Storm thought, giving the doctor's tracksuit bottoms and matching jacket a once-over.

Storm was about to question it when the door violently propelled backwards, bowling her over onto her arse - her coccyx screamed in agony.

A gun was thrust in her face.

"Stay the fuck down," Chester warned her.

Dr. Veech locked the front and then raced into the kitchen.

"What's going on?" Skye asked.

"Shut up, *bitch,*" Dr. Veech said, backhanding Skye across her face and flooring her. "You must be the fucked-up mother I keep hearing about."

Skye didn't answer. Her lip bled.

"*Well?*" Dr. Veech pressed, giving Skye a poke in her guts with her toes before kicking her full force under her chin, knocking her out.

"What's going on out there?" Chester yelled. "Is *he* here?"

"Settle down," Dr. Veech called back. "I laid the mother out. And no, it doesn't look as though he is. Ask his cunting daughter."

274

Storm whimpered as the cool gun muzzle was shoved into her mouth.

"Is your daddy here?" he asked.

She shook her head. Tears filled her eyes. *Not again,* she thought.

"Are you sure about that, sugar tits?"

Storm nodded, tears spilling down her face. She couldn't believe it. Why was her doctor doing this?

"Get that little fuck into the living room," Dr. Veech said. "I'll bring the bitch mother."

"Good."

"What will we do then?" she asked.

"We'll sit and wait like a happy family." He laughed.

Storm and her mother sat on the sofa, with Chester watching over them at gunpoint. Skye was out cold.

Dr. Veech went to the curtains and peeked through them. "Where's Huw?" she snapped, turning on Storm. "You said he'd be here, you little fucking weasel."

Storm sobbed. "Why are you doing this? You're meant to be my friend and doctor!"

"Please. I'm sick of your constant fucking whinging and how you think the world owes you a favour. You're nothing more than a sniffling little twat," Dr. Veech spat.

"I haven't done anything to you."

"Boo-fucking-hoo! You got in between me and your father, that's what you did. *You* caused us to split up because you couldn't stand it. Could you?"

"*What*? I didn't give a shit. You're mad!"

Dr. Veech silenced her with a hard slap. "Be quiet, or I'll slice you up and disfigure that pretty little face of yours," she said, thrusting her knife in Storm's face.

She pulled away from the blade. "Please, *don't.*"

"Tell us where your dad is," Chester said. "I have a bullet with his name on it."

"Don't hurt him."

"Why shouldn't I?" he asked, getting in her face. "He had me put away for a long time."

"He was a police officer – it was his job to put bad people away."

"I hope he's enjoying his retirement, because I'm going to give him a *permanent* leave!" he said, brandishing the gun in her face.

"You *bastard*," Storm muttered. "He's was doing his *job*."

"Tough shit." Chester laughed.

"Where the *fuck* is he?" Dr. Veech screamed. "It's gone eight."

"You know Dad. Never early."

"Fucking wise bitch," Chester said. "Going to blow her brains out in front of daddy."

"You sadistic piece of shit!" Storm said, getting off the sofa before being pushed back down by her doctor.

"I don't think so. Stay still or I'll ram this into you." She showed Storm the knife and put it to her throat. The serrated edge bit into her flesh, drawing a drizzle of blood.

A car door slammed.

Moments later, there was a hard knock at the window.

"*Dad*!" Storm screamed. "*Help*!"

"Shut up!" Chester said, pointing the gun at her.

"I'll go," Dr. Veech said. "He trusts me. Grab her."

Chester pulled Storm off the sofa and put his hand over her mouth. "Make a sound, and I'll blow a fucking hole through your face," he whispered in her ear.

"*Mmmm*!" She frantically shook her head.

The front door opened, and the doctor's soothing voice greeted her father.

"No, we didn't hear anything. Come in. Your daughter and Skye are waiting for you, Huw."

"Thanks. I thought you lot would have—" His words derailed when he walked into his living room. "Chester Nailfree!" he blurted.

"Hello, DI. Long time," Chester said, shoving Storm to one side and raising his gun. "I'll see you around."

He eased off three shots. The first shattered a picture above Huw's shoulder, with the second and third drilling into his chest.

"*Dad*!" Storm screamed, watching her father fold to his knees – blood dribbled from his mouth and pumped from his chest. He was dead before he hit the floor. A crimson pool gathered beneath him. "You motherfucker!"

Storm jumped up, but was tackled back down by Dr. Veech who whipped out her knife. "Get off me, bitch!" she screamed and pulled the doctor's hair. The blade tore at Storm, but she kept fighting.

As the women struggled on the floor, Chester watched and laughed. "Come on, Doc—"

Skull crashed through their living room window, showering them in glass. Dr. Veech and Storm looked up and screamed. The cannibal held Dylan's head in one hand, a knife in the other. He dropped what remained of the DI and grabbed Chester by his throat and squeezed – the jailbird didn't have chance to aim or fire his gun.

He wheezed and gagged. The bones and muscles in his neck crunched and snapped as the pressure intensified. The gun slipped from his hand and hit the floor. It slid in Storm's direction, who got a hand to it before the doctor could.

"You *bastard*!" Dr. Veech screamed, rushing over to Skull and punched her knife between his shoulder blades.

Storm watched in disbelief as Skull threw the dead Chester to one side and grabbed Dr. Veech by her hair. He then turned her around and forced her face towards the shattered window, impaling her on the jagged shards. Blood pissed from her mouth and nose – her body bucked.

"Don't you fucking move," Storm told Skull, who beat his chest and ran towards her.

She didn't hesitate in firing, taking him to the ground. To make sure he was finished, Storm emptied the gun into his head before letting the weapon crash to the floor.

Storm collapsed at her father's side and wept.

Chapter 26

She hadn't looked back. Hadn't dared. He'd told her to head as far away as possible, and that's what she'd done.

After four days of walking, stopping only to feed herself and the babies, Paula had discovered a cave and decided it would be their new home.

When enough days had passed, she knew nobody was looking or coming for her. Skull had seen to that. She was free. Paula also realised that Skull and Eight-Ball would never return. She'd heard gunfire and screams of pain as she'd run for safety with the babies.

The loss of Skull and Eight-Ball was painful. She'd cried herself to sleep every night since, but had to keep it together for the babies and the one that grew inside her. She had a family to rear.

Not only had Skull left her with child, but also with many new skills, like hunting and killing. She was a born-again warrior.

And, when the time came, she would go back to the valley and seek vengeance.

End

Experiment of an Ancient Breed

A Short Story by

David Owain Hughes

Elizabeth, who was named after her great-great-grandmother, had been the sole manager and proprietor of the Lamb and Flag pub for the past nine years. When she'd first acquired the establishment fifteen years ago, she'd been the joint owner, along with her brother. He died six years into running the place, forcing Elizabeth, who preferred to go by Liz, to take on full responsibility.

Paul, Liz's brother, had been taken ill unexpectedly.

"I'm sorry for your loss, Elizabeth. It seems Paul had a rare, and certainly unusual, blood disease that we've not seen or treated in this hospital," had been the doctor's cold, unforgiving words. "We'd like to keep your brother's body for a couple of weeks, run some tests and see if we can prepare for the next case we have involving the extraordinary illness."

She'd found his frankness astonishing. Had she not been emotionally drained at the time, Liz would have taken more than a few strips off him, but then he added, "It would be a good cause towards medical science . . .", swaying her judgment somewhat.

Her mind had reeled. *What if it's in me? What about Jason? The babies!*

"By all means, come in for a check-up," the doctor had said after she'd told him her concerns.

Six weeks later, Paul's body had been retuned, and the green light to bury him had been lit.

Liz hadn't had time to mourn. She had a business to look after along with her family: her baby twin girls, four-year-old nephew and younger brother, Jason, who all lived at the pub with her.

The first four years without Paul had been tough. A slog. Not just physically, but mentally, too. Had Liz not had Jason to help mind the children whilst she worked every hour God sent, then it would have been an impossibility to keep everything going no matter how good she was at spinning plates.

When Jason turned sixteen, Liz put him to work behind the bar – not that she had to do much arm-twisting. He'd been chomping at the bit to get involved ever since Paul had passed.

"It's not fair to take all the work on yourself, sis," had been his words after they'd buried their brother. "Let me at least do some bar work for you."

"No," had been her stern reply. "You can help me out by looking after the little ones – keep them entertained, warm, and their bellies full for me. That would be a massive help."

Jason coming of age had been a welcomed relief, taking away much of the strain that had been building and threatening to cave her in. When Liz realised how much of a good thing it was, she'd suddenly become scared, knowing that if her baby brother had been slightly younger, meaning there wouldn't have been aid for another year or two, then she would have gone under.

Stress would have killed her.

And if the stress hadn't, then giving up the pub would have. That act would have been like the hammer called Life slamming down on the one bullet in her revolver's chamber.

The Lamb and Flag was her lifeforce.

Not only that, but the place had been in the family for two decades – it had been passed down from father to son, mother to daughter, brother to sister, and so forth. And, with no immediate relations around her except for her nephew, brother and children, who were all too young to take the pub on, then it would have been sold to a stranger and lost to her blood forever.

Besides, working the Flag gave her a sense of purpose in life. It filled her with pride and get-go whenever she thought about how hard she'd worked to build the place up – to get back a lot of the trade and punters it had lost when it had been in the hands of her parents.

Her mother had placed blame for the pub's decline and descent into near rack and ruin squarely at her father's feet. "He's become a no-good lush and womaniser," she'd said. Whereby he had drained the profits dry, she had chased off the female customers by accusing them of fucking her husband.

When it looked as though the pub was going to close down, a miracle happened – her mother died and her father fell ill within weeks of her going. The doctors had labelled his sudden deterioration into an early grave as a 'broken heart'.

"Yeah, you see it all the time," the undertaker had told Liz and her brother. "When one dies, the other normally follows pretty rapidly. They start pining, see. A sad thing, the human heart."

He'd said it in almost a cheery way.

Liz could have sworn she'd detected a wry smile on the bone collector's face.

Not that she cared. She was glad to see the back of them, knowing her and Paul could start their new venture together and breathe new life into the battered, bruised business.

All it's going to take is a bit of elbow grease and some honest sweat and toil, she'd thought, standing before the pub with her brother.

They'd gutted the place, all four floors, getting rid of the olde-worlde décor, fixtures and fittings that had been there since their parents had taken over the pub forty years prior.

"This joint probably hasn't seen an update since it was built, sis!" Paul had commented. "Let alone a lick of paint or a splash of colour."

"You know how Mum and Dad were . . ."

"Frugal?"

They'd both laughed at that one.

All the booths, sofas, tables, chairs and the bar were also ripped out so they could modernise completely. They'd decided that they wanted to make the place hip and chic, so it would attract the attention of the younger crowd – they even put in stylish and expensive drinks, along with craft ale and a pool table.

When they were fully up and running, they decided to upgrade the rear of the pub and install an elegant kitchen so they could start providing meals.

"You don't go to a pub for food," their father had always argued. "The only grub that should be served is nuts and pork scratchings."

He's such a short-sighted fool, Liz had thought when her dad had responded with that after their mother suggested a chef be brought in. Even as a child she'd had good business acumen. Her mother had clearly had it too, because she was forward-thinking: serving food to bring in a healthy profit/income in an ale house around the time was uncommon.

But with him gone (her mother too, God rest her soul), they'd been free to turn their business into a booming success – something she knew their mother would have been proud of.

Things had been going swimmingly.

The place ran like clockwork, and there was hardly ever any violence or the need for the police to be called, unlike when their parents had run it. Liz could recall many occasions when there was trouble at their door late at night, which had been scary. Still, nothing ever came of it.

Liz had used to look forward to getting up in the morning and heading downstairs to the bar to get an early start. Life was good. Great, in fact. She had her brothers, nephew, baby girls and her own business. *What more could a girl ask for*? she'd thought.

But it had all crashed down around her ears after her brother died, and it had taken all her strength to keep the place from slipping under.

"You should get some staff in to help you," a drunk, loyal punter had once suggested.

But Liz hadn't wanted that – she wasn't particularly keen on the cook being there, but knew it was necessary. So she'd struggled on until Jason was able to fully help take control. As soon as he'd become of age, she'd made him a legal partner, too. She'd showed him all the ropes, from locking up and setting the alarms, to filling in orders and keeping the books.

"I want you to know all this stuff in case something ever happens to me," she'd told him.

And so she'd soldiered on with Jason, who helped her iron out all the creases that had occurred after losing Paul. It took them less than a year to get the place back on track, with the punters and money flowing in once more.

Since then, things had been peachy.

They were living the dream.

It's been a rocky road, she thought now, looking across the bar at Jason, who was serving someone with a pint of beer. *But I – no,* we – *have managed to pull through it. And look at us now!* "And to think I almost lost my dream job . . ." she muttered, looking about her.

"Any chance of some service here, *bitch*?!"

Ugh! Liz inwardly groaned. *But sometimes, just sometimes, the arseholes on a Friday night have a knack for getting you down,* she thought, turning to the man who had so rudely interrupted her chain of thought.

"Give me a fucking beer!" the guy demanded again, belching. His eyeballs resembled marbles: they were glassed over and rolled around in his skull. Liz couldn't tell if he was looking at her, or through her.

She wondered if he'd been eating tuna, and had a hard time in not pinching her nose closed. He didn't so much as stand there, but swayed, as though manipulated by a breeze. Liz couldn't understand how he hadn't collapsed or fallen backwards onto a table.

His face didn't look familiar, either.

He didn't fit.

"*Sir,*" she said in a calm yet firm tone, "I think you may have had enough to drink. I can't, and won't, serve you another—"

He slammed his fists down on the bar. The knuckles on both his hands were scuffed and bloody. "No fucking bitch is going to tell me when I've had enough!" he screamed, his voice breaking.

A hush fell over the crowd in the pub – only the jukebox could be heard.

Her tone took on an edge. "Don't make me have to call the police, sir!" Whilst he mumbled and drooled, she glanced over at Jason and saw he had his hand on the phone. All it would take was a nod off her, and Jason would speed-dial the police – they'd be here in minutes.

She shook her head and turned back to face the drunk.

"Call the fucking army or the prime minister, *whore*! See if I care!" He slammed his hands on the bar like a spoiled brat.

Whore? How dare he! She saw red, walked around the bar and grabbed the man by his ear. She twisted it and escorted him to the front door. He tried to protest

286

and wrestle free, but he was no match for her sober superiority. "And stay out! You're barred."

She went to the window. The man hung around outside, and then slipped down the alley connected to the pub. Inside, after a few people commended Liz on how she'd handled the situation, the place became raucous once more.

****

He eyed her from a barstool located at the counter. He was lost among the drunken barflies who sat all around him; his face was invisible, his person unknown and nameless. He knew her but she didn't know him, and that's the way he intended to keep it, right up until the point when he killed her.

Then he would tell her who he is.

He wanted to hear her scream his name; to see her cry, bleed and plea for her life.

He picked up his glass, put it to his lips and sipped at the whiskey. All the while he kept his eyes on her from over the rim of his tumbler. The scotch was sour and fiery, just the way he liked it and his women. It caused him to pull his lips, exposing his well-polished teeth and healthy gums.

"That's a damn good drink," he muttered, nobody hearing him due to the thumping music and the hubbub of laughter and chatter.

His stare remained on her.

He watched her every move, like he had done for the last six years; he'd stalked her, crept in her shadows. He knew when she ate, slept, shit and drank – he knew all there was to know about her.

Liz, he thought. The name sounded poisonous. *That's because it is fucking poison. Her whole fucking family is toxic.*

As he continued to glare, he rolled the glass between his palms. He enjoyed playing this game of cat and mouse. *Soon it will be cat eat mouse*, he thought. *Liz thinks she's so clever – thinks nobody knows about her and her lot. Well, I know. I made it my business to know.*

Most people around the city didn't pay much attention to the killings and the missing people, but he had. Especially after his son had been murdered, his body dumped and discovered in woods roughly ten miles away.

The police had called it an accident. They had said the lad, who turned eighteen on the night he went missing, had stumbled through the woods drunk and fallen. His head had been caved in. The authorities had also reported that the wildlife had picked the body clean – foxes and other wood-dwelling animals had ravaged his face and shredded his carcass.

There hadn't been much of his lad on the slab to identify. Had it not been for the tattoo on his left shoulder blade, he wouldn't have been able to I.D. his own flesh and blood.

The man sitting on the stool, burning a hole through Liz as he nursed his whiskey, went by the name of Tokyo. He didn't even want the drunks knowing his real name.

If someone should come asking questions, he thought, *it wouldn't take the cops much to put two and two together.*

Up to now, he was fairly confident his tracks had been well and truly covered - nobody had suspected a thing. Nobody had come knocking. And, since he'd killed three members of her family over two decades, he was certain he was safe.

She has no idea that I've been slowly tearing her family apart. He laughed into his whiskey as he raised the glass to take another few sips.

At first, he'd been happy with the police report. Like a man, he'd accepted it, and reminded himself that life can sometimes throw you a curveball, and that the senseless accident that had happened to his son occurred the world through on a daily basis.

Life, sadly, is fragile.

Not only that, the youngster had been drinking copious amounts. After all, it had been his eighteenth birthday.

But then word reached him that two of his son's friends had also disappeared that night – their bodies were never discovered. And, when he'd looked further into the matter, he found that a series of people had been going missing around the same time, and were still doing so.

Soon his son's case, the missing friends, and scores of others hooked him. Consumed him. It took over his life, forcing him to give up his job as he played private dick. In the process, he lost his home and wife as well – his life came away at the seams.

You've cost me more than you will ever know, you fucking cunt! he thought, glaring at the pub owner. If he could have killed her there and then, along with her other brother, he would have. *Going to keep biding my time. Soon. I just need to see the rest of her family before I make my final move. Then again, killing babies won't fucking bother me. They've all got to die.*

At the start of his investigation, he'd retraced his son's footsteps on the night he'd been killed. By now, he was convinced his son had been murdered and his body moved to the woods. His search was narrowed down after the police divulged to him the approximate time of his son's death – this meant he was able to eliminate some of the pubs he knew his boy had called at.

The Lamb and Flag had been last on his list, and after an uneventful quest for justice up to the point of visiting this final ale house, he had started feeling despondent.

Like in all the other pubs he'd been to, he'd shown Liz's parents a photo of his son and asked a series of questions. When he'd asked about viewing their CCTV tapes from the night in question, they'd agreed, but something about their vibe, body language and facial expressions told him something different. They'd also bumbled their way through some of his questions.

The husband had gone off in search of the tape.

"Surely you mark your tapes?" Tokyo had said to the mother.

She'd given him a forced smile.

As he'd expected, the husband had come back empty-handed. "I appear to have misplaced *that* tape, along with a few others. Would you like to call back in a few days?"

A smile briefly flickered across Tokyo's face. "Sure, why not?" he'd said, turning to leave. As he did, he could almost feel the weight of relief and panic lifting off them. After he walked out the door, he took a sneaky look through one of the windows and saw the pair arguing.

He knew then that something was up, and that they knew more than they were letting on.

The jig's up, kiddos! he'd thought, walking away and not returning to ask about the 'missing' CCTV tape.

Instead, he'd started looking into the couple – he did background checks and asked about them around the city. Not only that, but he watched them and held stakeouts outside the pub.

This went on for months, with nothing strange occurring. Also, he'd drawn blanks on finding out about them – who they really were, where they came from and if they had more family in the area. It got to such a point of boredom and frustration that he thought he had the wrong place and people; that they lived a quiet, peaceful life, and didn't want trouble. At that point of breakdown, he'd thought himself a stupid old bastard – he'd thrown his life away playing detective.

But then a few things happened. Two more people went missing – they'd been reported as being last seen at the Lamb and Flag pub. When he saw photos of the teen girls, he remembered seeing them enter the pub, but not leave.

Secondly, an old friend he'd asked to dig up details on the pub owners had finally found something. The information had been relayed to him on his answer phone whilst he'd been on a stakeout.

Beep: *"Looks like your friends at the pub there are hiding a huge secret, Tokyo. I'm not sure if you're old enough to remember the incident in Bridgend some sixty or seventy years ago, when a pack of cannibals living in the woods attacked some concert that was being held there? It was massive news at the time. Anyway, I won't go into it over a robot – if you want to meet for coffee, get back to me. Also, if you check the library archives, you'll find plenty of information."* Beep.

Tokyo had set up a luncheon with his friend at a café around the corner from where he lived.

"Your message more than intrigued me, Sam. Tell me the rest."

"Did you go to the library?"

"I did, but I couldn't find much – a lot of information was missing from the archived documents."

"Yes, I should have told you: the authorities tried to cover it up, but they did a poor job. I know the full story, and I'll probably have the answers to all your questions."

"But?"

"It's going to cost you."

"I'll give you five hundred for everything you have," Tokyo said.

"Make it a plump thousand and I'll also give you my services – you might need my help in what you're dealing with, friend."

The revelation had startled Tokyo. What was he getting into? How deep did the river of shit go? Who exactly were the people at the Flag?

His mind had swum.

"Deal," Tokyo had said, offering his hand. "Shall we go back to mine for more privacy? I have a bottle of Hennessey with ten years worth of dust on it."

Sam unfurled an age-old story before his brandy-glazed eyes, once Tokyo had slid his lifesavings across the table and into the small, bespectacled fella's greasy mitt.

"The tribe that came out of the woods were old – hundreds of years old, Tokyo. They attacked a concert and snatched the daughter of a police officer. The father went looking, along with a few other men. They thought they'd killed all the 'Man-Eating Fucks', which is what the trashy tabloids labelled them as. But they came back a couple of years after and went for the father and his daughter once more, succeeding in doing plenty of damage."

"But the* wood-dwellers were all killed off. What does this have to do with the Lamb and Flag?"

Sam was visibly shaking. "No," he whispered. "Between us, we've managed to unearth something quite extraordinary, my friend."

Tokyo had felt his patience wearing. "Right, but what does it have to do with my dilemma?"

"The tribespeople were killed off the second time, yes, but what people didn't know, and still don't, is that a woman had been snatched at some point in the two years the cannibals laid low. Also, one of the cannibals that survived the first attack had babies. When the cannibals made the second attempt on the police officer, or so I can gather – the story is rather sketchy, but it's all true – the woman was left behind with the offspring . She was also pregnant with the tribe leader's child."

"Are you trying to tell me this woman stayed in the woods and raised them?"

"No, but you're not far off the money."

"Then what are you—"

"She stayed in the woods for a number of years, allowing the babies she'd adopted to grow to teenagers and mate with each other. She then moved her 'clan' out of the woods and integrated them into society. She taught them to count, read and everything else a growing mind would need in the real world. The disfigured children were kept out of sight – they stayed at home with their mum and helped out. As the tribe grew, she shipped them out into the world to fend for themselves. I've heard that some have gone as far afield as the States, but I've yet to confirm this. Most of her children and grandchildren stayed here and continued to grow the tribe. Yes, Tokyo – they walk among us!"

"How do you know all this?"

"When I started digging, I had to go to other sources – people who are up on local legends, history and various other fields. Most of this has been dispelled, but I believe it's true, and the couple living at the Lamb are direct descendants. I also have a contact who was once close to the tribe, but I will never divulge his details."

"But…but, they're normal!"

"To look at, yes. But they still have the urges. It's built into them – it's something their 'normal' breeding will never stamp out."

"Jesus . . . If this is all true, then we're dealing with real-life monsters."

"We are indeed, sir. And I think it's our duty to rid the world of as many as we can, starting with the nest in the Lamb."

"But some of them are children!"

"Who will grow up to kill and devour our fellow man, Tokyo."

He nodded. "I certainly want vengeance for my son."

"And you will have it. So, will you help me destroy as many as we can, starting with that lot?"

Tokyo picked his glass up, reclined, and thought about it for a couple of minutes. He eyed Sam as he took delicate sips from his tumbler. "Yes, I will."

After hatching a plan together, Sam and Tokyo had visited the Lamb and Flag – because Tokyo had already exposed himself to the owners of the pub, he'd gone in disguise.

Their idea had been simple: poison.

They'd gone equipped with a couple of vials of untraceable killers: wolfsbane and cyanide. The former of the two was slower-acting than the latter, which they'd decided to give the father.

After biding their time within the establishment, they'd taken their opportunity after seeing the couple with drinks in their hands at separate periods in the evening. Once the cyanide had been dumped into the mother's coffee, they stayed to watch her die, which wasn't the spectacle they had been hoping for. In one way, it was a good thing.

A few minutes after taking a gulp of her drink, the woman collapsed, never to move again. The husband had been paralysed with grief. When they knew she was dead, Sam and Tokyo had left.

Within weeks of her dying, the father was reported to have lost his life, too.

Their plan had worked but it took Tokyo a few more years to claim his next cannibalistic offspring, as Sam passed away unexpectedly, leaving him in disarray.

At first, Tokyo had taken Sam's death as a huge blow. Luckily, the man had told him everything he would need to know, especially where all the other cannibals were across the country.

He never did find out if a few had made it to the States.

Well, they're not our concern! Tokyo had thought at the time.

After a few weeks of reflecting on Sam's passing, he'd started to see it as a blessing. Did he really want to kill the parents' children? And, more importantly, the children's children? He didn't think he could do it. Had Sam been here, then he probably would have felt obliged to.

Tokyo became dormant.

The way he saw it, he'd had his vengeance – his thirst for revenge had been slaked.

And then people started to go missing again, forcing him to take action.

Sam told me they'd kill. I should have listened to him. Had I, then lives would have been saved.

Before others were murdered, Tokyo took immediate action. He went back to the pub but didn't bother with a disguise. Along with him, he took the slow-acting poison and slipped some into the brother's drink when he wasn't looking.

The result had been perfect – he'd died within a few days of taking it, the blame being laid on a rare blood disease.

With him out of the way, Tokyo had then planned to wait for the perfect moment to storm the pub after closing and kill the reminder of the family in their sleep.

****

All this rushed through his mind as he watched Liz escort the drunk out of the pub and then spy on him through the curtains. He could see lines of anger pull her face this way and that.

Your next victim, cannibal? he thought, draining the last of his whiskey. "Another!" he snapped at the younger brother serving. *Jason? Yeah, that's right.* He looked at the lad and smiled. *I killed your brother, fuckhead.*

The drink was placed down on the bar, the money asked for.

When Liz pushed away from the window and walked towards the bar, Tokyo got ready to follow.

"Watch the bar a sec, Jay – I'm off to the loo," she said.

Tokyo caught her wink. When she shot by him, he got up and slopped out of the room behind her. He was careful to hang back and ducked into doorways and hidey-holes when she stopped. As soon as she started walking again, he was hot on her heel.

She led him to the back of the pub and walked through a door marked Staff Only.

"Fuck that!" Tokyo said, carefully opening the door and peeking around the corner. Liz disappeared out the fire exit at the end of a corridor. He rushed after her and followed her out into the night. He scrambled behind a bin and watched from the shadows. In the poor light, he could just about see her standing guard at the entrance to the alley.

What the hell is she doing? he thought, shifting into a more comfortable position.

Liz carefully peeped around the corner and saw the drunk pinball his way towards her. He was mumbling something, but she couldn't quite make out what.

A fool like him won't be missed! A nice treat for me and the family – it's been a while . . .

The man crashed through bins and almost went down, but a car kept him up as he fell against it. He laughed as he pushed himself off it and lurched forward. Now he was close enough for her to hear what he was saying.

"Fucking hotshot cunt thinks she can tell me wha— *HIC*!—what to do. I'll fucking show her." He bent over to pick up a bottle that was rolling towards the gutter. As he was doubled over retrieving it, he farted, which followed through.

The seat of his blue jeans faded to a watery brown colour. The stench floated through the air and assaulted Liz's nostrils, but she didn't bat an eyelid.

The drunk put his hand to his arse and felt the wet patch. "Fuck!" he said, sniffing his fingers. "Ah well, who cares." He burped again and walked towards the opening of the alley.

He didn't stand a chance against her fierce, ferocious strength.

She pulled the man into the alley, disarmed him, and threw him up against the opposite wall. His head struck the concrete, and he slid down it, leaving behind a bloody, slug-like trail.

"Fix me, will ya?" She stood half-in, half-out of the moonlight that slanted in through the alley's opening.

"N-n-no!" he cried.

She walked up to him and kicked him hard in the balls.

He instantly threw his guts up and pissed himself as he clutched his nuts.

She picked up the dropped bottle, which hadn't smashed, and held it before her. It had once held Beaumet Cuvée Brut. Liz put the top of the container to her nose and inhaled the fumes that had been left behind. "Must have been a bloody good year."

When she looked down, she noticed the drunkard was slowly pulling himself up the lane and out of harm's way.

Liz looked out the lane and saw the streets were dead.

Time for some fun. To let out some of that repressed family rage. Her face creased into a smile. "Where in the *fuck* do you think you're going?"

"N-n-no . . ." the guy continued to cry.

Liz stepped up behind him and grabbed his trousers with her free hand. In one violent movement, she ripped the garments from his body, exposing his shit-spattered anus and scrawny legs.

"You're fucking disgusting!" She turned the bottle around, knelt beside him, grabbed his sagging ball-bag and rammed the neck of the Beaumet up his arse.

He screamed, but not as loud as she'd hoped.

His puckered arsehole has been lubed by his crap.

She crushed his bollocks in her grip until they were nothing but mush as she fucked his arse. Standing, she breathed hard. When she noticed he was still alive, she got on her knees again and repeatedly smashed him about his head with the thick end of the bottle until it was nothing but a concaved mess.

Tokyo watched on, mortified, as Liz got her face close to the dashed-out brains and splintered bone, scooped it up and shoved it into her mouth. He put his hands to his ears to close out the awful sound of her smacking lips and sucky, chewing sounds.

Bile raced up his throat, burning it.

He crawled deeper behind the bin, fearing she would either see him or sense him with her wood-dwelling instincts that were buried within her.

Once she'd finished feeding, her face, hands and arms plastered in blood and dripping gore, the sexy, lath-like woman picked the man off the ground and threw him over her shoulder as though he was a rag dolly.

She then went back to the fire exit and slammed the door closed behind her. There was no trace to indicate anything had happened in the alley.

Sitting there, Tokyo found it hard to take control over his shivering body, but he did.

He didn't know how long he'd been there, but when a light flashed on from somewhere above, it startled him back to reality. From where he sat in a crumpled heap, Tokyo looked up – there was a glow coming from a second-floor window.

Something splashed against the glass.

"Oh, Jesus! What is she doing?" Tokyo crawled across the alley and pulled himself up with the aid of the ladder attached to the wall. He started to climb it, noticing it led onto a steel veranda that was opposite but looking down on the pub window that was lit up.

Tokyo tried to make as little noise as possible as he climbed the steel rungs to the top. His heart thumped against his chest. Sweat poured down his face, forming a liquid moustache, and dripped off the end of his chin.

I'm out of shape!

He huffed when he reached the top and pulled himself onto the balcony and into a shadowy corner.

"Oh. My. God," he muttered, looking through the window opposite. He put a hand to his mouth, aghast, as he watched Liz and her family crowd around the drunk she'd put on the dining room table.

The twin girls, who he'd thought were mere babies, were indeed grown women – teenagers, possibly – but he couldn't tell due to their hideous disfigurement: their heads were misshaped, with lumps and bumps at the back, and they had little hair.

Their mutant-like fingers dug into the drunk's ripped-apart belly and scooped out all the soft bits. They ladled blood into their greedy mouths with their huge, shovel-like hands.

"Nice, Nine-Ball?" Liz asked. "How about you, Billiard-Ball?"

The inbreds nodded.

"They're horrific," he whispered, continuing to watch on in morbid curiosity.

The man's entrails were yanked on, his tongue pulled free from his mouth. The twin who'd been referred to as Nine-Ball now had her hand up the man's back passage. Tokyo didn't know, or want to know, what she ripped out of him and put in her mouth.

Liz stepped out of the picture and back into it with a carving knife. "Who wants the pecker?!" she asked, smiling and flapping the man's limp penis with the blade's tip.

The girls started squabbling, Liz chuckled, and then someone else entered the room: a monstrously disfigured man who had to stoop so his head wouldn't drag along the ceiling.

"That can't be the nephew?" Tokyo blurted, slapping a hand over his mouth when he saw Liz step close to the window. She appeared to be looking straight at him, but he knew it was impossible.

Before she turned her back, Liz closed the curtains, blocking his view entirely.

His whole body trembled. He felt as though he was lucky to be alive.

This can't go on. I have to stop them. I was foolish to wait so long – why did I not listen to Sam and take them all when I had the chance?

The one positive to come out of this exclusive viewing of a cannibalistic feeding frenzy was that Tokyo now knew exactly what he was up against.

And I thought I'd be killing children. Fuck this, they all need to be wiped out.

He stood on shaking legs and stepped down the ladder's rungs one at a time. Once he was at the bottom, he rushed down the alley and onto the main road.

Tokyo didn't stop running until he made it to his front door, breathless, exhausted and terrified out of his mind. When he removed his front door key from his pocket and tried to slip it into the lock, he kept missing the snug slit due to his shaking hands.

"Come on, come on, for fuck's sake."

Unlocking the door, he rushed inside, slammed it closed and fell back against it. He wiped the beads of icy water from his forehead and puffed hard – his breathing came in ragged rips.

No time for resting, he thought, pushing himself off the door and making his way through the living room and down to the cellar. Once there, he went to his work bench and sought out the stuff he would need.

Tokyo removed a hammer and screwdriver from off the tool rack attached to the wall, along with a flashlight and saw. From there, he went to the wall opposite and dismounted his .410 bolt-action shotgun normally used for hunting wild rabbit. On a smaller bench beneath the gun was a tin of slug cartridges. He opened it and grabbed handfuls of them and stuffed them in all available pockets.

Finished, he grabbed a heavy-duty satchel and stuffed everything inside, including a half-empty bottle of whiskey he kept stashed under a floorboard marked with an *X*.

"I hope you aren't drinking down there? You'll have my broom across your backside if you are and I catch you!" his wife used to call down the cellar steps. Of course, she was only partly serious. "You know what the doctor told you, love."

Five years before his wife had left him due to his detective antics, Tokyo had suffered a mini stroke and had been told to lay off fatty foods, nicotine and booze. But when his son had gone missing, the stress of it and trying to find out what happened to him had brought it all back on – the drinking continued.

With the shotgun loaded, a slug of whiskey in his guts and a heart full of bloody murder and vengeance, Tokyo was ready to go back to the pub and finish what Sam and he had started so many years ago.

Tokyo took the cellar steps two at a time and headed out the front door. He was worried that if he stopped and thought about what he was about to do, then his nerve would fail him.

His jaw clicked as he clenched it. *Not a chance!*

The streets were deserted, which was a good thing. Before he'd exited the house, he'd slipped on his old high-visibility jacket, hardhat and duffle coat to disguise the shotgun on his back – if anyone should see him, they'd think he was on his way to work and wouldn't stop or think to question what he was up to.

Still, to be on the safe side, he took backstreets and lanes and stayed in the shadows where and when he could. In no time at all, he reached the Lamb and Flag. The pub was in complete darkness, as were the surrounding houses and businesses. There wasn't a soul on the street.

Tokyo made his way into the alley he'd been in earlier and walked up to the fire exit. Gently, he tried the bars. Locked.

He set his workbag down and drew out the work tools. He wedged the screwdriver into the door jamb where the lock was and started tapping it in deeper with the hammer. When it was in far enough, he pried it. Wood splintered around the bolt in the door, and, soon enough, it popped open with minimum effort and noise.

After replacing his tools, he went inside and closed the door at his back. Darkness enveloped him and panic lodged in his throat, but it was dispelled when his flashlight kicked in. He tried to slow his heartbeat and control his rapid, ragged breathing.

Tokyo felt he needed another shot of whiskey, but knew it was a bad idea. He had to keep his mind as clear and sharp as possible. He stood still for a few moments and shifted his torch around as he listened for any movement with pricked ears.

If they've had a good feast, they'll be sleeping soundly and won't hear me coming! he thought, moving forward at a slow pace and keeping vigilant.

He soon found himself in the bar area. Tokyo took his time, making sure to avoid the tables with glasses on them and the few chairs that blocked his path. When he got behind the bar, he spotted a knife block and drew the biggest blade. He then went through a door and found a staircase. He climbed to the second floor.

Once he was on the landing, he swept the upper floor with his torch and found another door. He went through it and found he was in the kitchen – his feet crunched as he walked about. When he looked with his light, he noticed he was treading in dried blood. His nostrils suddenly filled with the smell of iron.

Tokyo gulped down the bile in his throat.

His eyes glazed over.

"Jesus," he whispered, his torch beam falling on the drunk's remains on the kitchen table. There was nothing left but a husk. The eyeballs, nose, most of his cheeks, ears and lips were missing. His chest, like his stomach, was ripped open – there was nothing inside. In fact, when Tokyo peeked in, he could see the table through the gaping hole in the torso.

Small flies buzzed.

Stepping away, he aimed his light at the sink. In it was a pile of blood-spattered plates, utensils, pots and pans – even the kitchen units were plastered red.

More odours assaulted him.

"Can I smell shit and piss? Surely not!" he blurted.

Chunks of human flesh littered the floor, along with congealed pools of blood.

Shaking his head, Tokyo started towards a third door. Opening it, he saw it led into the living room.

There's got to be another set of stairs leading to the bedrooms, he surmised.

A floorboard creaked as he walked into the sitting room, which was rather sparse of furniture. No TV; just one sofa. A few baby toys lay scattered about the floor – a playpen stood erect in one of the corners.

There are no babies here . . .

Tokyo then found what he was looking for when he rounded a corner: stairs leading to a third floor. He went up them as fast as he could, not wanting to hang around much longer and take any chances.

He was faced with four doors at the top.

Ideally, he wanted to take out either the big fucker first, which he was convinced was the nephew, or Liz, the tribe leader.

Upon gently opening the first door, he was greeted by Jason. The sleeping lad was lying on his back with his legs dangling over the side of his bed. His sheets were in a knotted mess.

As Tokyo got closer, he could see the blood stains on the lad's face.

None of them are innocent. Just because he's a mere child, I can't let that stop me from taking him down. He must *die.*

Swiftly, Tokyo straddled the boy and clamped his free hand over the youngster's mouth. Tokyo was worried the lad would have impressive strength like his mother, but he didn't appear to. With his weight alone, Tokyo was able to keep Jason pinned to the bed as he slowly sawed through his neck with the knife.

He gargled and bucked.

Blood sprayed Tokyo's face.

When he felt a warm wetness spread beneath his arse, he knew Jason had soiled himself.

Jason stopped moving, allowing Tokyo to get off the dead boy. He didn't let what he'd done dawn on him, and moved back to the landing.

One down . . .

Tokyo headed back the way he'd come. He crept along the carpeted floor and gasped when he was forcefully shoved down the stairs.

He yelled as he rolled down them like tumbleweed, his legs smashing through the spindles that helped make up the banister's railing. When he hit the bottom and slid along the floor, he felt paralysed. The pain in his back and shoulders was beyond anything he had ever experienced, but he knew he had to get up, and fast.

From above, a light came on. This was followed by someone screaming and crying.

His vision was foggy, but he managed to see the huge blurred shape moving his way.

"*Fuck*!" Tokyo scrambled backwards on his arse, using his hands to help him. "No . . ."

The massive cannibal grabbed him and threw him against the playpen, which collapsed to the floor under Tokyo's weight. "Ugh!" he cried, feeling a rib pop.

He tried to scramble away again but was picked up like a rag doll and hurled across the living room. He crash-landed near a bunch of toys: cuddly bears, rattles and plastic keys – all covered in bloody fingerprints.

Tokyo crawled towards the kitchen.

If I can make it there . . .

His foot was grabbed and he was hauled into the kitchen – the drunkard's body was swiped off the table. Tokyo was scooped up and thrown down on it, which forced a violent coughing fit to ensue.

"*Jason*!" Tokyo heard a woman screaming, taking it for Liz.

Lazily, he opened his eyes and moved his head – the big cannibal had lumbered off towards the sink where a wicked-looking cleaver rested.

"*Argh*," Tokyo wailed, rolling off the table and slamming against the floor.

The cannibal looked over his shoulder but didn't stop his journey towards the meat-chopping utensil.

Tokyo tried to slip the gun off his shoulder. He screamed in frustration when he couldn't quite get to it. "Come on, man."

The cannibal grabbed the cleaver, turned, raised it overhead and stalked towards Tokyo, who was still scrabbling on the floor with his shotgun. Frantically, he wrestled to get the strap over his head as the beastly man moved closer.

He heard the cleaver cut through the air, and then felt it slam into his shoulder.

Tokyo screamed, but he didn't allow it to stop him getting the gun free and into his arms. Before the cannibal could knock the gun to one side, Tokyo cocked the weapon and fired. The shell bit through his opponent's collarbone, propelling him backwards. This gave him a chance to reload and fire again.

The second cartridge drilled through the giant's chest and threw him onto the table.

Tokyo reloaded and fired once more. The slug smashed through the overgrown cannibal's forehead, killing him, before the shotgun was knocked out of Tokyo's hands. The gun slid under the fridge.

"Mother-*fucker*!" Liz screamed in his face, and then slashed her knife across the bridge of his nose and cheeks.

Tokyo fell to the floor and spied the dropped cleaver. Grabbing it, he sprung to his feet and went at her. "Fuck you, cunt!" he screamed.

Before he could reach her, a set of teeth clamped down on his left shoulder, and then his right, forcing him to drop his weapon and crash to the floor.

He felt his flesh being torn away in strips, his blood guzzled.

"Enough, girls. We don't want to kill him just yet."

Tokyo rolled onto his back and looked up at the hideous girls' faces looming over him – strings of bloody saliva clung to their drooping lower lips and chins, bringing to mind strawberry laces. Their teeth were broken and misshapen, and their eyes were mismatched in colour. Like Liz, they were naked – their sagging tits were covered in boils and blisters, which bubbled and oozed.

"Bite fingers off," the one drooled.

"Chomp cock," said the other.

Both girls giggled.

"This fucking bastard killed our Jason and Bear," Liz said, looking down at her dead nephew with tears in her eyes.

"I murdered that fucking brother of yours too," Tokyo yelled, spitting blood everywhere. "Do your worst."

Liz's face changed. "Onto the table with him, ladies," she said calmly.

"*Wait*!"

"It's too late for pleading, fucker."

He was once again slammed down on the table, his clothes ripped from him. Their talons raked at his skin, face and privates. "Don't you want to know about your parents?" he yelled, feeling he had one last card to play to try and get out of the situation.

"What about them?"

"Spare me and I'll tell you all."

Liz called the girls off with a wave of her hand. "Tell me how you know so much about us first."

Tokyo relayed all the information about his son and Sam, and how they had unearthed the dark secret.

"It's true – we do hail from a long line of cannibals."

"Why?" he choked out.

"Kill?"

"No. Why expose yourself by living out in the open? Some of you have genetic failure—"

"Because we've been able to survive much better this way. Long ago, your kind used to hunt my family down in the woods and kill them. Now, though, there's no stopping us." She smiled. "You were foolish to come here tonight. Even if you had killed us all, it would have still been a failure – we have family everywhere. Globally."

His mouth formed a perfect O. "So it's true…"

"What of my parents?" She put the cleaver to his face.

He licked his dry lips. "We killed them, Sam and I. Poison."

She laughed. "You did me a service – they were old, useless and in the way."

A flutter of hope swelled in his belly.

"Still, they were my blood and gave me this workplace . . . Have him, ladies."

"Oh Jesus, *no*!" he begged. "Let me go and I'll—*Argh*!" he screamed as one of the girls bit down and through his cock, ripping it and his testicles from his body.

The second girl tore his nipples off and sank her teeth into the side of his neck. Whereas the first girl's fingers had started to burrow into his arsehole, the second teen's digits worked their way into his mouth and yanked on his tongue, tearing it free and feasting on it.

Then there were fingers in his eyes and up his nose.

He prayed for death but the pain continued for a few more torturous minutes before everything slanted and turned black. The last thing he heard was Liz's laugh.

The End

About Your Author

David Owain Hughes is a horror freak! He grew up on ninja, pirate and horror movies from the age of five, which rapidly instilled in him a vivid imagination. When he grows up, he wishes to be a serial killer with a part-time job in women's lingerie…

He's had multiple short stories published in various online magazines and anthologies, along with articles, reviews and interviews. He's written for This Is Horror, Blood Magazine, and Horror Geeks Magazine. He's the author of the popular novels "Walled In" (2014), "Wind-Up Toy" (2016), "Man-Eating Fucks" (2016), and "The Rack & Cue" (2017) along with his short story collections "White Walls and Straitjackets" (2015) and "Choice Cuts" (2015). He's also written three novellas – "Granville" (2016), "Wind-Up Toy: Broken Plaything & Chaos Rising" (2016).

www.hellboundbookspublishing.com/authorpage_hughes.html

www.facebook.com/DOHughesAuthor/?ref=hl

www.amazon.co.uk/David-Owain-Hughes/e/B00L708P2M/ref=sr_ntt_srch_lnk_3?qid=1458241417&sr=1-3

http://david-owain-hughes.wix.com/horrorwriter

www.goodreads.com/author/show/4877205.David_Owain_Hughes

twitter.com/DOHUGHES32

Other HellBound Books Titles
Available at: www.hellboundbookspublishing.com

Man Eating F*cks

A dark, incredibly entertaining excursion into the delightfully twisted imagination of David Owain Hughes....

An average teenage girl and her father find themselves caught up in a brutal nightmare at their local recreational centre, when an age-old enemy comes stumbling out of the woods to crash a heavy-metal gig; a gig that has all the promises of being killer. This is one blood-soaked gig you won't want to miss!

Praise for Man-Eating F*cks from Ty Schwamberger (author of The Fields, Deep Dark Woods & The Death of a Horror Writer.) "Man Eating F*cks is old school horror, but with a new, blood-soaked twist! David Owain Hughes effectively creates enjoyable and lethal characters in this tale that is sure to keep you up at night. This is the type of tale that you need to read with a light on…I'm serious. You better put your seatbelt on 'cause you're in for one helluva ride. Look out, Hughes might very well be headed to the major leagues after this twisted tale! Highly recommended!"

Psychological Breakdown
By
David Owain Hughes

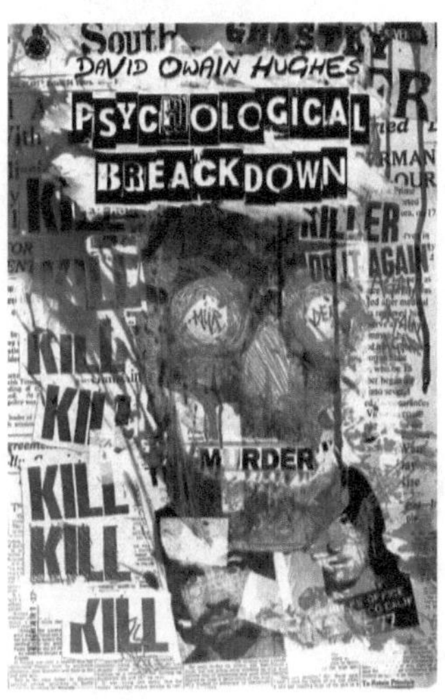

Within this tome lies eighteen tales of mind-bending terror, as Hughes delves into the human psyche and dishes out stories of what becomes of the broken minded, spirited and downright irked.

Part these blood-drenched pages at your own peril, for you will find diseased minds geared towards revenge and bloody chaos, with a few twists, turns and surprises thrown in for good, fucked-up measures.

Keep the lights on!

Puckered

Percy is kinky.
Percy is perverted.
Percy is a loner.
Percy is sneaky…

…But most of all, Percy wants to be left alone.

Whether it be a nagging mother or something from his past, it feels like he is always trying to escape something.
Will he be able to find his own peace, or will the real world catch up to him?
There will be blood.
There will be s**t.
There will be unusual sexual kinks.
But most of all, there will be murder…

Worship Me

Something is listening to the prayers of St. Paul's United Church, but it's not the god they asked for; it's something much, much older.

A quiet Sunday service turns into a living hell when this ancient entity descends upon the house of worship and claims the congregation for its own. The terrified churchgoers must now prove their loyalty to their new god by giving it one of their children or in two days time it will return and destroy them all.

As fear rips the congregation apart, it becomes clear that if they're to survive this untold horror, the faithful must become the faithless and enter into a battle against God itself. But as time runs out, they discover that true monsters come not from heaven or hell… …they come from within.

No Rest For The Wicked

A modern day ghost story with its skeletons buried firmly in the past.

From beyond the grave, a murderous wife seeks to complete her revenge on those who betrayed her in life; a powerless domestic still fears for her immortal soul while trying to scare off anyone who comes too close; and the former plantation master - a sadistic doctor who puts more faith in the teachings of de Sade than the Bible

When Eric and Grace McLaughlin purchase Greenbrier Plantation, their dreams are just as big as those who have tried to tame the place before them. But, the doctor has learned a thing or two over his many years in the afterlife, is*putting those new skills to the test, and will go to great lengths in order to gain the upper hand. While Grace digs into the death-filled history of her new home, Eric soon becomes a pawn of the doctor's unsavory desires and rapidly growing power, and is hell-bent on stopping her.

The Amnesia Girl

Filled with copious amounts of black humor, Gerri R. Gray's first published novel is an offbeat adventure story that could be described as One Flew over the Cuckoo's Nest meets Thelma and Louise.

Flashback to 1974. Farika is a lovely young woman who wakes up one day to find herself a patient in a bizarre New York City psychiatric asylum. She has no idea who she is, and possesses no memories of where she came from nor how she got there.

Fearing for her life after being attacked by a berserk girl with over one hundred personalities and a vicious nurse with sadistic intentions, the frightened amnesiac teams up with an audacious lesbian with a comically unbalanced mind, and together they attempt a daring escape.

But little do they know that a long strange journey into an even more insane world filled with a multitude of perilous predicaments and off-kilter individuals are waiting for them on the outside. Farika's weird reality crumbles when she finally discovers who, and what, she really is!

The Cabin Sessions

The Cabin Sessions is a confronting, hard-hitting dark psychological thriller, told with an acid wit. Themes of domestic and child abuse are explored through minds distorted by fear, and corrupted by hatred and delusion. A tale where redemption is gained in unexpected ways.

It's Christmas Eve when hapless musician Adam Banks stands on the bridge over the river that cleaves the isolated village of Burton. A storm is rolling into the narrow mountain pass. He thinks of turning back. Instead, he resolves to fulfill his obligation to perform the guest spot at The Cabin Sessions. He should be looking forward to it, but fear stirs when he opens the door on the Cabin's incense-choked air.

Meanwhile, Philip's sister, Eva, prepares to take a bath. It's a ritual. She's a breath holder. At twenty-eight she's returned to Burton to finish the business of her past; business she must attend to, if only she could make sense of it. Memories begin to surface concerning the innocence of her brother.

Blood and Kisses

The definitive short story collecting from James H Longmore - an eclectic mix of dark horror, bizarro and Twilight-Zone style tales of the downright disturbing.

Welcome to the long awaited collection from the writer of horror novels *'Pede* and *Tenebrion*; a forword by Richard Chizmar (co-author of *Gwendy's Button Box* and author of *A Long December*), 18 short stories, 5 flash fiction and even a poem - all skin-crawling, soul-shredding tales of terror, of the darkest things that skulk amongst the night's inky shadows, and of the everyday gone horribly awry.

Discover the alternative implication of technology becoming self-aware, enjoy the acquaintance of a charismatic new pastor who promises his flock a brand new place in which to worship his God, and spend a little time in the company of a nice young man who is inexorably caught up in his home town's terrible secret. Then there is Cupid's revelation that personally he has never experienced love, yet we discover that very emotion alive and not so well amongst the ruins of a post zombie apocalypse world, and we bear witness to a childhood innocence forever destroyed in a war-torn city. There is more, Dear Reader, much, much more; for within these pages we have devils, demons and ghosts, lycanthropes and demi-gods, all rubbing nefarious shoulders with vilest of Hell's offspring who have slithered from the netherworld to doff their caps and wish us all the sweetest of dreams…

The Big Book of Bootleg Horror 2

The second volume in HellBound Books' flagship horror anthology - this one bursting at the seams with even more fantastically dark horror from the cream of the rising stars in today's horror scene!

Featuring: Tracey A. Cross, Elizabeth Zemlicka, Shelby Thomas, Matthew Gillies, Spinster Eskie, Stephen Clements, Ken Goldman, Nathan Robinson, K.M. Campbell, Cody Grady, Sebastian Bendix, Leo X. Robertson, David Owain Hughes, Timothy McGivney, Kane Gordon, Todd Sullivan, Mike Mayak, Edward Ahern, Rose Garnett, Jaap Boekestein, Brandy Delight, Stanley B. Webb, D. Norfolk, and Thomas Gunther.

David Owain Hughes

**A HellBound Books LLC
Publication**

http://www.hellboundbookspublishing.com

Printed in the United States of America